ALSO EDITED BY GLENN YEFFETH

Taking the Red Pill:
Science, Philosophy and Religion in The Matrix

Seven Seasons of Buffy:
Science Fiction and Fantasy Writers Discuss
Their Favourite Television Show

Don DeBrandt

ANGELUS POPULI

Nothing in Joss's universe is left to chance, and so perhaps it's not surprising that Angelus, Buffy's high school nemesis, seems so familiar to every one of us over the age of fourteen. The cruelty, the mockery, the sheer pleasure he took in others' pain—all of us went to high school with someone like him. Of course, for most of us, the high school bullies we faced were pale imitations of the sublime evil of Angelus. For most of us....

A NGELUS.

Angel's dark side, the monster with the beautiful face. When I was preparing to write *Shakedown* (the fifth novel in the *Angel* series), I knew my portrayal of Angelus would be critical. I had to capture not only his ruthlessness, but the exuberant joy he took in his cruelty. I also knew it wouldn't be a problem, because Angelus was already a character I was all too familiar with.

See, I went to high school with him.

I grew up in a small town; too small, in fact, to have its own high school. It was decided that the students from my community—and a few other, nearby small towns—would be bused to a central, slightly larger town, where we would all learn together. I don't know about anyone else, but I learned a *lot*. Some lessons took longer to sink in, but it's amazing what repetition will do.

I learned to always carry the book I was reading with the back cover facing outward and the spine toward the floor; it made the book harder to identify, giving them less fuel with which to mock me. I learned that ignoring someone who's abusing you will *never* make them go away; it will only make them try harder. And I learned that adults, no matter how well-meaning, can't protect you from a determined predator.

Not that I was any stranger to bullying. I was always bright, already reading by the time I hit first grade; in a school populated mainly by farm kids, that made me a magnet for trouble. My parents decided to take the brilliant step of having me skip fifth grade, so I landed in a class where I didn't know anyone, was the smallest and youngest there and already had a reputation as a bookworm.

Did I mention my father was a teacher at the same school?

I love my father a great deal. He gave me my appreciation of books and words in general, and he's a decent, ethical human being. He was, unfortunately, the kind of teacher that good students love . . . and delinquents *hate*. And in an attempt to protect me, he taught me something it took a long time to unlearn: that if the bullying got too bad, I could always come to him for help.

This *did* protect me, to a certain degree; no one would actually lay a hand on me. Sometimes I wish they would have—a few schoolyard beatings might have toughened me up. Instead, I was attacked in all the other ways children can think up: name-calling, ostracization, having my stuff stolen or wrecked. And when it got too bad, when I felt like every kid I knew hated my guts, I'd tell my dad . . . which gave me a reputation as a snitch, as well.

But these were mainly farm kids. Simple people. Salt of the Earth. As Gene Wilder says in *Blazing Saddles*, "You know . . . morons." Thinking back on it now, they remind me of the vamps that Angel or Buffy would stake while on patrol: nameless thugs, not too bright, often dust by the opening credits. Bad guys, sure—but not particularly memorable or important.

Eighth grade was the last one legally required for my classmates to attend, and out of a dozen or so guys, a grand total of three—myself included—made the jump to high school. Neither of the other two used to bully me, so you'd think I'd be home free, wouldn't you?

Did I mention that when they started busing kids to the new school, my father went with them?

And now it was a whole new ball game. Same rules . . . but a different breed of player.

SUCK AND CESS

Let's call him Jock. He certainly was that, but it wasn't his physical strength that made him a threat to me. Jock was as different from the ignorant farm kids that picked on me in middle school as Angelus is from the blood-sucking cannon fodder Angel dispatches on a regular basis. See, Jock wasn't just a brute—like Angelus, he was good-looking, surrounded himself with others of his own kind and was smart. He only laid a hand on me once the entire time we were in school together, to punch me in the stomach when I didn't get out of his way fast enough, and even so he glanced around first to make sure nobody else saw him do it.

No, Jock preferred more sophisticated weapons. He was a master of sarcasm, of mockery, of innuendo. He wasn't above name-calling, but while previous attempts at saddling me with a nickname ranged from the infantile to the naive—what can you say about people so deeply ignorant they think "Professor" is an insult?—Jock's creations were vicious and deeply humiliating. They started with Bookworm; that mutated to Bookmaggot, then Bookfaggot. Shortened versions of any of these were also considered acceptable, with Maggot usually taking first place. Considering the amount of crap they made me eat, it was almost appropriate.

For the first time, I had to deal with someone who wasn't simply following a knee-jerk response, mindlessly attacking me because I didn't fit in, or even because of who my father was.

No, Jock's motivations were entirely different. Like Angelus, Jock understood exactly what he was doing—and he enjoyed doing it a great deal. He didn't hate me; if anything, I was a hobby he enjoyed. He got his friends interested as well, as people with hobbies do, and then there were the inevitable copycats who just wanted to jump on the bandwagon. Picking on me was almost trendy.

I endured this for two and a half years. During this time, no subject was taboo if Jock thought it would provide entertainment. Masturbation, bestiality and of course the all-time classic, homosexuality, were favorite topics.

And then my sister died.

She was six years old. She was born mentally handicapped and with epilepsy; her entire existence was spent in an institution, her personality never growing beyond an infant's. And no, Jock saw nothing wrong with mocking that.

On the day after her funeral, I walked into typing class and sat down. I felt dead inside. In those days they taught typing on big clunky Underwood typewriters, made out of metal and heavy as hell. I put my fingers on the keys and heard Jock, who sat at the table behind me, say, "Hey. I heard your sister died."

I stood up, grabbed the typewriter, turned and smashed it into his face as hard as I could.

It broke his nose and knocked out his front teeth, but that was incidental. It also caved in his right temple, crushing the skull and driving part of the frame into his temporal lobe. He was dead before he hit the floor.

Sure.

What really happened was I turned around, looked into his eyes, and said, "That's right." He must have seen something there—like I said, he was smart—and he muttered, "Sorry," and looked away. Lucky for him—for both of us, really—because I'd already rehearsed the other part in my mind. If he had shown so much as a smile, I would have done exactly as I just described. After two years of abuse, I just didn't care any more. Fortunately, it never became anything more than a fantasy.

Sometimes, when reality is too grim, fantasy is all we have. Fantasy lets us remake the rules to suit ourselves; it lets us right wrongs, change the world, transform ourselves. Supernatural fantasies, in particular, are great for this—you can use magic to juggle any circumstance, justify any outcome. You can literally bend reality itself, as in the episode "I Will Remember You" (A1-8), when Angel gains his humanity for twenty-four hours only to have the entire day erased as if it had never been. While ultimately it's for a noble purpose, he suffers horribly as a result.

Because not all fantasies are happy ones. Mine certainly weren't.

It wasn't the first time I murdered Jock, nor was it the last. I smashed his face in with a baseball bat. I tore his head off with my bare hands. I locked him a concrete cistern with a metal grate set eight inches from the top, filled it with water and watched him try to claw his way out as he

11-13-04
Alka Bennet *[signature]*

To Benjamin and Isabella

To Sharon,
with my good & excellent wishes,
Nancy Hoeder
11-13-04
M.D.

[signature] 11/13/04

Acknowledgements

Leah Wilson copy-edited every essay in this volume. Some essays she barely touched; for others she took out the thick red pen and went at it. In every case she left the essay smoother and cleaner without disturbing the author's intention or style. And she did it without pissing off a single author (well, mostly). If you find this volume a smooth read, you have Leah to thank.

Contents

FIVE SEASONS OF
ANGEL

Edited by Glenn Yeffeth

FIVE SEASONS OF
ANGEL

Science Fiction
and Fantasy Authors
Discuss Their Favorite
Vampire

BENBELLA BOOKS
Dallas, Texas

First BenBella Books Edition October 2004

BenBella Books
6440 N. Central Expressway
Suite 617
Dallas, TX 75206

Send feedback to feedback@benbellabooks.com
www.benbellabooks.com

Printed in the United States of America

10 9 8 7 6 5 4 3 2 1

Library of Congress Cataloging-in-Publication Data
Five seasons of Angel : science fiction and fantasy authors discuss their favorite vampire / edited by Glenn Yeffeth.—1st BenBella Books ed.
     p. cm.
   ISBN 1-932100-33-4
   1. Angel (Television program : 1999-) I. Yeffeth, Glenn, 1961–

   PN1992.77.A588F58 2004
   791.45'72—dc22

                                                    2004009626

Cover design by Todd Michael Bushman
Interior designed and composed by Paragon PrePress, Inc.

Distributed by Independent Publishers Group
To order call (800) 888-4741
www.ipgbook.com

drowned. I killed him in a hundred ways, and some of them were pretty creative. Fantasy was the only outlet I had for my rage.

That rage has, to a certain degree, shaped my creativity. My work has a dark edge to it, an edge honed by that period of my life; the torture scenes in *Shakedown* were certainly sharpened by it.

Joss Whedon has said that if he'd been happy in high school, he never would have created *Buffy*. I wonder, sometimes, who Joss's Angelus was.

I'm sure there must have been one—or, more likely, a number of them—and he or they all fit the same description: handsome, popular, athletic . . . and cruel. This is the kind of bully that all teenagers know but somehow adults are oblivious to; unlike the vamps that live in sewers and graveyards, they can pass as human—because they're *successful*.

Used to be, vampires were considered hideous, monstrous beasts, one step above ghouls; but the twentieth century version has evolved into something sleeker, sexier, more akin to a romantic anti-hero than a walking corpse. Anne Rice's Lestat or Frank Langella's Dracula are what we expect in a neck-biter today, and it's not just their physical comeliness that defines them.

More than anything, vampires have become a metaphor for the upper class. They dress and act like royalty, gain their strength and power by preying upon the common man . . . and if one of them takes a liking to you, he may even offer an invitation to join their ranks.

Aside from living in a castle, that pretty much describes the popular crowd in high school. And like the twentieth-century vampire, they get away with murder . . . because they're at the top of the food chain.

The Jocks of this world are all too real, while vampires are just a fantasy. But sometimes, when a fantasy takes shape in a crucible of abuse, it can take on a life—and power—of its own.

FEAR AND LOATHING

Angelus was pure evil. From 1753 to 1898 he roamed Europe, leaving a trail of destruction and horror in his wake. His first act as a vampire was to kill and feed off his own family; when it came time to increase his vampiric pack, he drove a young nun insane before turning her into a fellow creature of the night. He developed a taste for torture, both physical and psychological—it wasn't the kill that mattered, it was the amount of suffering he could inflict on his victim beforehand.

Jock didn't kill anyone I loved. He didn't tie me up and drive railroad spikes through my body. But he did systematically try to destroy any trace of pride or dignity I had . . . and he did so five days a week for over two years. As an experiment, I tried to count how many times he insulted me in a single day.

He hit thirty-five by noon, and I stopped counting.

What sets Angelus apart, more than anything, is his attitude. He's not just a killing machine, he's a party animal. He's always grinning, always gleeful; you know there's nothing else he'd rather be doing than turning somebody else's life into Hell.

And we almost want him to succeed . . . because he's *funny*.

When humor is used as an attack, it's specific and directed. It's no accident that all the adjectives used to describe this type of humor sound the same: razor-sharp wit, barbed comments, cutting remarks. This kind of humor always has an edge, and how deep that edge cuts depends on how far the comedian is willing to go.

It's all about pain. Ridicule is just a way to get rid of your own by forcing it upon someone else. It is an act of violation, and the people who employ it express the same savage joy in the act that all rapists seem to take. It's *that* attitude that Angelus projects so well . . . and as stand-ups from George Carlin to Chris Rock can attest, channeling it in the right way can make you very popular indeed.

But heaping scorn on society with a microphone in your hand isn't the same as slicing someone to ribbons in person. Only the end result is the same, at least for the comedian: people laugh. And in high school, it's infinitely better to laugh than to be laughed at.

I don't know what kind of pain Jock was trying to get rid of by launching it at me. I don't really care; it's hard to empathize with someone who's made it his hobby to destroy you. Perhaps Joss never understood his tormentors either—Angelus is portrayed as a being of elemental evil, one who enjoys the process of causing pain simply because he's so good at it.

And he *is* good at it. Unlike other fictional killers who come off as insane or disgusting, Angelus has the charm and wit to make us laugh. It may be a nervous laugh, we may not like ourselves for laughing, but laugh we do.

Part of it is simply that he's good-looking. Even when he vamps out, when his forehead bulges and his teeth become an orthodontal nightmare, Angelus is still sexy. Would we still think he was desirable if he sported piggish features, a beer gut and a bad haircut?

Of course not—because that's what *real* bullies look like, isn't it? At least, that's what we've been conditioned to think. Someone with Angelus's good looks couldn't be a bully, because bullies are *losers*. The virtue of physical attractiveness somehow justifies even the worst actions; on some level, we seem to believe people like that are just taking their due. The resentment we feel toward them is balanced by our desire to *be* them, to have what they have and do what they do. It's that crucial point, the ability to transform a victim into a fellow victimizer, that makes the modern-day vampire so attractive . . . and why we turn a blind eye to the cruelty of those we consider our betters.

CENTER OF BALANCE

I wonder sometimes why the undead always claw their way out of the grave with an extensive knowledge of the martial arts. It doesn't matter if the guy was a ninety-eight-pound accountant who never stepped foot in a gym when he was alive—as soon as he sprouts fangs he's doing spin kicks and somersaults like a Chinese acrobat. What, does Bruce Lee have a dojo in Hell?

Not that I'm complaining—the fight scenes in *Angel* are always well-choreographed and exciting. The spiritual aspect of certain Eastern disciplines also mirrors many of the underlying themes of the show; Angel and Angelus are the yin and yang of not only good and evil, but action and reaction, comedy and tragedy.

Angelus is very much the male part of the equation. He's aggressive, invasive; he has an agenda and he devotes all his energy to getting what he wants. He attacks both physically and psychologically, always moving forward, always a force of destruction.

Angel—like many heroes—is reactive. He responds to evil, rarely seeking it out. Cases used to come to him via the Powers That Be; now, he deals with the clients of Wolfram and Hart, the law firm that used to be his worst enemy. Most importantly, he doesn't just destroy monsters; he tries to make the world a better place.

And where Angelus laughs, Angel broods.

There are different ways to deal with pain. You can fight it, you can ignore it, you can try to transform it into something else—even a joke. Humor, when used as a defense, disperses the hurt, generalizes it; it's an inclusive process, one that everyone identifies with. When someone laughs at himself, he invites the world to laugh with him.

But a person with a self-deprecating sense of humor is still trying to lessen his pain by sharing it. Angel won't allow himself that luxury; he takes responsibility for *every* one of Angelus's actions. Despite the supernatural aspect of their relationship, he refuses to hide behind the rationalization that Angelus is someone else. Angelus is him, and as such Angel must bear the guilt of everything he's done. He insists on keeping all that pain to himself . . . and that pain is the force that drives their relationship. Angelus inflicts it; Angel internalizes it.

And the pivot on which that pain turns is Angel's soul.

PAYBACK, WITH INTEREST

Angel is doomed to suffer. He literally cannot experience a single moment of true happiness; if he does so, he loses his soul and Angelus takes over. He is not simply a tragic character; he is a character who is incapable of being anything *other* than tragic. He is trapped in a hell of his own making, where he remembers in vivid detail every horrific act he ever committed. Angel suffers, and perhaps worst of all, he cannot escape the conclusion that he *deserves* to suffer.

Angel's condition was an act of revenge—a gypsy curse, inflicted by the family of one of Angelus's victims. But it resonates, at least for me, on a much deeper level.

It's easy to wreak revenge through fiction. You're playing God, after all; you can do anything to your characters. If you want to take someone you hate and toss them into a volcano, go ahead. You can beat them, maim them, torture them and kill them with impunity. Writers do it all the time.

If you're a good writer, you can get away with even more. Disguise them well enough and you can hold your substitute up to the same kind of mockery that they put you through. No one but you will know who that slimy, despicable wretch represents, of course—that's what libel laws are there to prevent—but at least you'll have the satisfaction of tormenting your own metaphoric voodoo doll.

But a really good writer goes one step further. He doesn't just respond in kind, trading attack for attack. Instead, he takes the object of his anger and holds up a mirror. Makes that character see himself for what he truly is, the effect he's had on others' lives. Makes that character understand the cost his victims have paid for his entertainment . . . and most of all, makes that character *care.*

The metaphor Joss uses is the soul—but what Angelus really has imposed on him is a conscience. It's not that an ensouled Angel is incapable of evil; he's just as capable of choice as any other self-aware being. But that awareness has been expanded beyond his own immediate pleasure, and now includes both the consequences of his actions and empathy for his victims. Is there any punishment more just than this?

Maybe . . . but is punishing Angel for Angelus's actions fair? For that matter, if Angelus is a creature of supernatural evil, is he responsible for what he is? Is punishment even the right response to horror, or does it simply lead to more horror in a continuing cycle of revenge?

QUESTIONABLE ACTIVITIES

Angel crosses a lot of genre boundaries: action/adventure, horror, comedy, even teen drama . . . and let's not forget mystery. Angel began his current stay in L.A. as the head of a detective agency, and a detective is always asking questions, trying to get to the truth. In a sense all fiction does this, but the structure of a mystery allows you to do it in a very ordered way.

Angel's early cases would usually begin with a vision from the Powers That Be, prompting the gang at Angel Investigations to ask question #1: *who needs to be saved?* This would lead very quickly to questions #2 and #3—*where is this person?* and *what are they in danger from?*—and inevitably to the big one: *what is really going on here?*

Good fiction always asks good questions, and *Angel* is no exception. Beneath the obvious ones that drive the plot, it asks much harder ones: What is the nature of heroism? Is evil a necessary part of the human condition? Is committing an evil act for a good cause right or wrong? And perhaps most importantly: Is redemption possible?

The answers to these questions are slippery, but there is a central concept that rises again and again, a theme that resonates through the entire series.

Atonement.

Punishment is simply revenge. It is as self-serving as the original evil act and often just as vicious. Hatred focuses pain the way a laser focuses light, and vengeance is a house of mirrors. Payback does not decrease pain and suffering; if it did, there would be far fewer wars.

Atonement is an act of compensation, a counterbalance. When fire is met with fire, all that results is destruction; an act of creation is neccessary to negate it. This, far more than the guilt he endures, is Angel's true burden: not just to suffer for his past, but to be a positive force for the future. There is a world of difference between fighting *against* evil and fighting *for* good. This is the real battle at the heart of the show: to be a positive influence amidst violence and horror, to keep your eyes on the light when you must live in the dark.

If Angelus does represent the same kind of tormentor to Joss as he does to me, I admire his response. Despite the deep anger he must hold toward the character, Joss has chosen redemption over revenge. Sure, he's made him suffer—Angel spent most of a century living in sewers and eating rats, and another hundred years in a hell dimension—but ultimately, he has the chance to make good. According to an ancient prophecy, if Angel "fulfills his destiny," he will be rewarded by becoming human.

Becoming human. No more Angelus, no more living in the dark . . . and by extension, no more fighting supernatural menaces. To rejoin the human race as a weaker, sadder, but much better person.

Is there any better fate to impose on a bully?

RESOLUTIONS

Everybody has a breaking point. I reached mine about halfway through high school.

It had been a particularly hard day. One of Jock's accomplices—like Angelus, he had his pack—had pushed me to the point that both of us wound up in the principal's office. While trying to explain the daily cycle of humiliation and degradation I was being put through, I used the phrase, "at every opportunity, they're always tormenting me." The accomplice—let's call him Toady—just smirked and blandly denied everything I said.

Of course, my accidental bit of poetry didn't escape him. Later, he and two of his friends thought it would be *really* funny to march down the halls and chant it as loudly as they could.

Over, and over, and over.

"At every oppor-*tun*-ity, they're always tor-*men*-ting me. At every oppor-*tun*-ity, they're always tor-*men*-ting me. . . ."

Can you hear it? Can you hear Angelus's voice?

I couldn't hear anything else. It took every bit of self-control I had to just walk down the hall. I felt both detached and like I was going to explode. . . .

And then I did.

In my semi-zombie state, I bumped into someone. I was in such a precarious condition that the impact split my rational and emotional selves; even though part of me knew it was simply an accident and not a malicious act, I reacted as though it was. I threw my books into the air and started screaming at the guy. All the anger and frustration of the last two years came spewing out in curses and threats and pure rage.

And this is where the story takes a somewhat odd turn.

One of the things I've always admired about Joss Whedon's writing is his ability to confound expectations. He's very good at leading you a particular way, then adding a twist that takes you someplace completely different but makes perfect sense. It's a difficult thing to pull off in fiction, especially more than once.

Reality, though, will throw that kind of thing at you all the time.

The guy I was raging at—let's call him Will—was something of an anomaly. Like Jock, he was popular and good-looking, active in sports and academically successful. But he never seemed to take the same kind of enjoyment others did in taunting me; maybe it was because he and I shared an interest in writing—he went on to journalism school afterward—or simply because he was a decent human being. In any case, the only member of Jock's social circle that had ever shown me any kindness or tolerance was the one I blew up at.

He didn't mock me, or take the opportunity to kick the crap out of me. He just looked at me and said, "Go ahead."

And I couldn't. I was a scrawny little guy and he was an athlete—the only opportunity I was being presented with was to embarrass myself even further, and so I just kept shouting until I attracted the attention of a teacher and found myself back in the principal's office.

But this time, things were different.

There's a moment many of us remember, though it usually happens when we're quite young. A stranger hurts us, for no apparent reason, and when we try to tell them that, when we attempt to explain our pain in a clear and reasonable way, we are made fun of. Our pain is mocked. A horrible sense of betrayal and confusion settles in, and suddenly we don't look at the world in the same way any more.

Well, for the first time in my life, the exact opposite happened.

The principal started by saying flat out that he was tired of the campaign of harassment he'd seen waged against me, and wanted to know why it had started.

Will did his best to tell him.

It was the only honest discussion of the situation I'd ever experienced. Will said that people thought I was a snob, that I acted like I was better or smarter than them. Amazed that anyone could confuse introversion with elitism, I pointed out that I was under so much stress I was barely passing several of my classes. I think we were both surprised—but what happened next surprised me even more.

The principal called for a truce. Will agreed to actually talk to people and get them to ease up—but only if I agreed to try, too. To join in, to get more involved instead of just hiding behind the covers of a book.

I don't know if I can properly convey the importance of that deal. Will could have done exactly what Toady had—blown the whole thing off, nodded in all the right places and laughed about it with his friends afterward. The fact that he didn't, that he actually treated me like a human being, was incredibly important to me.

Twenty minutes after we left the office, one of Will's friends said they were "going to give me a chance," and laughed. Something inside me turned off like a switch.

I sleepwalked through the rest of the day—nothing mattered any more—went home and told my parents I was done. After a long discussion, my mother persuaded me to take a day off, and then give it one more chance.

When I went back, the first person to greet me said, "Hey, Bookie!"

So did the next. And the next.

I don't know what Will said, or who he talked to. But no one ever called me Bookworm, or Bookmaggot, ever again. When I saw Jock, he simply nodded at me.

Did I mention that Will was Jock's best friend?

I did my best to keep up my end of the bargain. I stopped bringing books to school as an escape; I wasn't exactly socially active, but I tried to be less stand-offish. The one time afterward that someone attempted to humiliate me, by leaving phony love notes on my locker, I read the notes out loud to my class, made fun of the writing style and joined in the joke. It didn't go on for long—it's not much fun when your target mocks you right back, and it was a serious tactical error to try to use the written word against me.

The motto of Angel Investigations is "We Help the Helpless;" I guess that's exactly what Will did for me. He wound up being our class valedictorian, and at our graduation party, both of us were there passing around a bottle of wine as the sun came up. He asked me to make a toast, and while the toast was lame—"here's to graduating and not getting caught by the cops"—I was deeply grateful for the chance to make it.

Yeah, there are Angeluses out there—but there are Angels, too.

I don't know if I believe in redemption, but I do believe in second chances. Some people would argue that you can't have one without the other, and maybe they're right; maybe Jock went on to reform his ways and became a decent human being. Truth, after all, is stranger than fiction, and who would have thought Angel would wind up running Wolfram and Hart?

Last I heard, Jock was a lawyer. . . .

Don DeBrandt grew up in the wilds of Saskatchewan and currently lives in Vancouver, Canada. His previously published novels include Angel: Shakedown, The Quicksilver Screen, Steeldriver, Timberjak *and* V.I. *He has two works of suspense fiction due out shortly, written under the name Donn Cortez: a thriller entitled* The Closer *and a mystery set at Burning Man called* The Man Burns Tonight.

Laura Resnick

"THAT ANGEL DOESN'T LIVE HERE ANYMORE"

There are two Angels, Resnick points out. And, no, Angelus isn't one of them....

"IT'S NOT DADDY," the mad vampire Drusilla says when Angel enters the wine cellar in which she and Darla are about to eat a bunch of lawyers in "Reunion" (A2-10). She adds in disappointment, "It's never Daddy."

She is, of course, alluding to the unique (and, from Drusilla's perspective, unfortunate) transformation which her vampire "sire" has gone through—twice in the course of his eventful existence—changing from the gleefully evil Angelus into the conscience-stricken Angel. The ensouled vampire who confronts Darla and Drusilla in that wine cellar, though troubled and walking close to the edge at that point in his unlife, is not Drusilla's "Daddy" as she knew him, but rather her sworn enemy, the individual whom her sire ultimately became.

This schizophrenia is a well-known aspect of Angel's characterization, and it runs so deep that Angel and the Fang Gang often talk about his alter ego, Angelus, as if he were a separate individual altogether. Yet there is an equally strong split in Angel's characterization which goes unaddressed: The Angel we know on *Angel* is a different character than the one we knew on *Buffy the Vampire Slayer*.

When Darla, Angel's sire and former lover (to use the word loosely), recalls bitterly in "Dear Boy" (A2-05) that Angel preferred "that cheerleader" to her, one is startled by the notion of Angel dating a cheerleader . . . until one realizes that it wasn't this Angel. It was *that* Angel, and he doesn't live here anymore. Like Angelus, *that* Angel is a different character.

The *Buffy*verse equates a soul with conscience, compassion and the ability to experience remorse and guilt ("Angel," B1-7). Vampires are soulless demons in Joss Whedon's creation, and that's why they do the evil they do. When Angel's soul was restored to him (or, rather, forced on him) by the gypsy curse in 1898 ("Becoming, Part 1," B2-21), he became not only an anomaly, but also a deeply tormented individual, remembering "every single one" of the many people he had tortured and murdered with pleasure for more than a century ("Darla,"A2-7). He became, in effect, a different person.

The ensouled Angel found himself viewing 150 years of Angelus's unspeakable brutality through the eyes of an individual capable of feeling horrified by, guilty about and ashamed of such acts. Rather than merely killing Angel, the gypsies chose to inflict an eternity of emotional anguish on him. Pretty shrewd, huh? (Note to self: Do not piss off gypsies.)

The effects of the curse sent Angel off the deep end for decades. Only when fate finally brings him into the orbit of Buffy the Vampire Slayer does he pull himself together and get a hobby—helping her fight evil. After what we gather has been a long period of wandering lonely and aimless (though the flashback scenes in "Why We Fight," A5-13, now indicate there may have been more to this period than has been let on to date), *Buffy*'s Angel finds a purpose in the world, a girlfriend and a crowd of human acquaintances (calling them "friends" would be a stretch). Just when his unlife starts feeling pretty good, though, we discover the catch. (You knew there had to be one, didn't you?) The gypsies built a secret escape clause into their curse: If Angel experiences a single moment of "perfect happiness," he'll lose his soul. The gypsies intended Angel to suffer, not to experience the *benefits* of having a soul (such as love and joy).

We find out about this tricky subclause when Angel and Buffy declare their mutual feelings and make love ("Surprise," B2-13), and then the poor girl wakes up the next day ("Innocence," B2-14) to discover that her sensitive, understanding date of last night is an evil demon this morning. (We've all been there, honey.) Angel spends the rest of the season as the soulless Angelus, committing unspeakably evil acts and hurting Buffy as often as possible; in this way, he resembles many ex-boyfriends, though few of them actually try to get the world sucked into hell ("Becoming, Part 2," B2-22).

Angel's soul is eventually restored to him, but the jig is up. Since love and intimacy turn him into an evil monster, he and Buffy can never again be together as a real couple. Ultimately, he leaves town (and Buffy) so that the girl he loves can move on to a life without him ("Graduation Day, Part 2," B3-22).

It's a bittersweet story of first love, and the gypsy curse works brilliantly in the portrayal of a teenage girl's dark, brooding, wrong-side-of-the-holy-water boyfriend and their impossible relationship. The rupture of first love usually *does* seem almost supernaturally powerful and bewildering to its victims; and young love often *is* defeated by seemingly unmanageable social, logistical and/or emotional forces. Therefore, I particularly like the "no happiness allowed" subclause in Angel's gypsy curse on *Buffy*, because it fulfills one of the most effective and most difficult roles of good fantasy fiction: It explores real human conditions through fantastic metaphors which universalize the characters' individual experiences to speak personally to us all.

However, the gypsy curse subclause which works so well in *Buffy* is a lead balloon in *Angel*—because Angel is a different character in *Angel*.

Buffy's Angel lurks around a high school, mooning over a teenage girl whom he takes ice skating, to the movies and to prom. An idealized love interest, he's hot and he wants her, but he never pressures her for sex. He's a bad boy who's polite to her mother. He hangs out at—and more or less fits into—a teen haunt like the Bronze, where high school girls (such as Cordelia) flirt with him, but he only has eyes for Buffy. He gets moderately (but never insanely) jealous over teenage boys who show an interest in Buffy, and his devotion to her is patient, exclusive and selfless.

In other words, *Buffy*'s Angel is an appealing character for a series about high schoolers. Socially and emotionally, this Angel is a reasonable love interest for the show's teenage heroine. He's just dangerous or forbidden enough to be all the more attractive.

However, these same statements cannot reasonably be made about *Angel's* Angel. When the character moves from a supporting role as teen love interest to center stage as conflicted adult, his characterization (though not his backstory) changes. Upon assuming the lead role of his own semi-*noir* series set in L.A., Angel becomes a more complex and more adult character. In the vampire mythology of the *Buffyverse*, Angel is essentially the same age on both shows, though the years keep passing. In the context of story and characterization, though, Angel ages significantly between leaving one series and starting another.

Buffy's Angel spends time in the teen-oriented Bronze; whereas in the first scene of *Angel's* pilot episode, Angel is in a seedy bar with a glass of booze, and his regular social haunt later becomes a demon (karaoke) bar. *Buffy's* Angel hangs out with high schoolers and gets his save-the-world instructions in the local school library from Giles, Buffy's father-figure; *Angel's* Angel socializes with adults in adult settings, is self-employed and gets his instructions from clients or from a higher plane (The Powers That Be). *Buffy's* Angel places his girlfriend at the center of his world; *Angel's* Angel is a troubled man seeking redemption for his sins.

One of the most obvious differences between the two Angels is their relationship to money. *Buffy* never once pauses to consider how Angel pays rent on the apartment he's living in when he first meets Buffy, nor how he pays the utility bills on the mansion he later inhabits. Though he clearly doesn't have a job, *Buffy's* Angel never frets about the cost of beverages at the Bronze, and there's never any explanation of where he gets the cash to buy the blood he consumes. Angel's finances are portrayed in a pre-adult manner on *Buffy*, which is to say that they're never contemplated at all. By contrast, Angel's financial problems are often addressed on *Angel*. He works for a living, and, like most adults, he worries often about money. *Angel's* Angel frets about restaurant prices, client fees, paying his employees, cutting costs, generating new business and keeping up with business expenses.

Angel's single-minded devotion to his girlfriend is gratifyingly pure and unwavering on *Buffy*. His sire, Darla, re-enters his life ("Angel," B1-7), and Faith the (other) Vampire Slayer gets seductive with him ("Enemies," B2-17); but Angel remains steadfast without difficulty, his emotional and sexual loyalty as clear as any girlfriend could want them to be. Only on *Angel* does Angel develop a real and enduring emotional bond with Faith which is in conflict with Buffy's needs ("Sanctuary," A1-19). Though still in love with Buffy, Angel's Angel is attracted to other women, such as a hunted waitress ("City Of," A1-1), an unhappy actress ("Eternity," A1-17), a dimension-hopping princess ("She," A1-13) and Kate the cop. Unlike *Buffy's* Angel, *Angel's* Angel doesn't find it easy to turn his back on his 150-year relationship with Darla; in fact, this Angel is openly obsessed with Darla, both sexually and emotionally. And without ever renouncing his love for Buffy, *Angel's* Angel falls in love with Cordelia.

Buffy's Angel confirms the young ideal of love when he tells Buffy he has loved only one person in his entire life—her—in "Earshot" (B2-18). *Angel's* Angel is a more complicated and ambivalent lover, one whose obsessions can be as strong as his loves and whose loyalties and desires can be in conflict even when his love is sincere.

Throughout much of *Angel's* second season, Angel is darkly, passionately obsessed with Darla, his female sire. He expresses this slightly Oedipal obsession in a variety of ways, including setting her on fire ("Redefinition," A2-11) and flinging her through a set of glass doors before spending the night having rough sex with her ("Reprise," A2-15). During the throes of his obsession, he abandons his job, he alienates his tiny handful of friends and he's an accessory to a massacre ("Reunion," A2-10).

Now is this really a guy we want to see dating a cheerleader? If you knew *this* guy was climbing into a sixteen-year-old's bedroom window regularly, as Angel did on *Buffy*, wouldn't you call the cops?

The darkness of Angel's vampire nature is habitually present, acknowledged and accepted in the adult character portrayed on *Angel*. In "Somnambulist" (A1-11), Angel admits that he's been enjoying the dreams he's been having of stalking and killing people. In "Blind Date" (A1-21) he longingly remembers the emotional clarity of killing without remorse for 150 years. In "City Of" (A1-1), Angel is hungrily distracted by a young woman's blood when he's trying to rescue her. In "Reprise" (A2-15), he becomes not only destructively depressed, but also sexually violent.

I find this a fascinating (and, yes, sexy) character. I also find it genuinely repugnant to picture this character dating a teenager. *Angel's* Angel is *not* a suitable love interest for a high school girl.

By the end of *Angel's* third season, as Angel struggles with the challenges of parenting his resentful, troubled and increasingly volatile teenage son

(Connor, who first appears in season three), middle-aged mothers and fathers are probably far more drawn to this character than their fifteen- to eighteen-year-old daughters, for whom *Buffy*'s Angel is a heart-throb.

So there is a distinct change in characterization between Angel's departure from Sunnydale and his arrival in Los Angeles. I enjoy both Angels in their respective settings, but I find the adult one far more interesting as the more complex and conflicted character.

Moreover, I would say that, if anything, the initially-stated purpose of the gypsy curse works even *better* for the adult Angel than for *Buffy*'s Angel. Angel's ongoing struggle in *Angel* is not only to redeem himself by being the world's champion; it's also to find a balance within himself between his vampire nature and his human soul, a fantasy metaphor for the familiar good-and-evil struggle which goes on inside each of us.

The gypsy-inflicted soul which creates this archetypal struggle for Angel—the human heart in conflict with itself—features prominently on *Buffy*, but only so far as it affects Buffy's growth as a Slayer and teenage girl. It's on *Angel* that this theme comes into full flowering and takes center stage, making use of the irony of Angel's victims (the gypsies) having victimized him, the challenge of Angel's resultant quest for redemption, the character's inevitable ambivalence about his condition (Angel is anguished, but nonetheless wants to retain his soul) and the unique nature and breadth of understanding which result from the anomaly of being a vampire with a soul.

On the other hand, whereas the *subclause* of the gypsy curse (one moment of perfect happiness makes him lose his soul) is an effective metaphor on *Buffy*, it's just a nuisance on *Angel*.

Buffy's Angel is such a well-fitted love interest for the heroine, the emotional connection is so emphatically portrayed as true love, that the story needs a truly remarkable and credibly unconquerable obstacle if these two characters are to break up *without* one or both of them turning into idiots, jerks or corpses. The curse's subclause succeeds in creating that obstacle; through no fault of their own, and with no diminishment of their true love, Buffy and Angel cannot possibly be a couple.

Angel's Angel, on the other hand, is a deeply troubled loner carrying a *ton* of emotional baggage. He has trouble relating to people. He resists intimacy. He's often uncomfortable with (and in denial about) his own emotions. He has dark moods, predatory instincts and is prone to violence. As portrayed in "Lonely Hearts" (A1-2) and "She" (A1-13), he's socially awkward, even to the point of rudeness. He's obsessed with a woman he doesn't like or respect (Darla). He's done many evil things which haunt him—and which would horrify any woman who got close enough to him to fully understand what he's done.

Do we really think this guy is so likely to have a great relationship that he *needs* a gypsy curse to keep it from happening?

Angel as the ideal love interest on *Buffy* needed a device to come between him and Buffy (given that Mutant Enemy had decided to spin him off into a separate show). But *Angel's* Angel—deeply flawed, emotionally scarred, psychologically tormented and hauling his past around like a ball and chain—would clearly have plenty of trouble with his love life without any outside help at all. Here is a character fully equipped to stumble, fumble, fail, learn, try again and falter anew in his love life without any help from a "no happiness allowed" subclause in a gypsy curse. *Angel's* Angel is a character who's going to have a hell of a time just getting into the same ballpark with happiness, never mind hanging onto it, getting comfortable with it or turning it into a lifestyle.

And the frustrating thing about this curse left over from *Buffy* is that it prevents *Angel's* Angel from *trying* to find happiness, as well as refusing to try, beating himself up for trying, failing at it, wanting it, fearing it or fleeing it because he's so conflicted. A plot device needed to resolve the story arc of a limited character is now severely limiting the story potential of a far more complex character. The character arc, explorations and experiences of *Angel's* Angel are necessarily restricted well beyond the true scope of his characterization by a story device invented for someone else.

So long as that pesky, inherited curse hangs around his neck like an albatross, Angel and *Angel* will be prevented from realizing their full potential, wherein the character can explore all the ramifications of having a human soul—including the pursuit of happiness and whatever that entails, though it may well be doomed.

Angel fan Laura Resnick is the author of fantasy novels such as In Legend Born, The White Dragon *and* The Destroyer Goddess. *This Campbell Award-winning author of forty sf/f short stories is also the award-winning author of over a dozen romance novels published under the pseudonym Laura Leone. She is a regular contributor to the* SFWA Bulletin, Romance

Writers Report *and* Nink. *You can find her on the web at www. sff.net/people/laresnick.*

Dan Kerns

ANGEL BY THE NUMBERS

I first became aware of Buffy and Angel 4.5 years ago. I have since watched the 144 episodes of Buffy and 110 episodes of Angel a total of 943 times. I've seen "Waiting in the Wings" (A3-13) 6 times, a personal record. The largest number of consecutive hours I've spent watching Angel is 13. The total number of hours I've spent in conversation with Angel cast and/or crew is zero. The number of minutes in the last hour I've wished I was Dan Kerns: 60.

I N MAY OF 1999, I stood 6 feet, one inch tall and weighed almost 195 pounds, a good 20 pounds over my "fighting weight." Back then I had sandy brown hair and blue eyes, my eyesight was 20/20 and my home phone number was xxx-xxx-8881. It was that phone that rang with an offer to work on an upcoming television series called *Angel*. (I had a cell phone but it rarely rang. Mostly because I rarely turned it on.) The show was a spin-off of *Buffy the Vampire Slayer*, a TV show I'd never seen and knew little about. Since the main character on *Angel* was in fact not a foxy actress but a man, and not only a man but a vampire (vampires mean lots of all-night shooting), it was with some trepidation that I accepted the position of Assistant Chief Lighting Technician ("Best Boy"). Since then, some pertinent numbers have accumulated.

I have worked on all 110 episodes of *Angel*. That's 8 shooting days per episode for 22 episodes and 176 shooting days per season for 5 seasons, for a total of 880 shooting days. Add to that 80 prep days and 55 wrap days. Subtract 6 missed days, one due to illness and 5 just because I wanted a long weekend in Vegas or wine country, and that gives *Angel* and me 1,010 days together at an average of 13.5 paid hours per day. An average of 15.5 hours elapse from the time I drag myself out of bed to the time I crawl back in.

Since the start of *Angel*, I've had 5 offers to work on feature films, all within the first 2 seasons. All were enticing; all were turned down. The frantic pace of episodic television seemed to agree with me, as did the prospect of 9.5 months of steady employment. But who knew *Angel* would last? After the second season, the Director of Photography, Herbert Davis, decided to leave. When the new DP, Ross Berryman, was hired, he received recommendations from 2 people that he interview me for the vacant Chief Lighting Technician ("Gaffer") position. Ross gave me one interview and my first chance in 15 years to be a Gaffer. I eagerly accepted.

As the Best Boy for seasons one and two, part of my job was to prepare sets for shooting and strike (or wrap) sets that were finished. Consequently, I rarely showed up on sets during the actual shooting. Not until I became the Gaffer and head of the Set Lighting department for season three, and took on the job of lighting the scenes, did I actually get to know the cast. Some of them didn't realize I'd been working on the show all along.

Lighting the set can be a very physical job in any capacity. In 5 seasons, I've sustained 16 minor burns, 7 bruised shins, one pulled groin, 3 hairline fractures, 2 sprained necks, countless bouts of low-back pain, 2 cuts requiring stitches (only one was actually stitched), one separated shoulder, one dislocated collar bone, one serious concussion and 2 nasty hangovers. It should be noted that very few of these injuries occurred on the *Angel* set, and all were my own stupid fault.

My Set Lighting department used 1,560 dimmer channels throughout 4 Paramount Studios sound stages (5, 6, 7 and 17), and hundreds of lights of various types and wattages. The strongest light ever used was 100,000 watts; the weakest was 5 watts. Our Set Lighting crew consisted of one Gaffer, one Best Boy and 4 lighting technicians. *Angel* has had 2 Gaffers (one was me), 2 Best Boys (one was me) and 10 regular lighting technicians. There were 2 lighting technicians who voluntarily left the show, saving me the trouble of firing them (names available upon request).

Angel is produced and owned by Fox Television, airs on the Warner Bros. Network and is filmed primarily at Paramount Studios. Its highest weekly ratings rank was 85; its lowest 113.

A typical episode of *Angel* costs $x.x million (that number, I'm told, is privileged information) to produce, some of which goes to me. There are currently 12 producing credits on each episode: 7 executive producers, 2 supervising producers, one consulting producer, one co-producer and one producer, Kelly Manners. Lest these numbers fool you, make no mistake: *Angel* is produced by Kelly Manners. All x.x million dollars stop right on his desk.

At least 2 of the executive producers have never seen the set of *Angel*. A business deal signed at the outset of the *Buffy the Vampire Slayer* feature film gave these two a financial stake in all things *Buffy*. They've received credit and sizable checks for the duration of *Buffy the Vampire Slayer* and *Angel* for doing absolutely nothing. (Names furnished upon request.)

Angel has had 30 different directors and 22 different writers.

Each season has 2 First Assistant Directors, who alternately plan and schedule each episode. *Angel* has had 9 different First ADs.

Angel began with 3 main cast members, has had as many as 7 and will end with 6, and only one, David Boreanaz, will have appeared in all 110 episodes. He is the only cast member to direct an episode. D.B., as he is known on the set, grew up in Philadelphia, PA, near the mouth of the Schuylkill River. I grew up near the headwaters of the Schuylkill 97 miles away in the small town of Port Carbon, PA. D.B. and I are both fans of the Philadelphia Flyers and Eagles.

Three main characters have been killed off during the *Angel* saga (Doyle, Cordelia, Fred), one was transported (Connor), one came back in alien form (Fred), one died on *Buffy* and came back to haunt *Angel* (Spike) and one former cast member, Glenn Quinn, actually died. Several minor characters have been killed or vanished along the way (Kate, the Groosalugg, Darla, Drusilla, Eve, Lindsey, Lilah), and some have returned as story lines or contracts dictate. Death on *Angel* is just part of life.

In 5 seasons, 4 cast members have married. I found out D.B. got married after reading about it in the paper. Charisma Carpenter came to work one Monday morning and announced that she had married her boyfriend in Las Vegas over the weekend. Alexis married Allyson Hannigan, *Buffy* regular, early in season five and honeymooned in Tahiti. The beloved Amy Acker married her boyfriend between seasons four and five in Napa Valley. Approximately 3,700 hearts were broken that day, of which one was mine.

There have been 2 births. D.B. welcomed son Jaden; Charisma named her son Donavon. Much of Donavon's gestation appears on season four of *Angel*.

For the character of Lorne, Andy Hallett has had to endure 4 hours of make-up—3 to apply, one to remove—241 times. Since becoming a cast regular he has purchased one Dodge Viper. He will not admit to any speeding tickets.

James Marsters has one black leather jacket. He has muffed only 4 lines of dialogue, all in rehearsal. He bears a scar over his left eye received in an altercation in New York some years ago. Details are sketchy. The scar is highlighted and accented with make-up for his character Spike. After *Angel* wraps, he plans to go back to his natural hair color as soon as he can remember what it is.

J. August Richards plans to grow his hair back.

The New York Yankees came from behind to win the 2003 ALCS and deny the Boston Red Sox a World Series appearance after D.B. put 7 "Shanshu" hexes on the TV we were watching in the lighting control booth. When I asked him how a Philly native could possibly root for any New York team, D.B. explained that as a boy his father took him to Yankee stadium for his first baseball game.

There were 4 conniption fits thrown by 4 producers the day Charisma Carpenter cut her hair without telling any of the aforementioned producers (names furnished upon request). I'd always thought she was sexier with long hair, though it took me 3 years to tell her that.

There were 2 occasions over 4 seasons that I'd worked up the nerve to ask Charisma out on a date. Both were foiled by the fact that 1) I already had a girlfriend, 2) she already had a boyfriend and 3) in the absence of the first two factors, I still would've never had the guts to ask her out.

There were 2 occasions that I wanted to ask Amy Acker out on a date. See above.

At any one time, there are 758 songs in J. August Richards' heart (titles available upon request), one of which is usually emanating from his mouth in a silky voice whenever he's not acting, eating or sleeping. I suspect he also sings in his sleep, but only his girlfriend knows for sure.

Two days of shooting were lost due to an ankle injury suffered by D.B. doing a stunt in season one; zero shooting days were lost for his knee surgery during season five. Years of playing hockey had finally caught up with him.

Only part of one night of shooting was lost due to a severe cut suffered by Alexis Denisof at his home. Details are sketchy and Alexis isn't talking. Some believe roses were involved.

Alexis did 12 takes of various angles high-kicking in dancing tights with Amy Acker (a classically trained ballet dancer) for an uproariously funny scene that was cut from "Waiting in the Wings" (A3-13). He did not require subsequent knee surgery.

A total of 18 minutes were lost because the entire cast could not stop laughing during their first rehearsal with the Angel Muppet.

I had never seen Andy Hallet's face until the cast and crew party following season two. I didn't recognize him until he spoke to me. There are 4 actors—Matthew James (Merl, who didn't appreciate my comparing his makeup to an asparagus), David Denman (Skip, named after one of our writer/producers), Jack Conley (Sahjan) and Vladimir Kulich (The Beast)—whom I've never seen out of makeup and wouldn't recognize if I saw them again.

James Marsters' band Ghost of the Robot completely rocks.

Amy Acker has gained zero pounds since her debut on *Angel*.

There are 2 American-born cast members—James Marsters and Alexis Denisof—who affect English accents for their characters. Alexis studied in England; James studied in New York, but watched a lot of Monty Python.

I own the intellectual copyright for the "GunnLight." The Gunn-Light is a light specifically adapted, placed and trimmed to highlight the delicately rough countenance of the character Charles Gunn. It never fails to bring an excited smile to J.'s face. Due to my development of the GunnLight, J. has graciously forgiven me the 82 points he lost in a computer Scrabble game because I gave him a misspelled word (word available upon request).

I loaned Alexis Denisof 12 lights and 6 different colors of gel to decorate his front yard for Halloween. He claimed that, in his neighborhood, not decorating was grounds for a thorough T.P.ing.

There was one serious fire on an unoccupied set (Cordy's apartment) that was quickly extinguished by 4 alert crew members. Its cause is still unknown. No one blamed Phantom Dennis.

Producer Kelly Manners has chewed 7,208 pieces of Nicorette and nearly that many rear-ends. He still sneaks the occasional cigarette.

Director of Photography Ross Berryman has raised his voice in anger or frustration zero times over the 66 episodes he has shot, despite at least 264 valid reasons for doing so, many of which were provided by me.

Production Designer Stuart Blatt created a Kelly Manners bobblehead doll and has managed to sneak it into 6 episodes. The doll has also traveled extensively. There has been one attempted doll-napping.

Stunt Coordinator and *Angel* stunt double Mike Masa has suffered zero serious injuries during his five seasons of bouncing off walls, falling off buildings, running through fire, crashing though glass and getting beaten up, blown up, chewed up, impaled and mutilated. He admits to several bumps, bruises, cuts, scrapes, headaches and one hairline fracture.

Special Effects Coordinator Mike Gaspar has blown up 2 buildings, one mine shaft and one car. He has made walls bleed, swords fly, glasses float, cars drop, flames spout, rain fall, heads tumble, sparks fly, bullets hit and blood splatter.

Property Master Robert Anderson estimates upwards of 475 swords, daggers, dirks, knives, crossbows, guns, stakes and various other implements of torture have been used on *Angel*.

Construction Coordinator Ted Wilson has used the same 4 walls to create 7 different sets 6 times. He currently owns 42 various types of saws.

Head Make-up Artist Dayne Johnson has created 57 styles of demons and countless cuts, gashes, boils, warts, horns, protuberances and crooked noses. He also shoots skeet with deadly accuracy, a fact not lost on the occasionally cranky actor.

My girlfriend Heidi Strickler has been a lighting stand-in for 2 main characters (Fred, Spike), 6 minor characters (Kate, Eve, Harmony, Darla, Faith, Lilah) and 16 demons. She has appeared on screen 7 times, once as a mother being protected by Angel (and subsequently eaten by Darla) in "Darla" (A2-7). Her car has appeared (parked and moving) in 19 episodes. She has used my car in 22 more. She has refused my offer of marriage 3 times. I stopped asking after season three.

Camera Assistant Adam Ward won $4,200 in the Christmas party money pool during season three and $10,000 on a Super Bowl bet placed in Las Vegas while shooting "The House Always Wins" (A4-3). He then built an addition to his house.

Best Boy Jerry Mandley has covered my mistakes and made me seem more efficient than I really am 86 times. He has brewed 475 pots of coffee and crafted 331 cappuccinos, most of which I drank. He has 3 beautiful daughters and has to travel 475 feet to go surfing.

Lighting Technician Ray Ortega travels 862 miles from his home in Santa Fe, NM, to work on *Angel* and lives in Santa Monica, CA, during the season. When asked if the time away from his wife and home were hard, he replied, "It's harder being broke."

The 7 regular members of my lighting crew—Jerry Mandley, Carlos Torres, Ray Ortega, Tom McGough, Matt Little, Jason Beck and Jeff Noble—have a combined 14 irritating quirks and 26 annoying idiosyncrasies. (Various behaviors available upon request.)

In addition to 204 quirks and idiosyncrasies (available upon request), I have 64 pet peeves, but my crew (see above) will claim at least double that. They tolerate all of them.

There have been 6,703 gallons of coffee consumed on the set of *Angel*.

There are 17 people working on *Angel* that I hope I never see again (names available upon request).

There are at least 17 people working on *Angel* who probably hope they never see me again.

The entire cast and crew of *Angel* did not miss the irony of the WB Network discontinuing our vampire show to make room for another vampire show (*Dark Shadows*).

Over 110 episodes, I have been given 5 nifty *Angel* crew jackets, 6 *Angel* sweatshirts, 11 *Angel* caps, 2 hats, one bathrobe, 17 T-shirts of various styles and descriptions, DVD sets of seasons one, two and three, one *Angel* tote bag with water bottle and blanket, one bottle of "Vampire" wine with 2 "100 Episodes of Angel" wine glasses, one *Angel* action figure, 3 calendars, 6 comic books, 2 Swiss Army Knives (one was confiscated at the Burbank Airport) and one red bandanna. The jackets have never been worn and still have the tags on them; if they show up on eBay someday, it means I needed to make the mortgage payment.

I have 342 versions of *Angel* scripts, most with lighting notes scribbled on them. I'm told they'll be worth a lot of money someday should it ever become legal to sell them.

I have won one first prize (one drink and 6 chicken wings) for best "Ho" costume at J. August Richards' "Pimps and Hos" birthday party. Photos exist. I fear they may someday derail my aspirations for public office.

I have read 132 books since the start of *Angel* (titles available upon request).

The Set Lighting crew has worked very hard to place and power 991 lights of various sizes only to have me tell them to turn the lights off or move them somewhere else. They have also completed 2,105 crossword puzzles.

I have approximately 1,116 fond memories of my time on *Angel* and about 42 not-so-fond ones.

I owe Director of Photography Ross Berryman 1,000 thanks for the opportunity he gave me and I beg 1,000 pardons for the mistakes I made that he patiently endured.

There is one Joss Whedon.

There is one David Greenwalt.

There are approximately 4.5 million devoted *Angel* fans in the United States, and double that worldwide.

In April of 2004, I still stand 6 feet, one inch tall, but I now weigh 178 pounds and am closing in on my "fighting weight." I still have sandy brown hair (though with considerably more gray) and blue eyes. My eyesight has deteriorated to somewhere around 20/60 (I like to blame staring into bright lights, but it's probably just age). My home phone number is still xxx-xxx-8881. (I still don't turn my cell phone on much.) The chances of a call to that number offering me a chance to work on a new episodic TV series starring 6 talented actors, with one fantastic producer and one incredible Director of Photography that will last 5 seasons and 110 episodes are approximately 12,721 to one. But I still hope.

(It should be noted that many of the preceding numbers are estimates, guesses, stabs in the dark or just plain wrong. Inaccuracies available upon request.)

CODA

Six A.M., just out of the shower and ready to crawl into bed. After 5 seasons, 110 episodes, 1,010 days, 9 hours in a dank alley in downtown L.A. in the pissing rain and grown men hugging and crying . . . it's over.

Angel is finished.

I hope I can sleep.

Dan Kerns served as Chief Lighting Technician ("Gaffer") for the final three seasons of Angel, after serving as the Assistant Chief Lighting Technician ("Best Boy") for seasons one and two. He is a native of Port Carbon, Pennsylvania, and currently lives in Burbank, California.

Roxanne Longstreet Conrad

WELCOME TO WOLFRAM & HART: THE SEMI-COMPLETE GUIDE TO EVIL

In business school I majored in Evil. They didn't call it Evil, of course; they called it "strategy," or "corporate finance," or sometimes "business ethics." Many of us have long felt there was something familiar about Wolfram & Hart. Thanks to Roxanne Longstreet Conrad, we now know why.

TO:	Champions, all dimensions
CC:	Seers
FROM:	TPTB
RE:	Wolfram & Hart Materials

The following was obtained by one of our agents at great personal risk of life and limb. (Actually, it wasn't so much "risk" as "loss," but them's the breaks in the fight against evil, people.) These are the contents of a briefcase, possibly from a low-level attorney new to the firm.

Our final analysis appears at the end of the inventory.

INVENTORY:

Item 1:   *One (1) Wolfram & Hart Employee Orientation Manual, blood-stained but apparently complete.*

W&H

WOLFRAM & HART

Welcome to a world of opportunity at Wolfram & Hart.

Wolfram & Hart is the largest law firm in the known universe, spanning all dimensions containing sentient life (and a few that are still in question). We employ millions across space and time, offering chances for fulfillment and job satisfaction as well as personal wealth and power.

OUR MISSION

To be the driving force for evil by providing top-quality legal advice and services to demons and mortals alike who seek to dominate and destroy good in all its forms

OUR VISION

Wolfram & Hart is committed to facilitating efforts that will enhance the death and destruction of the forces of good.

To achieve these goals, Wolfram & Hart will actively work to:

- promote integration of evil into the daily lives of sentient beings everywhere
- strengthen partnerships with hellbeasts and collaborate with hellgods, health care providers, governmental agencies, insurance agencies and other entities of an evil nature
- support locally-based responsibility for the downfall of the community—evil begins at home!

Our vision for the future is one in which evil is viewed as more than just the delivery of death and mayhem. Our broader public view also includes strengthening the fabric of evil communities in all dimensions. Problem solving for the apocalypse will not occur in isolation, but in concert with solving the social, economic and other challenges that exist in the evil community.

YOUR RIGHTS AND RESPONSIBILITIES

Your rights at Wolfram & Hart are of no real concern to us. You have the right to an attorney. (A small jest; you don't, actually, unless you hold some major blackmail material over a superior.) But you *do* have the right to succeed at W&H by any means necessary, which include, but are not limited to:

- treachery
- assassination
- coup
- cabal
- cross-functional team formation
- favoritism
- nepotism
- sexual harassment
- discrimination
- blackmail
- torture
- outstanding performance of your duties

Your responsibilities to W&H are simple: You exist to serve us. We may call upon you at any time, 24/7/365, both in your lifetime and beyond. Your contract requires surrender of your immortal soul to us, and that's not just boilerplate. It's a commitment we take very seriously.

HOW ARE WE DOING? THE W&H STRATEGY AND SCORECARD

Obviously, the rise of certain forces for good (hereinafter referred to as "the opposition") have threatened our dominant market position. W&H has faced significant challenges to create and develop the competencies required for this newly competitive market.

By implementing a new partnering relationship with our major clients (e.g., *The First Evil, Microsoft, Vardath & Yog-Sothoth, LLC*), W&H

has advanced the cause of destruction by rethinking its physical implementation processes. Using the Evil Vertical Integration Leverage model (EVIL), we have helped clients use their skills, methodologies, knowledge, capital and experiences to align people, processes and technology in support of its overall strategy within a Program Management framework.

We convened a diverse cross-spectrum of criminal analysts and best demons, along with W&H consultants with deep skills in the apocalypse facilitation industry, to engage in a five-year itinerary of meetings in order to leverage their personal knowledge capital, both tacit and explicit, and to enable them to synergize with each other in order to achieve the implicit goals of successfully architecting and implementing an enterprise-wide value framework across the continuum of destructive cross-median processes.

These meetings were held in intimidating, marginally-survivable settings, enabling and creating an impactful environment which was strategically based, industry-focused and built upon a consistent, clear and unified market message aligned with W&H's mission, vision and core values. This was conducive towards the creation of a total business integration solution and the visualization of a cross-universe strategic initiative.

In short, Wolfram & Hart helped evil change its essential paradigms in order to become more successful at driving evil to the bottom line, resulting in clear, measurable and provable results.

Please see the secure server for current cockpit charts and up-to-the-minute measures of our success, and remember that each point on the chart equates to the blood sacrifice of an underperforming staff member.

FACILITY RULES

- **Covered parking is strictly regulated.** Vehicles parked in assigned spaces without authorization will be fed to violators one part at a time.
- **Please note that our parking areas are clean and well-lit.** This is so that you can clearly see the ravening demons who randomly roam our grounds before they eviscerate you. (Please note: Your chances of being eviscerated are slightly less than being struck by lightning, but as we have lightning attractors placed randomly throughout the facility, this should not reassure you.)

- **Driving while on company business.** We encourage our employees to drive while intoxicated, impaired, insane, under the control of a demonic power and/or while on mobile phones. We strongly discourage the use of defensive driving, seatbelts and protective equipment, including helmets.
- **Wear your ID badges at all times.** These are color-coded to identify which areas of the facility you are allowed to access. At random intervals, we hold drawings for each color for a trip for two to an exotic destination, such as Jamaica or Quar-toth. Very occasionally, in the event of budget cuts, these drawings also allow you to participate in our headcount reduction program. If your access badge at any point fails to work, please don't try to run. It won't do you any good.
- **We have an aggressive weapons policy.** We encourage all employees to conceal weapons on their persons, and to use them if the situation warrants. However, please note that if you are discovered with concealed weapons on your person by an authorized W&H weapons sweep team, you will be sacrificed to the BloodGod (7th floor, next to the Casual Café).
- **Office hours.** Our office hours are from 9 A.M. to 5 P.M., but consider yourself on permanent call. Evil never sleeps, and neither should you. Please consider having your sleep removed at the earliest possible opportunity—visit our friendly surgical consultants on the 5th floor for assistance.
- **Dress code.** Obviously, we encourage business professional dress. If this is not practical because of your physical limitations (e.g., slug monster, Tarth demon, etc.) then please consult with HR on appropriate ornamentation. No clip-on ties. No bow ties, unless you are in the R&D division or IT Services. Remember: the snappier the look, the better chance you have of surviving the day. Pretty is as pretty does, but frankly, it does a heck of a lot better than ugly when it comes to Team Evil.
- **Neatness counts.** Even though we're evil, there are some virtues we adhere to. Please be sure to leave your desk clean and uncluttered at all times; we wouldn't want anyone to suppose there was actual *work* being performed. Personal items are not only discouraged, they are punishable by death. If you want to stand out from the soul-sucking, identity-crushing machine, get hired by the opposition. They'll let you waste your time and energy on Dilbert dolls and Precious Moments figurines.

EMERGENCY EVACUATION PLAN

In the event of an emergency (fire, mystical attack, rampaging coworkers, visiting Senior Partners finding the coffeepot empty) please sit down at your desks and do not attempt to evacuate the building. We're fully insured in the event of your death, dismemberment or de-ensoulment.

If you are asked by Senior Management to leave the building, please use the marked exits, which will either deliver you to outside safety or into the bowels of Hell, depending on the day of the week. (Calendars are still being formulated in committee.)

COMPANY STRUCTURE

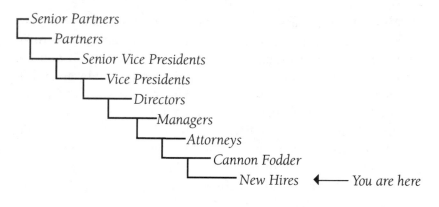

Senior Partners
Partners
Senior Vice Presidents
Vice Presidents
Directors
Managers
Attorneys
Cannon Fodder
New Hires ◄——— *You are here*

COMPENSATION

We pay you extremely well. Greed is part of our corporate vision, and we want you to always be dissatisfied with what you have. Angling for more money is not only encouraged but modeled by our corporate Subject Matter Experts (SMEs).

And when they say "You can't take it with you . . ."? Well, with the W&H Compensation Portability Package (CPP), you absolutely can. We have banks in all demon dimensions, as well as afterlife monetary exchanges at very advantageous rates.

BENEFITS

Working at Wolfram & Hart brings an exciting array of choices for your personal enrichment. We have divided these into two categories: Mandatory and Optional.

Mandatory Benefits

- **Health insurance for you and your dependents.** W&H provides complete health coverage to you and your entire family, free of charge. (Please note that you must use the W&H HMO system for all medical and dental services. In-house surgical services are provided on an outpatient basis only, including transplants and bypasses. In the event that your condition is life-threatening, you will be terminated and placed in an organ redistribution program.)

- **Vacation.** W&H cares about you! We assign you a generous four weeks of vacation a year, to be taken in one-day increments at the discretion of your manager. No carryover of vacation is allowed. Vacation accrues at the rate of .25 days per month, after a six-month probationary period, and may not be taken in the same calendar year as any sick leave. Vacation must be scheduled a minimum of two years in advance and may be canceled according to the needs of the business.

- **Sick Leave.** W&H has a simple, effective sick leave policy: Don't get sick. If you do, come to work anyway. You are allowed zero sick days a year for the first five years of employment. If you survive past five years, you will be allowed one sick day per year, but if you take it, you will be terminated for cause, or worse, referred to our HMO.

- **Retirement Plan.** We plan to retire you. Probably soon.

Optional Benefits

- **Weight Management.** Not that we'd hire you if you were physically imperfect, but in the event that you put on a few pounds in the service of evil, you can opt for our Weight Management Program (WMP). Few survive, but you're welcome to try. If you do, we'll put you to work as a liaison in our Entertainment Division, where advocates for bulimia and anorexia are always welcome.

- **Health & Wellness Plan.** Please see Weight Loss and Sick Leave for information on our great incentives.

- **Spa.** W&H offers a weight room, sauna, hot tub, Olympic-sized pool, tennis courts, handball, racquetball, Pilates, aerobics, yoga and volleyball in our state-of-the-art in-house spa. Dues are minimal, unless you're unattractive, in which case the gym is full.

- **Discount Program.** We offer discounts at our affiliated retailer partners, including Calvin Klein, Wal-Mart, Gucci, Old Navy and GAP, among many others. Unsure whether a store is included in our program? Check out their television ads. If it's annoying or pretentious, it's on our list.

Due to adverse business conditions, we do not currently offer dental or vision care. If you'd like to have your teeth removed, we offer an outpatient service in our Health Services clinic (anesthesia not available) and an attractive eye transplantation program which will not only correct your vision problems, but allow you to see horrific hell-visions as well. See your HR Professional for details.

HARASSMENT POLICY

We encourage it.

DISCRIMINATION POLICY

That, too.

DIVERSITY POLICY

Obviously, W&H wants to embrace diversity in its policies and people. We believe in a work environment that is staffed by a diverse workforce—from seers to cyborgs, from vampires to vengeance demons. Although the majority of our employees in a given dimension will be native to that dimension, we are always open to transfer programs, provided that transfers do not result in (a) the dissolution of the known universe or (b) parking problems. If you wish to embrace diversity in a more personal way, get a room.

SEVERANCE

After surviving your probationary period, you may be eligible for severance pay. Severance pay is based on a sliding scale of the body part severed, and whether or not it was required in the normal performance of your duties for W&H.

TERMINATION

Wolfram & Hart regrets the necessity of terminating any employee, but if it becomes economically or strategically advantageous, we will not hesitate to shuffle you off this mortal coil and into our *Afterlife Program*. Once you are enrolled in the *Afterlife Program*, you will enjoy all of the benefits of being dead without any of the tedious decomposition. You will be required to continue your duties without pause, rest or relief for eternity. See the section on Compensation for exciting news about how *you* can get paid even when dead!

DISCIPLINARY ACTION

At W&H, we have a zero tolerance policy for rule-breakers, unless it results in profit for the company. Here are some examples of misconduct and the required disciplinary action.

Misconduct	Penalty
• Failure to maintain a desired level of satisfactory performance	Death
• Misuse of work time	Death
• Excessive absenteeism	Death
• Failure to comply with W&H policies and rules	Death
• Repetitive disregard of stated rules and procedures (parking, safety equipment requirements, etc.)	Death
• Disregard of authorized work requests	Death
• Lack of cooperation	Death
• Failure to follow work instructions	Death
• Failure to stay at assigned work location	Verbal warning

IN SUMMARY

We want your stay at Wolfram & Hart to be the best—and *last*—job you'll ever have. You can make that happen by complying with all rules and regulations, submitting without question to our every whim and making generous contributions to the charity of our choice (generally, drug dealers or houses of ill repute, but we're also open to investigating new, needy beneficiaries).

Work hard. Play hard. We believe in a healthy work-life balance, especially since the work-afterlife balance will be so much more difficult. We promote excellence, so please, be excellent or be prepared to explain to Senior Partners.

And remember, in the words of Dr. E.L. Kersten, founder and COO of Despair, Inc. (www.despair.com): "You can do anything you set your mind to when you have vision, determination and an endless supply of expendable labor."

Now get to work being evil. We're watching you.

INVENTORY:
Item 2:   *Folder with W&H logo containing a Case Study and Brochure. The following are the contents of the folder.*
CASE STUDY

WOLFRAM & HART

If crime doesn't pay . . . you need better lawyers.™

Client:
We never divulge the names of our clients. But if we did, you'd recognize this Top 100 Evil as a household name with power over your every thought and deed.

Project:
Apocalypse facilitation and prophecy realization through the strategic implementation of a Champion Retasking Program (CRP)

Executive Summary:
A diverse team of W&H specialists worked in close cooperation with outsourced demonic specialists to accomplish the goal of our client: the downfall of The Vampire With A Soul℠, Angel, CEO of Angel Investigations, LLC.

Transforming the Soul of a Champion:
Accomplishing Evil Through Controlling the Provider and Deliverables

BUSINESS CHALLENGE

The CRP (Champion Retasking Program) had several key barriers to success.

Although the Champion in question, Angel, was previously a KOE (Key Operational Expert) in the field of platelet redistribution (under the brand name of Angelus^{SM}), Angel underwent a marketing shift several years ago which led him away from the key goals of our organization. Angel also diluted his focus by forming underperforming alliances with the Slayer® as well as various other organizations and individuals with agendas incompatible to those of our client.

Our client's requirement:
Repurpose Angel to regain his focus and realign him with key Apocalypse® goals.

Wolfram & Hart's Special Projects Division was retasked from other high-level duties to personalize and hard-target the strategic initiatives related to the Angel CRP. The team (composed of key best practice specialists and high-performing demon consultants) formulated a multi-step, long-term roadmap to:

- Locate and reincarnate the Key Performer (KP) who represented the best fit for the task
- Engineer a win-win solution by which the client and W&H would emphasize the KP's unique ability to combine deeply focused expertise with venue-specific best practice knowledge to construct solutions of sustained value
- Eliminate underperforming alliances from the Angel solution mix

A key feature of the KP project was the need for the KP to interact with multiple parties and interests across the evil community and to ensure that she was appropriately involved in, and had ownership of, the eventual outcome.

HOW WOLFRAM & HART HELPED

First, our Special Projects Division acquired the necessary tools, people and processes to bring our KP into the overall plan, by means of a massive Raising Ritual™. Facilitated by the SME (Subject Matter Expert) Vocah, we accomplished three major preliminary objectives:

- Created a Journey Management Roadmap which will address the risk of involvement by TPTB®
- Achieved acceptance and involvement from subsidiary demonic powers and major buy-in from high-level Evil Facilitation Consortiums
- Architected a major transformational approach to measuring success by introducing the *Transformational Scorecard*^{SM}, which tracks body count as a key indicator of a successful Apocalypse Facilitation

> "By combining time-proven arcane rituals with bleeding-edge technology solutions, W&H delivered key value to the client in achieving a complete success[1] in the CRP arena."

INNOVATION DELIVERED

The Wolfram & Hart Team delivered high value to our clients by managing, facilitating or contributing to the following deliverables:

- Raising of the Key Performer, Darla, from the Outer Darkness, by use of our patented, proven Raising Ritual™, which maximizes the focusing power of ritual sacrifice by use of our best-of-breed technology, tools and committed people power. Members of the W&H team contributed not just intellectual excellence but also physical mutilation to facilitate this success[2]
- Positioning our newly-risen KP to operate with maximum impact, focusing her on providing high-impact, high-results somnambulistic operational input to the targeted Champion
- Removing the Champion's support structure in order to leverage a sea change and repurpose him from providing Help to the Helpless (his previous, underperforming goal) to providing Indifference to the Helpless. This was an important redefinition, allowing the Champion's unique ability to combine deeply focused expertise with venue-specific best practices knowledge to construct solutions of sustained value to the cause of evil.

---

[1] "Complete success" is defined as achievement of our stated goals and completion of our step-by-step project plan, with key deliverables met along the way. W&H accepts no liability for the long-term durability of the CRP.

[2] Lindsey McDonald, a key associate on our team, stepped in when our consultant became overburdened and drove the project through to its conclusion. W&H provided him with substantial severance pay to compensate him for the regrettable loss of key assets during this process.

- Launching of our proprietary *Soul Downmanagement Plan*[SM], which culminated in the Champion sacrificing his principles, disavowing his former affiliations, and—most importantly—facilitating the deaths of mortals.[3]

At Wolfram & Hart, we are proud of our role in facilitating the downfall of a Champion. While considerable challenges remain, we continue to engage with our clients to leverage block-and-tackle, best-of-breed solutions to the most challenging problems facing the evil industry today.

[Also included in this folder was a full-color brochure advertising Wolfram & Hart's solutions management systems, people and processes, the contents of which, when translated from business speak, basically said "We take your money and give you copious reports on what we did with it." It was not value-added.]

INVENTORY:
Other items in the briefcase:
- One (1) PDA containing W&H telephone contact list, meeting schedule and downloaded porn
- One (1) tin of Altoid mints
- Twenty-two (22) business cards for "Lyle Ryan, Esq., Contracts Enforcement Division"
- One (1) Beretta 84FS Cheetah compact double-action pistol, 13-round staggered magazine and frame-mounted manual safety with hammer decocking device (loaded)
- Two (2) PowerBars, peanut butter and chocolate
- One (1) invoking crystal
- One (1) Hand of Glory (unlit)
- One (1) shopping list, listing ground beef, Hamburger Helper®, Dran-o®, ice cream and a package of chamomile tea
- One (1) set of keys to a 2003 Lexus SC2004
- One (1) laminated card with the W&H logo, reading, "In the event of my death, please contact Wolfram & Hart's Employee Reclamation Division at 1-800-GET-BODY, or online at www.w&hafterlife.com"

---

[3] Several W&H key players contributed biomass to this great bloodletting, including the former head of Special Projects, Holland Manners, who remains on *Afterlife Retainer*[SM] with our firm and can be summoned from his eternal torture upon request.

TPTB: FINAL REMARKS

Only an organization of pure evil could come up with material this fiendishly effective.

First, they clearly offer much better employee awareness and motivation than we do, and they retain nearly 100% of their staff (both pre- and post-mortem). We, on the other hand, are constantly losing our staff to disaffection, depression and death. Since we lack the massive advantage of an Afterlife Program, we're really in the underdog position.

One other key advantage W&H has: verbing. Their ability to mutilate and bend the English language to their diabolical ends has us at a key disadvantage. How do we compete with a firm that "transitions its learnings" instead of "conducts training"? How can we possibly win market share in the big, bad world when they are "co-visioning" and we are only "planning"? We simply must improve our capacity to obfuscate. Evil is indirect. In order to compete, we must vague up our language considerably.

To that end, we propose the following mission statement for the future:

Our Mission:

To be the driving force for good by providing top-quality champion advice and services to the helpless of all dimensions who seek to vanquish evil in all its forms

While this is eerily close to the mission statement of Wolfram & Hart, it is also equally close to the mission statement of the State of Indiana Department of Social Services; it seems to be a basic function of mission statements to generalize. We do not believe this is cause for concern.

We instruct Champions to take the following immediate steps to rightsize their organizations:

- **Minimize involvement with "the little people."** Outsource individual problems and focus on the "big picture" issues, such as world-destroying Apocalypses.
- **Hire more British operatives.** We believe this gives a touch of class to an otherwise hopelessly out-cooled team.
- **Move to bigger quarters.** Evil respects the appearance of success much more than actual success. If at all possible, move your operations to (a) upscale office space, (b) hidden lairs with secret

entrances, so long as they are accessible to the disabled, or (c) sublease space from a major corporation to offset security and data management issues.

Should these steps be ineffective in winning more market share, please consider a Trojan Horse strategy of actually joining the opposition in order to learn their methods and strategies.

Distributing these learnings and architecting a hybridized solution set may be our only viable long-term option to offset loss of perception and the potential of negative market value impact associated with attacks by the opposition.

Sincerely,

TPTB [their glowing mark]

/cc

Enc.

Roxanne Longstreet Conrad is the author of a whole bunch of books, most recently the Weather Warden series (under the pen name of Rachel Caine) and the mainstream mystery novel Ex-ile, Texas. She continued to BenBella's Seven Seasons of Buffy anthology, and is co-editor for the upcoming Stepping Through the Stargate: Science, Archaeology and the Military in Stargate SG-1, along with partner in crime P.N. Elrod. Visit her Rachel Caine website at www.rachelcaine or her "alternate personality" at www.artistsinresidence.com/rlc.

Steven Harper

JASMINE:
SCARIEST VILLAIN
EVER

Angel has had its share of creepy villains. The neurosurgeon from "I Fall To Pieces" (A1-4) who could disassemble his body, was very creepy. Also very creepy was the demon from "Expecting" (A1-12), who impregnated women with demon offspring that had a gestation period of, what, two days? But Jasmine was the creepiest. Steven Harper knows why.

I USUALLY IGNORE STREET EVANGELISTS, but this one caught me off guard. I do have an excuse—my girlfriend had just agreed to marry me. Spring breezes carried the smell of apple blossoms, puffy white clouds coasted through a perfect blue sky, and my mind was not bent on evading ambush in front of the library. Before I completely understood what was happening, a clean-cut twenty-year-old in khakis thrust a pamphlet into my hands and threw a wide, white grin into my face.

"Are you happy?" he asked.

My treacherous mind, still occupied by wedding thoughts, tossed me an image of a kneeling groom who was completely ignorant of the fact that a mischievous friend had painted "SAVE ME" in white on the bottoms of his shoes. My imaginary congregation was trying not to snicker. Memo to self: check shoes before wearing.

"Saved?" I said. "No."

"Then you aren't really happy," the evAngelust said. "You just think you are."

This little *bon mot* jerked me out of my fluffy-cloud haze. I looked at the earnest young man's face, both startled and puzzled. "Sorry?"

"You aren't happy," he repeated. "You just think you are."

I looked down at the pamphlet in my hand and at last it dawned on me what was going on. Half a dozen responses went through my head—punch, kick, bite, spit—but in the end, I just handed him his pamphlet back and walked away. In the distance, I heard the crackle of paper and a male voice saying, "Are you happy?"

That evening over dinner my fiancée—whoa!—and I laughed about the incident, though it also sparked a bit of debate. How do you know you're happy? I once had a philosophy professor who asked, "Suppose that for your entire life, you thought that two and two made five. Then one day you learned that they actually make four. Did you really *know* before that two and two made five?" As a class we agreed the answer was no—you only *thought* you knew. So couldn't you only *think* you're happy, only to learn that you haven't been? Hmmmmmm.

Of course, feelings aren't facts. You can't prove they exist the way you can prove mathematics. Still, my fiancée and I got an entire evening's conversation out of it. Worth thirty seconds with an evAngelust, I suppose. Not much later, we forgot the incident.

Thirteen years after that, Jasmine came along.

For those of you who've forgotten, Jasmine was an inter-dimensional Power-That-Was, born as a child to Connor and Cordelia. Jasmine sprang full-grown from Cordy's womb and took on a human form that looked amazingly like that first officer lady from the show *Firefly*. Angel, certain Jasmine was an evil demon, tried to kill her—only to fall down at her feet in loving ecstasy. Connor did the same, as did anyone else who saw her face or heard her voice. The entire city of Los Angeles fell to her charms, followed closely by the state of California. The world was next. And she filled me with more cold, creeping horrors than any other Joss Whedon villain ever has.

I'm going to assume you're happy. Perhaps you're even ecstatic or elated, though maybe you're just pleased or content. Hell, my thesaurus lists thirty-two synonyms for "happy" (counting "gay," which is another essay entirely) and only twelve for "unhappy," so my assumption of your upbeat mood has the English language on its side. But how do you *know* you're happy? How do you know you've really experienced joy? Isn't it possible there's some *better* form of happiness out there, one you haven't yet touched?

Jasmine answered that question—there is. You aren't really happy yet if Jasmine hasn't saved you because the only true happiness is what she gives you. Don't worry, though. All you have to do is look upon her and bliss is yours forever.

That bliss doesn't come without a price. Once you see Jasmine, you lose all will to do anything but serve her. Still, you'll have no cause for concern—you'll be purely happy every moment. It doesn't matter that you gave up your job or your family or your home. You're happy to do it.

There's a second hidden cost, too. (When isn't there?) Jasmine gets . . . hungry. Every day, she consumes between eight and twelve people. But they're happy about that, and eager to be eaten. Besides, isn't it worth the price? Jasmine promises—and seems able to deliver—an end to death by violence. With her in charge, we will have no wars, no genocides, no holocausts, no murders, no spouse abuse, no child abuse, no drive-by shootings and no suicides. These and other forms of violence kill hundreds of innocent people every single day, people who don't want to die. Wouldn't it be better to trade hundreds of reluctant deaths for a dozen willing ones?

This is the first reason Jasmine frightened me so much. The desire to answer *yes* is horrifyingly powerful, even logical. She offers a better world at an affordable price. Scary to the marrow.

"To truly be a part of something," Jasmine says in "Sacrifice" (A4-20), "you have to surrender to it completely." This is the second reason Jasmine is so frightening. To have this perfect peace, we have to surrender to her. And we *want* to surrender. Not because we choose to, but because Jasmine makes us want to. She doesn't ask if we want her better world—she gives it to us anyway. No biggie, really. Parents—older and wiser than their offspring—make their children do things they don't want to do to ensure their physical and mental well-being all the time. My mother never asked me if I wanted immunization shots, for example, and I would have given her a definitive *no* if she had done so. But I have to admit it's nice to be free of polio, rubella, measles and mumps. And wasn't it worth the one in ten-gazillion risk that the immunization would do me harm? Jasmine and her followers would certainly think so.

And the love you feel is *real*. How scary is that? When Fred and Angel are exposed to Jasmine's blood, it breaks the spell and they see her for what she is—a repulsive demon bent on gentle, loving world domination. But once Fred and Angel undergo this realization, do they become angry? Upset? Ticked? No. They're *depressed*, depressed at losing Jasmine and the associated bliss. They weren't really happy with Jasmine—they only *thought* they were—but it doesn't matter one tiny bit.

Remember the first time you broke up with that special someone? You have this person who makes you deliriously happy, who makes your heart swell and your spirit soar. Every moment you spend together is romantic, delicious foreplay. The love and passion intensify. And then comes that horrible day when you realize things aren't as wonderful as you thought. He snores. Or maybe she wheezes. He doesn't do housework. She eats these weird, stinky cheeses. He doesn't listen. She has a rude streak. Whatever it is, something pushes you over the edge and you realize you aren't in love anymore. You break it off. But what's this? Where's the sense of relief? The feeling that you escaped a horrible fate? All you feel is a terrible loss in the pit of your stomach, and it keeps you awake at night staring at the depressing darkness. You knew that two plus two made love, until you, like Fred and Angel, found out they actually make four. You'd give anything to have your old innocence back. Meanwhile, Jasmine smiles quietly to herself.

Pardon me while I shudder.

From the beginning, we, the television audience, know that Jasmine is going to be bad for us. Beautiful naked women don't spring forth from wombs and send their mothers into comas without some kind of bad mojo going down. And there's something . . . *sinister* about Jasmine's perfect serenity. Part of it we can chalk up to Gina Torres's wonderful acting. The rest, however, comes from Jasmine's very premise.

Notice how in the beginning she never actually tells anyone to commit violence in her name, yet doesn't go out of her way to discourage it. She merely acknowledges it. When Fred is accidentally exposed to Jasmine's blood in "Shiny Happy People" (A4-18), breaking Jasmine's hold on her, Jasmine professes continued affection for Fred even as Gunn and Wesley show their willingness to hunt Fred down and hurt her.

JASMINE: There's nowhere to run, dear [Fred]. My love is all
    around you.
WESLEY (TO JASMINE): What do you want us to do?
JASMINE: You already know.

Being surrounded by love never sounded so sinister.

The rest of Jasmine's followers also find violence in her commands. There are plenty of people around her who are willing to take Jasmine's message of peace, love and acceptance and twist it into something violent.

Does this sound familiar to anyone else? It should. Bump my street evAngelust up a few notches and you have a perfect match for Gunn, Wesley and the other followers. Jasmine and her devoted are clearly meant to be a mirror image for Jesus and some of his more far-flung fanatics.

Before we go any further with this line of thought, let me point out that I didn't write, direct or produce a single episode of *Angel*. I'm only pointing out what I'm seeing in someone else's work. So please don't plaster my house with Chick pamphlets, okay? Besides, mirrors show everything the same but *backwards*. Take a look at what follows.

Jasmine. Jesus. Okay, you've already noticed that the names are similar. So are some of the things they both say:

JASMINE: With my help, all things are possible ("Shiny Happy
    People," A4-18).
JESUS: With God, all things are possible (Mark 10:27).

Jasmine later admonishes to Connor that his pain is not his own, that she wants all of it. In a similar vein, Jesus says, "Peace I leave with you. . . . Do not let your heart be troubled, nor let it be fearful" (John 14:27). And when Angel visits Jasmine's home dimension, one of the scorpion-creatures says of her, "Love is sacrifice" ("Sacrifice," A4-20). Rather similar to, "For God so loved the world that He gave His only begotten Son, that whoever believes in Him should not perish but have everlasting life" (John 3:16). The words are different, but the concept is the same.

Christian doctrine also preaches that Jesus' blood washes away sin. Jasmine's blood washes away Fred's false belief. Fred even encounters Jasmine's blood while trying to hand-wash that very substance off one of Jasmine's shirts.

Meanwhile, Jasmine's followers take on a wild-eyed fanaticism similar to the kind that powered the Inquisition. When people like Fred turn out to be unwilling to hear Jasmine's message, her followers react first with disbelief, then hostility. They see unbelievers as dangerous. Wesley, still under Jasmine's influence, describes Fred as a siren who'll lure people away from Jasmine onto "the rocks of heresy." Fred becomes to Jasmine's followers as Jews and witches were to the Inquisition—someone to be hunted down and exterminated.

To remain safe, many Jews took their beliefs underground. Fred, for her part, goes into the sewers to hide. The sewers are also where Angel, Gunn, Wesley and Lorne eventually go once they're free of Jasmine's spell, and there they find more unbelievers—a street gang that hasn't yet heard of Jasmine. A true underground movement.

Fred seeks remedies in books, and she visits the Magic Bullet Bookstore to find one for Jasmine. In that bookstore, Fred shoots Angel (note the relationship to the store's name) and exposes him to Jasmine's blood, a great deal of which puddles onto the floor. Jasmine orders the store owner to burn his own building so others won't be exposed to the truth. The Inquisition is, of course, famous for burning books—and people—that ran counter to the Church's beliefs. Scary, isn't it?

Jesus, of course, was not a demon. Jasmine, as I said, is a mirror image of him—the same but backward. According to Christian doctrine, Jesus was the final human sacrifice. Jasmine demands sacrifice of everyone *except* herself. I don't think that Jesus of Nazareth would have advocated violence on his behalf. Certainly one of his more famous sayings is, "Put your sword back in its place, . . . for all who draw the sword will die by the sword" (Matthew 26:52). Jasmine, on the other hand, doesn't stop her followers from committing violent acts. On the contrary, she deliberately turns a blind eye to her followers' violent tendencies. She knows Wesley intends to kill Fred, but doesn't say anything to stop him. When the bookstore owner asks if he should leave after setting fire to his own building, Jasmine simply walks away. Connor hits Wesley, and Jasmine admonishes, "Connor, please. I don't want to see that" ("Peace Out," A4-21). She doesn't tell him to stop, you'll notice; she only says she doesn't want to see it.

This is what makes Jasmine the most frightening: Her followers reflect attitudes shared by any number of people in the real world. We've seen so many people who look at a peaceful religion and see a mandate for violence. Villains like Glory, the Mayor and the Master from *Buffy* are

intriguing but ultimately safe because we know they can't exist. Jasmine is terrifying because she *does* exist—or people like her followers do.
  And they definitely aren't happy—they just think they are.

———————————

Steven Harper lives in Ypsilanti, Michigan, with his wife and son. He teaches English in Walled Lake, Michigan, and he is appalled that the school requires him to teach Romeo and Juliet, *which contains horrifying violence and shocking dirty jokes. His students think he's hysterical, which isn't the same as thinking he's hilarious. He is the creator of the Silent Empire series for Roc Books, including* Dreamer, Nightmare *and* Trickster. *Currently, he's working on* Offspring, *the fourth book. His books were nominated twice for the Spectrum Award. Visit his web page at www.sff.net/people/spiziks.*

Jean Lorrah

A WORLD WITHOUT LOVE: THE FAILURE OF FAMILY IN *ANGEL*

Was your mother a little cold when you were growing up? Your father distant, or too demanding? Was your family unsupportive, combative, dysfunctional? Well, boohoo. You think you had it bad? Just be glad you didn't live in the Angelverse.

A S THE TELEVISION SERIES *Angel* ended its fifth and final season, the only character left from the opening episode of the first season was the title character, Angel. Compare that to *Buffy the Vampire Slayer*, the show which spun off *Angel*: Buffy, Giles, Xander and Willow were present in the first episode of the first season and in the last episode of the seventh season. Is the attrition rate in *Angel* mere coincidence, caused by the vagaries of the entertainment industry, or is it the byprod-

57

uct of a theme of the show—a theme that clearly differentiates this series from its parent?

In my essay, "Love Saves the World: the Nontraditional Family in *Buffy the Vampire Slayer*," published in *Seven Seasons of Buffy*, I argued that in the original series a major theme is the self-made family Buffy creates, and that it is the love between the members of that nontraditional family that makes it possible for them to triumph repeatedly over evil—even when evil resides within one of their own.

When *Angel* first began in 1999, it appeared in the opening episodes that Angel would build a similar family in Los Angeles. After five seasons, however, we see that not only did it not happen, but that it was never intended to happen. Not only can Angel not create a stable nontraditional family—he always has a team of helpers, but they change over time—when he is given a real, blood-related family (through the machinations of evil law firm Wolfram & Hart, an inauspicious beginning if there ever was one) the result is high tragedy that first echoes and then surpasses the Greek tragedies of Sophocles and Aeschylus.

The Darla-Angel-Connor-Jasmine arc runs for three years, from the first raising of Darla in "To Shanshu in L.A." (A1-22) to the annulment of Connor's history as the doomed child of two vampires in "Home" (A4-22), surely one of the most ambitious story arcs any television show has ever attempted.[4]

Reading the commentaries on the Internet, I am surprised that fans do not seem to have noticed the theme of incest in the arc, especially taking into account Cordelia's involvement. Darla is Angel's "sire," that is, the vampire who turned him into a vampire. Angel is Drusilla's sire. When Wolfram & Hart bring Darla back as a human woman and Angel refuses to turn her, they get Drusilla, who persists in calling Darla "Grandmother," to sire Darla.

Angel is seduced by Darla, formerly his sire (mother), now his granddaughter. Little wonder the act does not bring him happiness— upon wakening afterward, he has his epiphany in the episode of the same title, abandons Darla and his flirtation with evil and attempts to

---

[4]Though Angel's current position as CEO of Wolfram & Hart's L.A. branch is the direct consequence of the arc, by the last episode of season four Angel's "granddaughter" Jasmine has been killed and the "problem" of Connor has been solved—not just solved, but entirely removed, at least for everyone not Angel or the viewing audience. Connor's appearance late in season five tied up emotional loose ends, but even without it, the arc would have remained complete.

return to Angel Investigations. (His return recalls not Greek tragedy but the parable of the Prodigal Son: he asks to return not as the boss, but as an employee.) His turn towards the light is too late, however—Connor's life, unbeknownst to either parent, has begun.

Meanwhile, the second season diverts into the Pylea arc ("Belonging," A2-19; "Over the Rainbow," A2-20; "Through the Looking Glass," A2-21; "There's No Place Like Plrtz Glrb," A2-22). These episodes, which might appear to be just comic wheel spinning to fill the nine months that must pass before Darla can be brought back, underscore the "failed family" theme of *Angel* and foreshadow the trouble to come. Pylea is Lorne's home dimension. We learn, while there, that he left Pylea largely because of the rift between him and his family—he is an embarrassment to them, especially his mother. In Pylea they rescue Fred, who joins Angel Investigations and proves to be the only one in the group with a loving, functional family. In "Fredless" (A3-5), Fred's parents appear—and when Fred is ashamed to see them everyone assumes they must have mistreated her, showing what everyone else's home life has been. This is the sole example in the series of unconditional love of parents for their child in a normal family. It reassures us that, outside at least, there is a world where loving families exist. Not for Angel, however: only two episodes later, Darla appears, pregnant with Angel's child ("Offspring," A3-7).

Angel Investigations has been trying to determine the meaning of a prophecy concerning the imminent arrival of a being who will have a profound impact on the world. At the time it seems the subject of the prophecy is the impossible child of two vampires, and the phrase "there will be no birth, only death" is played out as Darla, experiencing love for the first time in her existence, stakes herself, sacrificing her life to save her child's. (Love on *Angel* seems always to mean sacrifice.) No sooner does Angel have his son than the revenging Holtz, whose family Angel destroyed when he was Angelus, seeks to take the child.

Note that Holtz did not begin as an inherently evil person. He made an enemy of Angelus because he was a vampire slayer (small "s"), which in the *Buffy*verse is ostensibly a heroic occupation. Angelus did not simply kill all of Holtz's family, but turned the man's beloved daughter into a vampire, forcing her father to kill her. Angelus made the classic mistake of leaving Holtz nothing to lose.

As Holtz stalks Angel and the baby he names Connor, Wesley discovers another prophecy: "The father will kill the son." When Angel begins to be attracted to Connor's blood, Wesley fears the worst. What Wesley doesn't know is that Wolfram & Hart have spiked Angel's blood supply with a sample taken from the baby. (The allusion is to another Greek tragedy, Medea, in which Medea cooks up the children she had with the man who cheated on her and feeds them to their father.)

Not knowing why Angel craves his son's blood, Wesley takes the child to protect him—and walks right into a trap. Holtz takes the child and departs into another dimension where Angel cannot reach him. There, for sixteen years, Connor regards Holtz as his father and is brainwashed with the pure hatred Holtz still feels for Angelus. Holtz never does understand the difference between Angelus and Angel—or else he does not care. He believes that Angel cannot possibly raise a child to be anything but a monster. The irony is that through the pact Holtz made in order to have another chance at Angelus, as well as through the force of his own desire for revenge, the boy does indeed become a monster.

Even though Angel eventually finds out why Wesley took Connor (the machinations of Wolfram & Hart again—the Senior Partners function in the story much as the Greek gods used to, manipulating humans to work out their plans), he does not forgive Wesley until well after Connor and Holtz return. With that return the pre-ordained tragedy continues on its course.

Angel and Cordelia have been slowly but obviously falling in love. Angel has good reason to fear such an event, but Cordelia is not Buffy, especially after she chooses to become part demon in order to prevent her visions from killing her. When Connor returns, Angel and Cordelia work together to try to win the boy's love to his real father—Holtz, of course, has taught Connor only about Angelus, not Angel.

By the beginning of season four, however, we are much less certain of Cordelia's motivations. When she inexplicably returns from higher planes, she has amnesia—and when her memory is restored at the end of "Spin the Bottle" (A4-6), it is not the Cordelia we know, but an entity set on working out its own plans. It could be argued that it is not until after Cordelia becomes pregnant that she is possessed by the creature we come to know as Jasmine, but I find her behavior to have been erratic from the start, and as Skip explains to Angel later that season in "Inside Out" (A4-17), "Nobody comes back from paradise." Angel, however, does not pick up on these behavioral cues—by "Long Day's Journey" (A4-9), he is far more concerned with what Cordelia is doing with Connor. Angel knows that the woman he loves has seduced his son, but not why.

This betrayal has a greater feeling of incest than any earlier playing with who sired whom among the vampires. Just before she "ascended" in the season three finale ("Tomorrow," A3-22), Cordelia was on her way to tell Angel she loved him at an appointment at which Angel was planning to tell Cordelia that he was in love her. And images such as the one at the end of "Dad" (A3-10), where Angel and Cordelia lying facing one another on Angel's bed withthe infant Connor between them, have reinforced in the viewer's mind that Cordelia is the only mother Connor actually knew. Not to mention that although he spent sixteen years growing up in a hell dimension, to Cordelia Connor was a babe in arms less than a year ago. If he had stayed in this dimension to grow up, Cordelia would certainly be old enough to be his mother.

In "Soulless" (A4-11), Angelus taunts Connor (who would not know the Oedipus reference, so it is purely for the audience) by saying, "Doesn't it freak you out that she used to change your diapers? I mean, when you think about it, the first woman you boned is the closest thing you've ever had to a mother. Doing your mom and trying to kill your dad. Hm. There should be a play." The play, of course, is *Oedipus Rex*, but Angel's family is more dysfunctional than Oedipus's! Oedipus didn't know the man he killed was his father (in fact, as all he did was hit him with his crutch, he probably didn't even know he had killed him), and there was no premeditation in his act. It was a simple, clean blow, and Laios got off easy by dying in the road. Connor, on the other hand, plotted vengeance against his father. He intended for Angel not to die a clean death, but to go slowly insane, trapped eternally at the bottom of the sea. Oedipus did not know that Jocasta was his mother when arrangements were made for him to marry the widowed queen, but Connor knew exactly who Cordelia was and took great pleasure in winning the woman Angel loved away from his father.

The culmination of all this anguish is the birth of Jasmine, the fully grown progeny of Cordelia and Connor, grandchild of Angel and Darla. In the episode "Inside Out" (A4-17), Angel learns from the demon Skip that virtually everything that has happened for the last several years has been manipulated by a higher power to bring Jasmine into being.

Jasmine is a far more interesting villain than the usual run of vampires, demons and other beasts. She is a beautiful woman whom everyone, male and female, automatically loves. People willingly do anything she asks. She does not appear either ugly or powerful, like the typical monsters. Only those who mingle their blood with hers can see her for what she truly is—that dysfunctional family theme again: When the blood of Jasmine is joined with the blood of someone else the result is not love, not progeny, but hatred and death.

In the end, Connor vanquishes his "daughter," but his and Angel's relationship cannot be repaired. Angel is forced to make a devil's bargain with Wolfram & Hart to alter history. As a result, Connor is no longer the child of two vampires—to everyone but Angel, that timeline never happened.

There are clear reasons within the Angel mythic structure that this arc could not end in reconciliation between father and son. It is not Angel's soul that prevents him from creating a loving family, but the curse that came with it. (Spike now also has a soul, but no curse with it—and Spike, soul or not, easily integrates into family wherever he goes.) Angel cannot build a family based on love—at least one that lasts—because love is the one emotion truly forbidden to him: His curse dictates that if he experiences happiness, he will lose his soul, and for Angel happiness has constantly been represented as bound up with love. It is the physical manifestation of his and Buffy's love, giving into it, that undoes him the first time. When the Shaman they hire in "Awakening" (A4-10) walks Angel through the process of attaining true happiness in order to loose Angelus for questioning, we see Angel's concept of love has grown in complexity—he must have not only Cordelia's affections, but also Connor's forgiveness and his family intact (Wesley and Gunn working again as a team)—but it is still love, if familial rather than romantic, that is the key to Angel's happiness.

But that fantasy was only that—a fantasy. In Angel's world, people don't come together in a crisis—they break apart. Bonds fail. Angel's whole history has been a series of partings: first from Darla, Drusilla and Spike, then from Buffy, and all of his demon fighting resources cannot save Doyle, or Cordelia, or Connor, or Fred.

If we look at the opening credits of every Angel episode, we see a graphic representation of Angel's eternal isolation. Yes, there are some changing shots of Angel interacting with the cast of each season, but the end of the montage never changes. Our final image of Angel remains that dark silhouette walking away from us into the night. Angel alone.

Jean Lorrah is the author of the award-winning vampire ro-mance Blood Will Tell, *creator of the Savage Empire series, co-*

author (with Lois Wickstrom) of the award-winning series of children's books beginning with Nessie and the Living Stone *and co-author (with Jaqueline Lichtenberg) of the cult classic Sime~Gen series. Her most recent new novel is* Sime~Gen: To Kiss or to Kill. *Look for Jean's Savage Empire series from Ben-Bella Books.*

Abbie Bernstein

IT'S NOT EASY BEING GREEN AND NONJUDGMENTAL

When Lorne was first introduced to Angel, I was definitely underwhelmed. A big, green, singing, sardonic, night-club-owning demon was the last thing Angel needed. Turns out I was wrong....

"THIS IS BEYOND MY KEN—and all my action figures." This line, applicable to so many situations, was uttered by Lorne in "Offspring" (A3-7). Lorne talks like that, a lot, and it's one of the reasons he makes a striking impression. Coincidentally (or maybe not), the line also sums up my feelings on being asked to do this essay. Even though I write constantly, and over the past three years have churned out a fair amount of material relating to *Buffy the Vampire Slayer* and *Angel* while working for Titan Publishing, the company that puts out the licensed magazines on both shows (and *Dreamwatch Magazine* as well), I haven't done writing of this type before. Even more disconcerting, I was asked to make this "personal," which goes counter to my non-fiction

AND MY BARBIE—

instincts—don't put yourself as a barrier between reader and subject! I believe that the first draft of this read sort of like a crime report by Joe Friday (just the facts, Ma'am . . . Sir . . . Thing . . .). But, okay, let's try to get personal. . . .

I have watched *Buffy* and *Angel* from Day One of both shows and enjoyed them hugely, without having any idea at the time that I'd wind up writing so much about them and their related personnel. Enjoyment and admiration turned to powerful enthusiasm for *Buffy* in season five, and then to evangelical passion with *Once More, With Feeling* ("I don't care if you have never seen this show before in your life, I don't care if you've been actively avoiding it – you're going to watch this musical!"). *Angel* I liked pretty steadily throughout first season – but the bomb hit at the start of season two. If somebody was going to set an Abbie-trap for the purpose of gluing me to a TV set, I don't know what could have succeeded more than Lorne.

As a child, I loved *The Wizard of Oz* (both books and film) with its array of non-human characters cooperating in friendship, and loved the *Planet of the Apes* films. I was especially taken with Zira and Cornelius, the characters played in heavy prosthetics makeup by Kim Hunter and Roddy McDowall. (Now that I think of it, the *Oz* characters are also in prosthetics, Dorothy and Toto excepted.) I also spent a good deal of my adolescence hanging out in discos (watching much more than doing, but still . . .). And a trait I really love in a character is the ability to, without in any way sounding self-righteous, express a sentiment that can best be articulated as: "Hey, you! That rod? Remove it from your ass!"

I am not someone who often outgrows old passions. So imagine my reaction to a demon, happily open to almost everything the universe can conjure up, singing disco music, exuding friendship, affectionately calling people on their bullshit—and oh, yeah, played by a guy in prosthetics. So I loved Lorne pretty much at once, even before his character started to develop beyond simply being a colorful means of dispensing exposition and tweaking Angel's personal gloominess.

What, then, does Lorne do for me, for Angel the character and for *Angel* the show?

Let's take those in reverse order. Originally, Lorne wasn't brought on to perform any long-term function on *Angel*. The fairly famous story of Lorne's creation is that Joss Whedon, already socially acquainted with Andy Hallett, saw Hallett singing at a karaoke bar and a few months later came up with the idea for a psychic demon who reads people's auras when they sing. Hallett had to audition for the role, but was clearly the best choice. Hallett says in an interview (okay, mine—*Angel Magazine* U.S. # 3, U.K. # 5) that he believes Lorne's nightclub Caritas is based on the now-closed Studio Café and Lounge in Hollywood: "It was just a madhouse. It was not just like the typical karaoke bar where everybody's kind of getting sloshed and no one's really paying attention. When you were up there singing karaoke, you were the entertainment, and people would jam on the dance floor. The part I loved the most about it was it was such an assortment of characters. I love thinking that Caritas stemmed from that environment. I remember the night Joss was there, and he'd brought Marti Noxon and several of the other writers from *Buffy*. I got up to sing 'Lady Marmalade,' and I was feeling so into it I had to kick off my shoes from the stage and my shoes went flying across the room and into one of the guys who was playing darts. Seeing Docksiders go flying across the bar and hitting Jim, I can see why Joss would have been like, 'Oh, my God.'"

It's not a good idea to confuse actors with their characters. Sometimes this isn't a problem. For instance, James Marsters, much appreciated by both fans and the genre press for his attention to, enthusiasm for and articulateness about every aspect of *Buffy* and *Angel*, is so utterly unlike Spike in manner, outlook, speech and even movement that he's almost unrecognizable off-set, even with the bleached hair. Hallett, however, has a lot in common with Lorne beyond just the ability to sing as though his voice is supernaturally powered. He's the first to acknowledge this—asked (same interview) if he's become more or less like Lorne over four years of playing him, he laughs, "Way more—do you see much difference between us?"

Hallett doesn't have horns and isn't given to psychic flashes. However, he treats human beings like human beings, instead of dividing the world up into real people, work associates, fans and (ack) the press. I'm not sure how much what Hallett is like in real life affects how Lorne is on the show. Never having interviewed Whedon on the subject of Lorne, I cannot speak with any authority on what exactly he saw in Hallett that went into writing the character. As an actor, Hallett can radiate utter malice when the situation calls for it (Lorne is legitimately scary in "A Hole in the World," A5-15) and if this is a part of his real-life persona, it's nowhere on display. Conversely, he can convincingly act warmth when he doesn't feel it; Lorne is a combination of clever writing and an astute performance, not painting Hallett green and letting him loose on the set. But it's hard to argue with the fact that he does have his Lornelike attributes. Consider the following:

It's September 2003. I have interviewed Hallett on several occasions over about two years, we have a very cordial reporter/subject association and it's time for another interview for the *Angel* magazine. It's the end of the shooting week for Lorne's big season five episode, "Life of the Party." Hallett gets home from a long day of shooting and returns my call to set up an interview time. It is by no means late, but I am taking a nap when the phone rings, and I sound sleepy when I answer the phone. Hallett apologizes profusely for waking me up, and I explain I was only taking a nap because I felt sick earlier. Hallett replies, entirely sincere, "Can I bring you anything?" He has just arrived home after spending twelve hours or longer working in prosthetics makeup, he's presumably made himself comfortable and he's volunteering to go back out to a drugstore and proceed to—well, at this point, he doesn't even know where I live—for someone he doesn't know very well, all because he perceives that the person on the other end of the line may need help and he may be able to provide it. I thank him, explain that I'm okay now and don't need anything brought to me, and conclude that Hallett is one of the kindest people I've ever met. (We do the interview the following day. It goes great.)

Lorne, full name Krevlornswath of the Deathwok Clan of the dimension Pylea, is a character who sticks with you, and not just because of his appearance (although this makes him hard to miss). For one thing, most of the characters in the Jossverse who at least start out as comedic figures—Cordelia, Anya, Harmony, Andrew, even Wesley—are funny because of their extreme self-involvement. They don't care, don't know or just plain don't comprehend what anybody else around them is going through. (One exception to this is Spike in his soulless stage, who does comprehend but sincerely doesn't give a shit about what anyone else is going through, unless the other person is Buffy or Dru.) Lorne is just the opposite—he's funny because of his intense *attunement* to others.

However, what does a character who is keyed into everybody else do for the show? Lorne's initial purpose looked like it was to be a colorful (literally and figuratively) and humorous device for dispensing exposition and *deus ex machina* bits of mythology to further the story, hopefully without us noticing too much that this is yet another variation on that ancient archetype Morrie the Explainer.

Theoretically, *Angel* didn't need Lorne or any other new character to tell Angel to stop being so rigid, because they already had somebody doing that job: Cordelia Chase. There is a whole other essay (heck, a whole volume) that could be written on Cordelia's function on *Angel*. Again, this is not one of the topics that has come up when I've interviewed *Angel* writers or even interviews I've read, so I can't say what the creative folks were thinking. What I got out of it as a viewer was that Cordelia doesn't really object to Angel's glumness at first; when she does complain, it's generally on the grounds that she is personally inconvenienced/endangered by Angel's unilateral vision.

When Cordelia's personality begins altering to accommodate her rather sudden (and, in my opinion, uncharacteristic) surge of sensitivity, she develops compassion but loses her sense of humor about it—so now Angel is (still) grimly serious about life, the universe and everything, and Cordelia is grimly serious about Angel's grimness. With this dynamic, we get either someone who isn't noticing that Angel is in pain the way that we notice it, or someone who does notice, but is actually now upping the pain index herself.

The show looked like it could use a third option. Lorne doesn't do grim often and, while he will object to Angel's broody fixations on the grounds that they can prevent the vamp from going out and doing what needs to be done, mostly Lorne wants Angel to relax a little because the vamp just looks so uncomfortable with that rod up his rear.

A case in point is "Happy Anniversary" (A2-13). Angel has fired Cordelia, Wesley and Gunn, disgusted himself by letting Darla and Dru kill a roomful of Wolfram & Hart lawyers, has even tried unsuccessfully to lose his soul by having sex with Darla and is generally radiating enough bad vibes to scare off greater Los Angeles. Lorne, knowing all this, still comes trotting into the lobby of the Hyperion Hotel, singing "The Star-Spangled Banner" and ready for a road trip. Now, strictly speaking, Lorne has a bigger agenda than either snapping Angel out of his funk or getting some companionship—there's an apocalypse afoot, and Lorne needs Angel to do the heavy lifting in preventing it—but the demon won't let Angel simply stew on recent events. Lorne endures Angel deriding him and borderline threatening him as he repeatedly returns to the heart of the matter: What's eating Angel? This persistence would be understandable in someone who has a friendship with Angel, but at this point the vampire and the Pylean demon are simply acquaintances—Lorne has no direct personal investment in Angel's well-being. Nor is it necessary in the larger sense for Angel to be on an emotional even keel for him to save the world. He's perfectly capable of fighting

Lubber demons while thoroughly morose.

Lorne's reason for wanting Angel to cheer up is so simple that with a human character it would probably play as one-dimensional unbearable sweetness. Lorne actually wants everybody to be happy. Part of what keeps Lorne from being one-dimensional is that he understands all too well that it's impossible for everybody to be happy all at once, since some beings' happiness depends on the destruction of other beings, who of course won't be very happy if the first batch of beings accomplish their goals.

Having a character around who actually looks at the universe in this way—that there's more going on than our heroes' agenda of the day, no matter how noble—provides a sense of perspective that *Angel* needs. Angel, for instance, is almost incapable of seeing things in a light that might let him feel good about himself, which means that he's usually got to interpret events very narrowly. Wesley is afraid to be caught looking silly or ignorant or, worst of all, helpless, so he is sober, wise and so stoic that he can't, say, ask for support when he comes across a prophecy that says, "The father will kill the son." We all know how that turned out. Without outside perspective, the characters are all still interesting—sometimes even fascinating—but we (okay, I) wind up wanting to yell at the screen, "Stop thinking of this just in terms of what it says about *you*, you big insert-expletive-of-choice-here!"

Lorne actually fits the pattern on *Angel* (especially for male characters) of rebelling against his upbringing—but Lorne's upbringing was anti-empathy, anti-nurturing and pro-xenophobia. Every time Lorne sees both sides of things, he's sticking it to his mother and the whole of Pylea and darn proud of it.

Lorne's mom has a tendency to say things like, "We ate the wrong son" ("Through the Looking Glass," A2-21), and wail that, in the taverns, she is called "mother of the vile excrement" ("There's No Place Like Plrtz Glrb," A2-22). Lorne did run away from home (and home dimension) to get away from this, but ultimately, he seems to deal with family issues better than many of his pals do. Angel killed his own father; Spike killed his mother *twice* (and the suppressed memory was used to turn him into a supernatural weapon for awhile on *Buffy*, though he's coping better these days). Wesley unloaded a pistol into what he thought was his father ("Lineage," A5-7)—it turned out to be a cyborg, but the intent was there. Lorne regrets his disastrous relationship with his mother, but once he faces it at the end of season two, he thereafter can look at it clear-eyed while still feeling sympathy with what this can do to a person.

When Angel's grown son Connor (another sufferer from parent issues) calls Lorne "Demon" in a threatening, insulting manner ("Benediction," A3-21), Lorne is stung, but then empathizes with why Connor may be so grouchy: "Since you were raised in a hell dimension by a psychopath, and since that happens to be a topic I know a little something about, we'll just let that slide." Connor then amends his words to "filthy demon." Lorne, whose patience is neither superhuman nor superdemon, becomes annoyed and alarmed enough to eventually leave town. (Not incidentally, this may have also really alienated a large section of the audience. Characters can get away with being horrible to Angel—witness Lilah, Lindsey, on occasion Wesley and of course Spike—or Wesley—Gunn punches him, Cordelia won't speak to him and Angel tries to suffocate him—and still be adored, but be mean to Lorne and people hate you.) Even so, when Connor is visibly distressed by Faith's apparent impending death in "Orpheus" (A4-15), Lorne gently encourages the youth to take the comatose girl's hand.

Lorne is somewhat anomalous in the Jossverse because he's almost humiliation-proof. This by no means implies that he doesn't wind up in awkward situations: Lorne has been shot, had his brain drained and even been decapitated (which he survived), to say nothing of being knocked out and/or tied up times beyond counting. When these sorts of things happen to the other characters, they tend to blame themselves for lamentable self-deficiency. Lorne, however, matter-of-factly accepts these incidents as a consequence of 1) being in opposition to violent types and 2) not being a very good fighter. Lorne's not stupid—he understands the advantages of being a good fighter—but he sees it as just another quality, like an ability to read auras: nice if you have it, but nothing wrong with you if you don't.

The flip side of this is that Lorne doesn't hold it against others when their skills don't match his. For Lorne, singing and music has a spiritual, perhaps even sacred quality. Hearing music in his head made him a freak in his home dimension, and Lorne concedes that when he somehow first encountered music (we don't know how this occurred, and it's possible Lorne doesn't know, either), he thought his head was full of ghosts. However, instead of concluding there was something wrong with him, he went through a portal to get to more music, which he describes as "beautiful and painful and right" ("Over the Rainbow," A2-20). If someone can make beautiful music, Lorne gives the ability his utmost respect, even if the person in question is evil. In "Dead End" (A2-18), we learn that Lorne has actually missed Lindsey McDonald's presence at Caritas, despite Lindsey's unwholesome status as Wolfram & Hart's golden-boy lawyer. Even so, Lorne doesn't hold it against anyone in the slightest if he or she can't carry a tune in a bucket (a good thing, too, or Lorne's association with Angel would have ended as soon as it began).

Unlike most of the other characters, Lorne generally doesn't even beat himself up when he fails at things that are normally his strong suits. In season four, when his psychic abilities go badly askew (due to possessed Cordelia's supernatural whammy), Lorne makes several serious mistakes—in "Calvary" (A4-12), he wrongly reads that Angel's soul has been restored to Angelus. Lorne is sincerely sorry and refers to himself as being "reliable as a cheap fortune cookie," but instead of moping around, he briskly sets out to get his mojo back in working order. One big, notable exception to this rule is Lorne's reaction to Fred's death in "Shells" (A5-16)—he's so devastated by his small part (he failed to correctly read Knox) in what's happened that he can't face anyone else and goes off to drink alone.

Usually, though, Lorne is the serenity prayer in action: He accepts what he can't change, works to change what he can and is usually wise enough to know the difference. Tellingly, when the caged Angelus is verbally flaying all of the other characters in "Soulless" (A4-11) and "Calvary" (A4-12), Lorne is the one person the vampire doesn't taunt. This is partly because Lorne sensibly stays the hell away from Angelus, but a more encompassing explanation is that even a master head-messer like Angelus would be hard-pressed to find actual shame within Lorne to exploit. (Go ahead, fantasize about superstrength and immortality. To me, knowing you're imperfect and still being okay with yourself would be the best superpower ever.)

Lorne has plenty of opinions, and acts on them, but he doesn't get them confused with right and wrong. When he punches out Eve and threatens to kill her in "A Hole in the World" (A5-15) if she refuses to help save Fred, he doesn't pretend there's any moral basis in what he is doing; he just wants his friend to get well. Lorne's not a saint or a cure-all; he just generally knows the difference between his personal feelings and the workings of the universe.

At a press event for Angel's hundredth episode, Joss Whedon referred to Lorne as "the conscience of the show." Sometimes a series with Angel's multiple ambiguities needs somebody to remind everybody else where they're trying to go. The authoritative-sounding Powers That Be types generally aren't trustworthy (and—a bigger crime in the Joss-verse—they're not very entertaining, either), and most of Angel's friends are locked into the whole good/bad, right/wrong, black/white mindset to some extent. Lorne doesn't see things in black and white, or for that matter, very much in gray—to him, everything is some shade of Technicolor. His nonjudgmental outlook gives him the moral authority to speak about what's going on, and his manner makes him not only tolerable but actually engaging when he does it.

What Lorne does for Angel the character is force him to take himself less seriously. For many reasons, "Smile Time" (A5-14) is my favorite *Angel* episode ever. Angel, temporarily transformed into a Muppet, winds up more comfortable with his feelings than he's been for ages in his own body. While he's not able to elicit such a literal transformation, Lorne does seem to be able to bring forth Angel's inner Muppet, if only a bit at a time. From the beginning, Lorne talks to Angel in a way that no one else would dare or even imagine doing. It just wouldn't occur to, say, Cordelia or Wesley to ask Angel *why* he picks Barry Manilow's "Mandy" to sing at karaoke, much less sit opposite the brooding vampire, confident of getting an honest answer (in "Judgement," A2-1). Nobody else in his right mind (certainly no other male) would blithely refer to Angel as "Angelcakes" and expect to walk away in one piece. Angel visibly bridles, but he's so thrown at this form of address that it takes him forever to even articulate an objection—when at last the vampire barks, "Stop calling me pastry!" the line has been years in the making (and it's wasted on Lorne, who continues with the blithe sweet talk). The undead hero who can face Hell without blinking and take down whole dimensions of bad guys can be halted in his tracks by a word or two from an unthreatening but observant demon. Lorne usually knows just what to say to force Angel to take a moment for self-reflection, which always takes a little of the ill wind out of the vampire's sails.

Angel often seems to take comfort from Lorne's outlook, even when the vampire can't entirely buy into it. Although Angel is getting better about it, he still has trouble accepting that other people know what they're doing when they trust him; he thinks they don't understand about Angelus, they haven't really envisioned his dark side or they're being blinded by their own goodness. He doesn't have to worry about any of this with Lorne—in terms of dealing with demons, Lorne is a big boy. Angel believes other demons—Darla, for instance—probably understand him better than his human friends do, but the demons are all pulling for Angelus to reappear. Until the appearance of souled Spike on the scene, Lorne is the one person Angel interacts with regularly who both has a full comprehension of Angel's demon nature and is rooting for Angel's better self to stay on top. If Lorne metaphysically knows what he's talking about, perhaps this means Angel isn't totally screwed. Even when Angel isn't consciously thinking in these terms (he seems to have other things on his mind most of the time) and the show isn't reminding us of this fact (also most of the time), Lorne provides a hefty dose of psychological backup simply by being himself and staying on Angel's side.

Even when Angel hallucinates, in both "Deep Down" (A4-1) and "Soul Purpose" (A5-10), it is Lorne who Angel's subconscious casts in the role of confidante and truth-teller. In "Soul Purpose," this function goes as far as dream-Lorne warning Angel of the very real parasite lodged on the vampire's chest. In "Awakening" (A4-10), most of the characters wind up in Angel's *Raiders of the Lost Ark*-esque fantasy, the better to create a moment of perfect happiness that will bring Angelus to the surface, but Lorne is absent from the scenario—Angel's psyche balks at using Lorne to deceive itself.

There's a hint that Angel, for all his longing for a clear-cut world, wishes he could see things Lorne's way. It's not clear if Angel actively admires Lorne's flexibility, but he certainly counts on it. Hence Angel has no hesitation in bringing the pregnant Darla to Lorne, who is solicitous even knowing how destructive Darla is ("Offspring," A2-7). Lorne is horrified by Darla's attack on his good friend Cordelia, but still unhesitatingly offers his bed as a resting place for Darla when she goes into labor ("Lullaby" A3-9).

Generally, Lorne's biggest priority is to try to get everyone to get along. For most of his time in Los Angeles (though not much of the time we know him), the club Caritas is Lorne's baby, and he has gone so far as putting an anti-demon-violence spell on the place to make sure everyone behaves peacefully, whether they want to or not—which allows him to give respite and hospitality to individuals and species that otherwise are too naturally violent to get along with anybody. He gives everybody a breather—and who needs a peaceful break more than those who are habitually violent?

When Team Angel lands at Wolfram & Hart, Lorne is all in favor of throwing the firm's annual Halloween party in "Life of the Party" (A5-5), even though this means socializing with the mostly scum-of-the-earth clientele, human and other. It turns out that Lorne's subconscious firmly disapproves of (and, as the subconscious becomes a separate physical entity, firmly dismembers) demons who wear clothing made from skins of Pyleans and humans. Consciously, though, Lorne will always argue for everyone setting aside what has happened in the past and what may happen in the future in order to get along in the present. When that's just not possible, Lorne will do whatever the situation requires. He's willing to fight a squad of National Guardsmen while armed only with a hockey stick ("Peace Out," A4-21), face down a gun-toting demon hater ("That Old Gang of Mine," A3-3) and even accompany the others to fight the formidable Beast ("Apocalypse Nowish," A4-7). But Lorne knows what he's really good at is helping people to get along and that sometimes this is actually the most important thing he can do. As Lorne tells Angel straightforwardly in "Life of the Party": "You know, Angel, I don't have superhuman strength. I'm not a fighter. Quantum physics makes me nauseous. I barely made a passing grade in mystical studies. But I'm on your team. This is something I can do. I believe this has a purpose." Angel doesn't disagree with him.

The paradox for Angel is that the souled vampire is a lot better at saving the world than he is at changing it. Because he can understand why everyone does what they do, Lorne sees the world as it is, with all its darkness, and believes the place is worth saving in its current condition; improvements would be nice, but they're not absolutely necessary. If saving the place without fixing it is sufficient, then Angel is not a failure. While this has never been overtly discussed in the text, Angel seems to be encouraged by in the fact that someone as perceptive as Lorne can hold this view.

Lorne also helps Angel feel like he belongs, or at least that he's no more out of place than anybody else. In "There's No Place Like Plrtz Glrb" (A2-22), Lorne observes to Angel after an especially ghastly encounter between Lorne and his mother in Pylea: "I had to come back here to find out I didn't have to come back here. You know where I belong? In L.A. You know why? No one belongs there. It's the perfect place for guys like us."

And Angel, who usually can't believe a bright side exists, much less look on it, replies: "That's kind of beautiful."

Lorne winds up allowing *Angel* to wave its flag of ambiguity right up through the end. As season five wears on, Lorne does suffer a crisis of confidence—he just doesn't feel that he actually can cheer anybody up or guide them to any path worth taking; his heart isn't in it—but unlike most of his friends, he doesn't have a crisis of conscience. When Angel, at the time convincingly playing the part of someone corrupted by power (he's faking it, but must fool his intimates as well as the bad guys), tries to equate his newfound lack of morality with Lorne's non-judgmental attitude, Lorne won't buy into it: "Can I not be the poster child for your nervous breakdown here?" ("Power Play," A5-21)

Lorne is not with his erstwhile comrades in the final moments. This is not physical cowardice on his part, as he accompanies the untrust-worthy Lindsey into a melee that could get them both killed ("Not Fade Away," A5-22). Ultimately, Lorne does something totally against his na-ture, because Angel has asked it of him and because he recognizes that it's needed to keep evil from tilting the scales further—he bluffs his way into Lindsey's confidence (or at least his blind spot) and kills him in cold blood. But this is not the way Lorne wants to go about his existence. He has never gotten used to his friends' ideas about sacrifice of others for the greater good—Wesley's near-sacrifice of Faith in "Orpheus" (A4-17) and Angel's actual sacrifice of Drogyn in "Power Play" (A5-21) appall him—and he's not comfortable, not *himself*, deciding who ought to die. So Lorne leaves the fight—and Angel—not to save his own life (indeed, he walks out into a potential apocalypse leaving his gun behind on the barroom floor), but to be able to hang onto his sense of self. *Angel* the series is about shades of gray, and you can't get much grayer than a char-acter who is determinedly non-evil, yet in the end does not follow the course taken by all of his hero friends, because it is not *his* course. The character of Lorne allows *Angel* to state convincingly that there are no absolutes, even (or perhaps especially) when so much is at stake.

Finally, what does Lorne do for me? Since much of the time I feel so odd I might as well be bright green, there's comfort in seeing someone who has long ago given up on blending in without giving up altogether. I have a mediator's nature, so it feels good to see this quality presented as something denoting sanity rather than cowardice. Lorne often gets to sum up what's going on in a scene in a way that makes me laugh out loud, and when he sings, it sounds great. Mostly, for all the reasons I've given for what Lorne does for *Angel* the series and for Angel the charac-ter, he does what all our favorite characters do for us—he engages my imagination and makes me feel less alone.

Abbie Bernstein began working as an entertainment journalist at the age of 12 as a movie reviewer for the Gardena Valley News. *Since then, she has written for a wide variety of publications, including the official licensed* Buffy the Vampire Slayer *and* Angel *magazines. She is currently the Los Angeles liaison for Titan Publishing (which publishes the* Buffy *and* Angel *magazines, among many others). Bernstein has also written and directed two short films,* Inconvenience *and* The Rumpelstiltskin Incident, *written the one-act play* Slaughterhouse *and directed and produced the three-hours-long-total "Making of Robin of Sherwood" documentaries for Network Video's* Robin of Sherwood *DVD releases. Bernstein has a shared story credit on an episode of* She-Wolf of London *and was paid at various times by Paramount, 20th Century Fox, Columbia, Universal, United Artists and TriStar to write a number of feature screenplays, none of which have been made. Her short story "Ragnall Redux" is included in the* Hot Blood XII: Strange Bedfellows *"erotic horror" anthology volume. She was born, raised and continues to reside in the Los Angeles area. She has a sense of humor, but you'd never know it from this bio.*

Chelsea Quinn Yarbro

ANGEL: AN IDENTITY CRISIS

If anyone knows vampires, it's Quinn Yarbro, creator of the beloved Saint-Germain vampire novels. Her detailed and comprehensive understanding of history and folklore are legendary. So when Yarbro turns her attention to a vampire like Angel, my ears perk up. Only trouble is, it turns out Angel isn't really a vampire at all....

L IKE WEATHER AND WATER DEITIES, vampires are found in folklore throughout the world. Almost all cultures, past and present, have a sun god (although there is a small company of sun goddesses), and almost all cultures, past and present, have vampires—improperly dead former mortals who subsist on the living, ninety percent of whom cannot cross running water, walk about in daylight or cast shadows/ reflections. Almost all cultures, past and present, also have were-creatures: living mortals who can or are compelled to take animal forms, or have periodic bouts of delusionally animalistic behavior—often, but not always, associated with the full moon, or, in Asia Minor, earthquakes or other disturbances in the ground. In most folklore throughout the

79

world, vampires are distinguished by their solitary and solipsistic behavior—packs of vampires are the folkloric exception, not the norm—
which requires a self-awareness that includes vast self-knowledge and a
comprehension of their acts, along with a singular lack of guilt or shame
for their predation.

This distinction is one of the significant psychological differences
between were-creatures and vampires, for were-creatures—and they are
not all wolves by a long shot—seem to suffer a kind of psychotic break
during their altered state. Actions are often only partially remembered
by the human component of the creature and what is recalled is usually
abhorred (with the notable exceptions of the Japanese were-fox geishas,
who harken back to pre-Buddhistic animistic traditions, are mischievous but fairly benign and take delight in their vulpine state; Canadian
Ojibwa were-loons, who give literal voice to auguries; were-seals in Scot-
land; were-tigers and goats in India; and were-reindeer in Lappland and
Finland, as well as a host of others around the world); the were-creature
often devotes tremendous human energies to undoing the harm he or
she has done in the creature-state. Were-creatures often run in packs—
the exception being the sexually demanding female were-creature, who
works completely alone—which undertake mob-like destruction, rap-
ine, pillage and other anti-social acts. In other words, vampires are traditionally psychopaths and were-creatures are traditionally psychotic.

Most technologically sophisticated cultures view these archetypes as
being more metaphorical than actual, and most less technologically sophisticated cultures regard these archetypes as literal, but in all cultures,
these archetypes remain durable, operating in well-known contexts that
have their own specific rules and limitations.

Which puts Angel in a bit of a fix, since although he is very clearly
identified as a vampire, he has an element of were-creature in his psychological make-up that creates many problems for his dramatic manifestation. This is what makes the show so puzzling, and often so hard
to resolve, for with or without a soul, Angel is atypical of his archetype,
and this atypicality is ill-defined. Some of the difficulties may have begun with *Buffy*, where Angel was presented from the first as being unlike
other vampires—this meant he had to behave dissimilarly to those of the
greater part of his ilk, from his appearance to his conduct, so that the
audience, at his first appearance, did not say, "Aha! A handsome-but-for-
lorn vampire!" but rather wondered who he was and why he was hanging about. In the beginning, his ambiguities were real assets to develop-

ing the character as a contrast to the usual ravening Sunnydale throng.

That these ambiguities spilled over into *Angel* was only to be expected, but in doing so they have created their own problems. With Angel at the center of the story, developing a strong sense of his difference becomes increasingly ticklish; he lacks the conceptual context provided on *Buffy*—the strong abnormal/good vampire versus standard/bad vampire dichotomy—which necessarily results in poorly defined limits to his nature and behavior. By extension, finding the right villain is much trickier in this sort of situation than when the folkloric psychology is firmly in place and does not require constant shoring up, for suiting antithesis to thesis in such oddly unsettled parameters can make the satisfactory conclusion of story elements next to impossible. This may account for the striking inconsistency of tone that has marked the show from its beginnings: *Angel's* range included dark comedy, moody morality play, metaphorical adventure, urban myth run amok, neo-Gothic satire, surreal social commentary, high fantasy heroic saga, sardonic psychodrama and Byronic romance, to name but a few of the stylistic influences that have cropped up in the series. Not that a show must necessarily be strictly one thing—that would be powerfully boring—but *Angel* has lacked what *Buffy* so signally possessed: a core attitude, a stance from which all high-jinx are addressed. That essential deficit makes assessing each particular episode of *Angel* especially difficult. Oddly, and delightfully enough, the one character who has most consistently exemplified this kind of coherence is The Host (Lorne), whom Andy Hallett plays with such unabashed relish.

In terms of dealing with Angel's anomalous vampirism, Angel's season one interactions with Lindsey were by far the most unvaryingly sustained stylistic and attitudinal episodes in the series to date. The writing from episode to episode maintained a nice mix of edginess and droll humor, with a David (Angel) and Goliath (Wolfram & Hart, represented by Lindsey) conflict at its center, very nicely acted by David Boreanaz and Christian Kane. But the focus was lost along with Lindsey's hand, and the conflict jangled away into Them-vs-Us, which works like gangbusters in World War II stories and westerns but is less successful when dealing with turncoat vampires and an ultimate corporate evil in a low-fantasy (fabulstic real world) Los Angeles.

Wolfram & Hart, by the way, is a wonderful dramatic device, full of all kinds of menace as well as the monolithic implacability of corporate conduct, a literal and figurative monument to nefarious dealings.

It is clearly an opponent monstrous enough to demand Angel's constant monitoring, and deserving of a dire fate. It gives protection to the fell and unscrupulous and champions the causes of iniquity. So why is Angel now smack in the middle of it? Granted, it is a very bold move dramatically, but it also serves to muddy the waters even further. Angel has already shown himself to be highly susceptible to negative influences—Gypsy curses seem to work malign wonders on him, and he has slipped the traces of Angel into Angelusism with some regularity. While suspicious of his position (a very wise precaution, under the circumstances), he persists, exposing himself and his associates to who-knows-what dangers even though he knows the Senior Partners are gunning for him. With everything that has happened between Angel, his associates and Wolfram & Hart, the reasons offered thus far for their close association seem inadequate to excuse the risk being taken; the pay-off, nebulous as it is, does not equal the dangers to which Angel and his companions are exposed.

All of this narrative difficulty appears to hark back to the were-creature nature of Angel himself, and his were-other. For Angel's alter-ego, Angelus, is more like a were-creature's psychotic state than a vampire, a device that permits Angel to behave reprehensibly but still maintain the sympathy of his audience, as if he had an evil twin rather than a predatory aspect of himself that he had the power to control but failed, to do so. It also puts an element of uncertainty in Angel's behavior, a hint of something potentially *wrong* that could have significant consequences for all concerned. While this can be a useful dramatic device, it tends to skew the folkloric integrity of vampire behavior all cattywampus, so that Angel is not as convincing a vampire as, say, Spike has been, with and without a soul. Among other things, there is no apparent reason why a soul creates the partial amnesia Angel experiences when Angelus has been causing trouble—the soul certainly doesn't warp recollection for Spike, whose memory is, if anything, sharper with his soul than it was before he had his soul restored. The limited recollection and intense chagrin are far more typical of were-creatures than vampires.

The other memory factor that is largely missing from Angel's character (and the one I find the most disconcerting) is a sense of age, of passing time. As presented in script after script, Angel seems to be relentlessly late twentieth/early twenty-first century, a man for whom World War II is ancient history and whose social context does not appear to extend back before Disco. Except for his bouts of post-Angelus perturbation, Angel behaves as if he is unconnected to his former life; it is as if every Angelus incident severs him more completely from his past. He may mention the past, but he does not seem to connect with it.

If this is the case—that his Angelus phases cause him to lose memory—it could be pointed up dramatically to good effect. As it is, the memory loss is just another one of those problematical aspects of Angel's behavior. Black leather coat, white hair and swagger notwithstanding, Spike implies an historical continuity that proffers his present appearance as just a stage of his life: a way in which he can be understood by those around him, a trashy-classy fashion-statement and a way of showing his adaptation to his surroundings, not a baring of his innermost self. In *Buffy*, Spike took on a lot of the big questions of vampirism in taut scripts that contained an awareness of the impact the past has on the present, socially, culturally and personally, which is one of the reasons that, despite an unabashed enjoyment of predation that was almost feline, he was likeable from the first. He also was given a great many opportunities to debate ethics—of course he didn't call them that—and responsibilities that were directly linked to the underlying premises of the series. On *Angel* he became a kind of dark-humor comic relief, less inclined to discuss issues of the nature of existence—which, given his early predicament, would have been wholly appropriate as well as useful in terms of Angel's theme-and-variation character—than to pop up to deliver sardonic observations. James Marsters did this very well indeed, but being put in this role tended to limit the wide range he had already demonstrated as an actor and to vitiate a character whose complex emotional nature provided strong dramatic counterpoint to the mortal problems on *Buffy*.

Of course it is a television show and can make its own rules and break them at will, but when dealing with such enduring archetypes it is disappointing to not see the archetype explored to its full extent. If the show was striving for something more than forty-two minutes filled up amid commercials, a greater effort was needed in conception and execution. When you are bucking folklore, most deviations require careful explanation, and it is just that explanation that is lacking in *Angel*—not just for Angel himself, but for many of the other characters as well. Also, having established rules, it is best not to break them too often, and if you do break a rule, to have a damn good reason for doing so. Again, this was one of *Buffy*'s strong suits, and it is especially disheartening to find it so absent from *Angel*. Even with solid performances by the actors, there is only so much they can do when the internal logic of their universe is tampered with, or ignored altogether.

To enlarge on that point: One of the reasons *Buffy* worked so well was that there was always an explanation of what they were up against, and something about what kind of baddie it was (even when the description made little sense, either scientifically or in occult terms, it was provided a place in the *Buffy* universe) and how it could be identified and defeated. The explanation was often modified in the course of the story, but the elucidation was almost always present, and the deviations, when they occurred, were accounted for, including an indication as to why the variations existed. In *Angel*, even with Fred and Wesley, or Cordelia in her prophetess manifestation, on hand to decipher what's happening, they hardly ever had much to offer beyond incomplete theories and obscure references that made Giles' tomes seem, in retrospect, concise and explicit. *Angel* generally left the manifestations of evil without context, which may be very like real life but makes for unsatisfactory drama. The show unfortunately also tended to layer Bad Things one on top of another, with no accounting for their multiple presences, even if such presences were intrinsically contradictory.

As Tamara Thorne says, "You can only have one piece of bolonium per story—it can be a big piece or a little piece, but an audience will only accept one; after that, you're screwed." The bolonium can be conceptually huge (there is a place called Middle Earth . . .) or quite small (there is a gold watch that can stop time for the person holding it . . .), and many events may devolve from it, but there can be only one. Folklore is very much the same way, particularly given that all folklore exists in a cultural framework. There is nothing wrong with shifting folkloric parameters or making new sets of rules for a folkloric universe—storytellers have been doing it for millennia—but once embarked upon, such realignments must be rigorously adhered to or the credibility of the universe is lost, and with it the strength of the folklore from which the new universe was derived.

Easily the most contextually confounding story-line thus far was the whole father/child interaction—or lack thereof—with Conner. (I must interject at this point that this is where my interest in the series failed and I did not see most of the episodes until I agreed to do this essay. I've watched the last season, but have not been as engaged as I had hoped to be.) The amount of sleight-of-hand the writers had to come up with to create the Hamlet-like youth was mind-boggling, doubling back on itself in a manner that pushed the willing suspension of disbelief to operatic levels. To start with, one of the most consistent folkloric characteristic of vampires throughout the cultures of the world is that since they are dead, vampires cannot create or bear life: In almost all folklore—the exceptions being in Southeast Asia and in Lappish heat-vampires—lacking proper life, male vampires are impotent and female vampires cannot menstruate or become pregnant (in northern Greece until the 18th century, sterility was one of the signs of potential vampirism and could require the suspect to be staked before burial). In this regard, Conner's existence is problematic from the start, and the fancy footwork that follows only compounds the rapidly mounting deviations. So the show can deal with teen-aged angst, the infant is spirited away to a hellish dimension with a disproportionately rapid passage of time and schooled in dogma and loathing; then, primed with fury, he is returned to Los Angeles at the height of post-pubescent testiness to put paid to his father, whom he regards as an interloper at best. All he lacks is a skull to talk to. His departure might have provided an opportunity for a more cohesive direction for the series, but that has failed to emerge: I wish the producers and the writers could have agreed on a core stance other than, "There is this soulful vampire living in Los Angeles and acting like the Lone Ranger . . ." that would have informed the series, as was done with *Buffy*. I wish the producers and writers could have decided what *Angel's* rules of vampirism/were-creaturism were, and then stuck to them. I wish there had been some competent, powerful women on the show whose power was not ultimately damaging to her. I wish the series would have tackled some larger issues than was generally the case.

Most folkloric archetypes have not survived into the twenty-first century as active in the cultural consciousness, at least not in technologically advanced cultures. The two that have—vampires and were-creatures—endure for a reason, and those reasons deserve exploration and respect. *Angel* had a unique opportunity to do this, if only the show—or the character—could have found its identity and decided, at last, what it was.

A professional writer for more than thirty years, Yarbro has sold over seventy books (including her Saint-Germain vampire series) and more than sixty works of short fiction. She lives in her hometown—Berkeley, California—with two autocratic cats. In

2003, the World Horror Association presented her with a Grand Master award.

Sherrilyn Kenyon

PARTING GIFTS

Doyle is gone, but not forgotten.

EW SERIES HAVE EVER CAPTURED an audience the way *Buffy the Vampire Slayer* and its spin off, *Angel* have. Each episode and show gifted us with truly memorable and often lovable characters, but out of all the great lines and moral-yet-oddly-immoral characters who came and went, none were more beloved than Doyle.

Frances Doyle only appeared in nine episodes, yet he left an indelible mark on those of us who watched and loved the show from the very beginning. Indeed, his death was like losing a real friend. For years now, I have grappled with why Doyle had to die so early in the first season only to be replaced by characters who, to me at least, weren't nearly as high caliber. Not to mention why the loss of that one character almost made me stop watching the show entirely. I didn't, but those remaining first season episodes that followed left me cold.

Part of the reason could have been that the show was feeling out its new and separate identity from *Buffy*. After all, it's quite a challenge to build a whole new series based on another one without rehashing the same characters and situations over and over again. In this, I give Joss Whedon and the show's writers eternal respect. They did a remarkable job of giving *Angel* its own unique look, characters and plots.

To me Doyle was one of the keys to setting up that separation. He was much darker and edgier than any of the *Buffy* characters, especially at the time the show originally aired. In many ways, he was more real. I also found it odd that, while it wasn't until several seasons into *Buffy* that a major "good" character was killed off, Angel started out with that very scenario. Was it an attempt to add more of an edge to the show? Was it a way to remind viewers that L.A. isn't Sunnydale, and the old ways of doing things need not apply? Or were the rumors about Quinn's personal and professional difficulties true, and just made him too hard to work with?

In the first episode, when Doyle meets Angel, he tells Angel that the reason he's been sent to him is to make sure that Angel is "connected" with the world. In truth, I think the writers and Whedon gave us Doyle so that we as viewers were "connected" to the show.

Very few people can relate to the completely self-centered Cordelia, though to be honest, that first season of *Angel* her character was a lot more likable and sympathetic than she had ever been on *Buffy*. At the end of the day, however, she was still the same selfish, judgmental Cordy who thought she should be a socialite, not a social worker. Angel was still the withdrawn and brooding vampire that we grew to love on *Buffy*, and I think Spike parodied Angel brilliantly the first time he appeared on the scene in "In The Dark" (A1-3): Angel is just too perfect, and rather grating in his Batmanesque "I fight for right and no other reason" mentality. Doyle was the balance between these two characters: one the epitome of "gimme," the other was the epitome of martyrdom.

Or the way I see it, those first episodes were a complex and interesting study of Freudian theory. Cordelia was the Id, the whiny "give me what I want and I want it now" part that we all possess. Angel was the Super Ego, the altruistic, "I do what I do because it's right" part. And Doyle was the ego that mediated between them.

Never was this more evident than in "I Fall to Pieces" (A1-4), where Cordelia is nagging Angel yet again that they need to get paid by their clients because she has "Designer needs" and wants a raise. Angel refuses to take money from people who are in trouble, but Doyle makes the point that Angel should charge for his heroics not because the three of them need the money so much as because the clients will then feel that they no longer owe Angel for his services. Doyle explains that charging a fee will give their clients dignity, allowing them to go on with their lives without feeling indebted.

It was Doyle who provided the true humanity of the series and who allowed it to gain its loyal following. It was him alone whom I related to as a human being.

Angel, while a great character, was very difficult to relate to. The "I want nothing for my services, I'm just repenting my life gone bad and will never again know happiness" attitude isn't something most of us can commiserate with. Now granted, most people have had their brooding moments—ongoing teenage angst has pretty much plagued us all. But how many of us have killed everyone we came into contact with, including our family, and were so evil that even the most evil baddies feared us? (Hopefully not many.)

Cordelia wasn't much better. She represented the worst in all of us, but was entirely unrepentant. Unlike Cordelia, most people are too embarrassed to admit that even while all manner of hell is breaking loose (literally), they still think they should be the focal point of the world.

Doyle, however, was different. He was an average Joe, aside from his being half demon—but even then, how many of us possess some sort of darker side or a part of ourselves that we don't wish to face? Some inner "demon" that we don't want to let out? Yet, just like with Doyle, somehow our higher selves over shine our darker natures.

How many of us, again like Doyle, rise to the challenges life hurls at us, face them, defeat them and then aren't rewarded for it? Case in point, in "Lonely Hearts" (A1-2) Doyle rushes to protect Cordy's reputation and gets banged up. Angel rushes in mid-fight and kicks butt, which for a vampire against humans is easy to do. Doyle fights as a man. But the end of the fight, it's Angel who gets all the attention, while Doyle is completely ignored.

Doyle is our human selves, our humanity. And he was Angel's. It wasn't so much that Angel needed to connect with the world; it was we who needed to connect with Angel. To have a vested interest in what happened to him, and to Cordelia, and everyone else who crossed our screens thereafter.

More than just the plucky sidekick, Doyle not only allowed Angel to find the people he needed to help, he allowed the viewer to find the parts of Angel and Cordelia that they needed to see in order to care about them. It is his infatuation with Cordy that gives her a human side. Up until the moment when she confronts him in "Hero" (A1-9) and tells him that she doesn't care that he's a demon, I could take or leave her. But in that instant, she transformed from a vacuous bitch into a woman.

More than that, she became a real friend: someone we could care about without wanting to pop her in the head and tell her to grow up.

In "I Fall to Pieces" (A1-4), when Angel realizes that he is intimidating and that he scares people, he sends Doyle to watch over their client and to bond with her human to human. As Doyle said, "People need people."

And we, as people, needed Doyle.

Doyle, unlike Angel and Cordy, was always imperfect and caring. Cordy was at times imperfect and Angel was often caring, but Angel was never imperfect, nor was Cordy ever caring—at least not until the final Doyle episode, when she makes a breakthrough that shows she can actually feel for someone other than herself.

Doyle was also complex where Angel and Cordy weren't. I tuned in every week hoping for more Doyle tidbits. His backstory was far more interesting than either Angel or Cordy's. Part of this was, yes, because it was unknown—we knew Cordy was a rich girl turned poor and Angel was an ever-suffering vampire—but it was also because Doyle's story wasn't played for humor, like Cordy's was, or for melodramatic pathos, as Angel's so often was. Doyle's past was real, and affecting, in a way neither of his fellow characters' could be.

And so, when he commits suicide to save the family of demons in his final episode ("Hero," A1-9), it is far more moving than any of Angel's heroics. As Doyle so eloquently said, "I get it now." We don't know just how much of a hero we have within us until we are faced with a hard decision.

In that moment of truth, our smarmy, smart-mouth bookie became a hero—not to make money or gain fame, or to redeem his wicked soul. He did it because he cared, and because it was the right thing to do.

So I have to ask: Why did they kill off the only truly human character? Why kill off the one character who really piqued the audience's heart?

Maybe the actor Glenn Quinn no longer wished to play Doyle, but, myself, I think it was more the fact that most shows don't wish to upstage the main player with a secondary one. After all, the name of the show was *Angel*, not *Doyle*.

I didn't want to believe that theory. But when they brought in Wesley, who was essentially Barney Fife (a comparison I can't help making, since Barney was the name of the demon Wesley was chasing in his introductory episode, "Parting Gifts," A1-10), it seemed to substantiate my fear.

While I have nothing against Wesley, I have to say that he was always one of my least favorite characters on *Buffy*. I often referred to him as a "Gilligan"—you know, the character who, if he lived in real life, you'd have to kill him simply as a moral imperative. The bumbling, I-can't-do-anything-right-and-constantly-have-to-be-bailed-out character. At least he wasn't a blond, buxom female, though his character serves the same purpose.

I firmly believe that if Wesley had shown up originally instead of Doyle, the show wouldn't have succeeded. Wesley, while easy to laugh at, wasn't easy to relate to. Not like Doyle was.

The last episode where they show Doyle, "Parting Gifts" (A1-10), is very aptly named: Doyle's legacy wasn't so much his visions to Cordy as it was his lasting humanity, a humanity that allowed us to care about the other characters, because we cared about Doyle and Doyle cared about them.

New York Times *best-selling author Sherrilyn Kenyon has been a devout* Angel *fan from the beginning. She lives outside of Nashville, Tennessee, with her husband and three sons. Versatile and prolific, she has successfully published in virtually every known genre and subgenre. Writing as Kinley MacGregor and Sherrilyn Kenyon, she is the best-selling author of several series, including* The Dark-Hunters, Brotherhood of the Sword, The MacAllisters, Sex Camp Diaries *and* BAD. *For more information, you can visit her online at one of her websites: sherrilynkenyon.com or kinleymacgregor.com.*

Michelle Sagara West

WHY
WE LOVE LINDSEY

One of the many great pleasures of the Jossverse are the amazing moments he gives us—scenes of such power and intensity they seem to transcend television. Buffy and Angel's post-coital bedroom scene in "Innocence" (B2-14). Doyle's goodbye speech in "Hero" (A1-9). And Lindsey's "evil hand" scene in "Dead End"(A2-18). I always thought Lindsey was a great character, but it was that scene that convinced me of how great. For some, Michelle Sagara West included, he was the best thing about Angel.

WHEN JOSS WHEDON SPUN DAVID BOREANAZ off into his own series—to the near universal anguish of Buffy/Angel shippers everywhere—he said that *Angel* would be a darker show with a less easily defined morality; if *Buffy* was the tale of coming of age, in which morality and responsibility were of necessity tightly entwined, he wanted *Angel* to be something a bit more grey.

But it's hard to do that when you're building on an established premise, with established characters, in an established world. At best, you leave your watchers wondering about the validity of earlier assumptions; at worse, you end up with inconsistencies that rob earlier shows of strength and merit. Plus, in *Angel's* case, you're trying to build a whole show around someone whose loudest legacy is a good, deep, pout.

Still, I watched *Angel*, partly for the guilty pleasure of Cordelia Chase—whose acerbic personality and total lack of tact were delivered in such an inimitable fashion (and just how much she was missed was made clear to me in the hundredth Angel episode, "You're Welcome," A5-12)—and partly because I wanted to see exactly how Whedon and his team would carry through on their hopeful premise.

For the most part, to me, they didn't. For all the reasons stated above, I don't blame them: Having established a universe in which the rules were fairly clear vis a vis good and evil, it's really hard to backtrack without slapping a lot of people in the face. And in the one case where they did succeed, the exception proved the rule: Lindsey McDonald, of Wolfram & Hart.

Lindsey McDonald started out as the series equivalent of an office clerk—or worse, an unnamed lawyer with the now infamous Wolfram & Hart offices. I remember thinking at the time that casting lawyers as the source of all evil was kind of funny, if not exactly original, and wondered where the writing team was going with it. I certainly didn't give Christian Kane a second thought after that first episode.

He got a second chance at partial obscurity when Faith came to the big city, fresh from losing her latest encounter with Buffy on so many levels she was primed to explode. Lindsay took advantage of that, and sent her after Angel—which, as he later acknowledged, was perhaps not his brightest move. But again, in this episode, he was the corporate face of evil. Nothing that really glimmered.

So why, then, is it Lindsey McDonald, of all of Angel's many friends or foes, that captures the heart of Joss Whedon's stated intent?

Episode twenty-one, "Blind Date." The fact that Lindsey is cold-blooded is not in question; in "Blind Date" he gets splattered with a colleague's blood during a review meeting, and he doesn't even flinch. He's certainly not concerned about the fate of most of his various clients' victims—and wasn't horribly upset when Angel shoved one of those clients through a floor-to-ceiling glass window from a fairly significant height. He's a good evil corporate lawyer.

But he has his limits, and in "Blind Date," he reaches them when he realizes that one of his Wolfram & Hart clients is about to assassinate a group of refugee children. It's the first time that he shows any compunction about anything he's been told to do—and it takes him, inevitably, to Angel.

Angel is not sympathetic. Fair enough.

He basically tells Lindsey that Lindsey's concern isn't about the soon-to-be assassinated children; it's all about himself, his fear of W&H, his inability to dig himself out. This has odd undertones of the Sam/Gollum encounter in *Lord of the Rings*, when Sam's heated rebuke destroys what seems possibly the *only* genuine sign of penitence Gollum shows. Then again, if you give me about five minutes, I can find *Lord of the Rings* parallels in almost *anything*, so this may be just me. Lindsey certainly isn't Gollum.

But he is at a crossroads.

His immediate boss, the fatherly and pragmatic Holland, is aware of this. Aware that his almost-surrogate son is having a crisis of faith. Although Holland discovers Lindsey's betrayal of the firm, and his alliance with Angel, he doesn't order an execution—as he did with a man who was secretly in negotiations to go to a *different* law firm (which brings up the question of just how many demonically evil law firms there *are* in L.A.). Instead, he tells Lindsey to take the measures he needs to take to see him through this crisis.

And Lindsey's response?

He works with Angel. He goes to the children's safe place, and while Angel fights the blind assassin, he gets the children out. This episode was the only episode of the first season—with the exception of the first Faith episode—that knocked my socks off.

Kane's Lindsey, coming up from a background of poverty and despair, has learned that the game is all about money and power—and this is probably the first time he's ever looked at the underside of that power and seen that the price paid *isn't* just monetary. But he knows hunger; he's lived it. He's seen his family house signed out from under him. He's seen self-righteous people like Angel who've had it all, who've come from money and who've had the *luxury* of morals.

He's no worse a man than Angel was, before Darla; he's probably not a better man, either. He's just . . . a focused, driven, ambitious man.

And until this episode, he's either held Angel in contempt, or seen him as just another obstacle on the way up.

When, having saved the children, Lindsey returns to Holland, it's not as the lackey—it's almost as the penitent son. And as a reward for his "noble" initiative, Holland promotes him. It's not about Right and Wrong, Holland says; it's about Power—who has it, and who doesn't. The implication—that those who have power can do as they like, even perhaps saving children—is left unspoken.

It's the moment at which Lindsey hovers in the open door of a new office and a position that he's always wanted, Holland's words ringing in his ears, that the show absolutely fulfills Whedon's earlier promise of a more adult show with less clear fault-lines of right and wrong. And when that door closes with Lindsey on the inside, it's a gut punch, and an utterly believable denouement to something that might have been: redemption.

Lindsey's darkness, Lindsey's desire, are utterly believable—and in the real world, or in the adult world of this dark L.A., they *sing*.

Lindsey, in that moment, is what *Angel* the show struggled through its first season to be.

But of course, Lindsey made his choice. And instead of leaving the nuance of that choice to stand, the next episode swings him right back into the heart of darkness, his commitment to W&H cemented. Because of Lindsey, Darla is resurrected, and if Lindsey loses a hand in the bargain, it's because he's facing Angel.

There's a palpable sense of loss in that episode—because we've seen clearly what Lindsey *could have* been—but that's all the final first season episode offers. It's in the second season's Darla arc that Lindsey comes into his own and becomes a human mirror for Angel.

Why a mirror?

Let's look at Angel/Angelus. He was a son who hated his father, and his anger made him a wild, self-indulgent man. When Darla offered him eternity, he accepted it willingly; he didn't fight it, didn't run from it and didn't really look into its face until he was forced to, centuries later, by a gypsy curse. He certainly wasn't any Buffy Summers.

Neither is Lindsey McDonald. Angel pre-vamping and Lindsey both care a lot about themselves.

Lindsey doesn't live in the world that Angel occupied then, but lives in the one he occupies now, and his descent is not so abrupt, his rise not so dramatic. But from the moment that Darla is welcomed into the Wolfram & Hart fold, she compels him in the same way she compelled Angel, centuries ago. He sees her as she is—he generally sees clearly—and in spite of it, or perhaps because of it, he's not afraid of her. If she offered him what she offered Angel—and she can't, being human—it seems pretty clear to me that he would have accepted it, and followed her in much the same way. Then again, this *is* Julie Benz we're talking about.

Lindsey is understandably unhappy about the loss of his hand, and even though he knows the Senior Partners have plans for Angel, he's perfectly happy to watch Angel go up in a cloud of dust. He's also happy to see Angel in torment, and Darla clearly knows how to do just that. Lindsey is by her side as she plots a course for her Angel, and if he doesn't understand that her goal *isn't* revenge, it doesn't matter. She tells him he's fun—for a human. But she's homing in on Angel, as Lindsey watches.

Holland is aware of Lindsey's attachment to Darla and warns him that he should foster "healthy" attachments. Holland isn't above playing Lindsey's attachment for what it's worth, though, and when Darla begins to lose her mind, and her demonic detachment, he plays Lindsey for a dupe, because he knows that an increasingly desperate Lindsey will go to Angel in an attempt to save Darla's life.

Darla *is* dying. Lindsey is drunk when Angel knocks on his apartment door; drunk enough that he invites him in a number of times before Angel actually steps across the threshold. Lindsey gives Angel medical proof of Darla's advanced condition, and because he's drunk and obviously unhappy about it, Angel finally allows himself to believe what he refused to believe: Darla is dying. Lindsey tells Angel that Angel can save her—and Angel knows what that "salvation" means in a way that Lindsey can't. Lindsey says, "You never loved her," and Angel says "I couldn't," adding that he doesn't believe Lindsey is capable of love, either. Lindsey acknowledges that this might be true, but if he had the power to grant her eternal life, he *would*.

And in the end, against both Darla's will and Angel's, he *does*, ushering in Drusilla and once again vamping our girl.

Drusilla is happy about this, because she'll be a mother; Lindsey wants to remain for the "birthing," but Holland ushers him out, telling him it should remain a "family" affair. Besides, they all have a social function to attend, and it's with a backward glance at the coffin that houses Darla that Lindsey is finally pulled away.

Angel comes too late, echoing Lindsey; they both want to be present when she wakes, but again, want to save her from different things. They're different aspects of the same person—but one of them has been damned, and one hasn't, yet.

Angel fails his first save, and Darla escapes, confused and enraged. In the end, her vampiric nature reasserts itself, and her anger at having to live with a soul, at having to live with horror and remorse, drives her straight to the same social function that Lindsey and Holland are attending.

There, in a room full of lawyers, Drusilla and Darla put on their best game faces, and feed on fear—on everyone's fear except for Lindsey's. The smile he gives Darla when she walks into the cellar is a small smile, but on Lindsey's face, a telling one (and a really, really attractive one, just to be clear). He isn't afraid of her. She asks him why, and he doesn't know. She even teases his neck with her teeth—without biting—and tells him that he could die here. That he probably *will* die here. When she asks him why he doesn't care, he's still smiling. He tells her he does care, but he doesn't mind.

Because he sees her as Darla, and he always did.

When Angel arrives on the scene, and he's standing in the door looking at the gathered coterie of terrified lawyers, Lindsey watches him in silence—it's only when Angel turns his back on them all, locking the doors from the outside, that Lindsey once again *smiles*. Another moment in which they're in their strange synchronicity.

But Darla doesn't kill Lindsey. And she doesn't kill Lilah (more's the pity), because they might both be useful to her later. She does play with Lindsey, telling him that she "loves" him before laughing in his face. It doesn't change what he feels for her.

Proof of this comes when Angel attempts to kill Darla and Drusilla with fire. Lindsey finds Darla and brings her home, hiding her from both Angel and Wolfram & Hart. Darla has her own plans for Angel, which involve a ring, the Wolfram & Hart seventy-fifth year review and a demon, but she doesn't share. Instead, she asks Lindsey why he always takes a shower when he comes home from work, because he's never dirty; his response: "I always am." It's insight into Lindsey, or perhaps a clear nod to the fact that he doesn't lie to himself, either.

Perhaps if he could, or did, Darla would love him; she rolls her eyes when his back is turned, but she plays on his love for her by telling him that he's the only one she can count on. He promises he'll never leave her.

Angel and Lindsey meet again during the aforementioned seventy-fifth year review. Angel homes in on a disguised Darla and strips her of that disguise; Lilah screams at security to "stake the bitch" (a distinct case of pot calling kettle black—but Lilah's evil is somehow vastly less seductive and interesting to me than Darla's), and Lindsey belts her, managing to get Darla out of the offices before she can be killed. He's only angry at Darla for not telling him about her plans—because if she had, he might have been able to help.

Lindsey has become all about Darla; Angel has spent the entire Darla arc in that same frame of mind. They are both obsessed with her, with saving her; it's only their definition that differs.

But when Darla returns to Lindsey clearly unhappy in a way that she's never been unhappy, Lindsey finally accepts what he's never given voice to: She's still in love with Angel, or with Angelus—someone she's never, ever going to get back. He asks her to tell him everything, and the implication is that she doesn't. There's a big distance between them on the large couch that can't be bridged.

Lindsey goes out after Angel—and, significant to me, he doesn't do it in his Wolfram & Hart daywear; he rides out in his old pick-up truck, in jeans, work boots and a flannel shirt. This is primal Lindsey; this is the man beneath the suit, the man beneath the ambition, the person that Wolfram & Hart can't—quite—obliterate. He's the man who's walking the dark edge, and he's struggling with each step.

He doesn't take a gun, he takes a sledgehammer—and he runs Angel over a few times before he gets out of the truck to beat on him. He wants to know everything that Angel did to Darla. Everything.

And Angel refuses to oblige him. He turns the tables, and only when he has the upper hand does he tell Lindsey what's on his mind: he's sorry that Darla will never love him. He's sorry that Lindsey will just have to live with that. He's sorry that he didn't try harder when Lindsey first came to him. He's sorry that Lindsey made the wrong choice. Of course, he punctuates these apologies with punches, but there's still a ring of truth to them. In fact, there's more than that. Lindsey is treading danger-ously close to Angel's path—the mortal Angel, pre-Darla—and Angel doesn't have it in him to be a good guide.

Angel smashes Lindsey's fake hand with the sledgehammer before racing off to save Cordy, and says that Lindsey should be glad Angel had an epiphany—because otherwise, it would have been his good hand. Lindsey, beaten, has had an epiphany of his own.

But it takes the next episode, and the closing of the first Lindsey arc, to really underscore this. Lindsey is offered a significant and expensive opera-tion by the company, and he accepts it; it leads to a new hand, a functional one, replacing the hand that he lost to Angel at the end of the first season.

Interestingly enough, the first thing he does once he has it is take his guitar and head out to Caritas, Lorne's old digs. There, he plays for a very appreciative crowd—which is to say, everyone but Angel, who's doing his best not to be impressed. Lorne points out that there's no violence on the inside of the bar, and Angel . . . well, Angel pouts. This should not come as a surprise.

But Lorne tells Angel that Lindsey is the key to Cordy's current vision, and the two are forced into another awkward pairing as they attempt to discover who the donor of Lindsey's new hand was. Except "was" is the wrong tense.

It's clear to me that Lindsey would never countenance the murder of children, regardless of where he now stands in the hierarchy of Wolfram & Hart. It becomes clear to Lindsey that there are other things he can't countenance, and that those things will just keep coming, when he faces the donor, recognizes him and listens to what's left of the man plead for the mercy of death.

Angel tells him it's his choice, and Lindsey pulls the plug. They blow up the hidden laboratory, leaving it a fireball, and Lindsey goes back to work for the final decision on his place in the firm.

This time, as in the last time, he is offered a promotion, and *this* time, he makes a different choice. It's not—quite—a clean act of redemption; nothing about Lindsey has ever been that black and white. But in as much as adult life is never that clearly defined, it's as close as Lindsey is going to be allowed to come, and it's a fitting closure to his role in the series.

Has he been a villain? Yes. And a hero. And everything in between. He's what Angel might have been, had the writers a bit more leeway left from his role in *Buffy*.

So what role does Lindsey have left to play?

Why did the writers bring him back late in the fifth season game? To be another opponent for Angel? To be the Bad Guy?

I'd like to give the writers more credit than that.

Looked at from Lindsey's point of view, Angel has always had everything that Lindsey has ever wanted. Power, strength, Darla (love), purpose—everything. The only thing that he *didn't* have was the corporate respectability that defines mundane power. He opposed Wolfram & Hart at every opportunity, and in the end, he was even *right* about that; Lindsey was forced to see the law firm through Angel's eyes, and he left the life he had struggled so hard to obtain for himself.

And for what?

In the end, Angel has *his* job. It's not the job itself that galls—although he says something to that effect to Eve. Angel, who in theory fought against everything Wolfram & Hart stood for is now *running* the whole show. If Lindsey didn't exactly look up to Angel, he did hold some respect for Angel's position—and it's all been revealed as hypocrisy and lies.

He *could* just accept it lying down . . . or he could make his own plans, and Lindsey has always, in the end, gone his own way. He wants to take Angel down, and he makes his plans for this, using a somewhat lost Spike as his dupe, and using Doyle's identity as a way in. Beyond a second confrontation with Angel, beyond his desire for Angel's destruction, it's not clear what Lindsey does want—but I find the desire entirely within character.

Lindsey is focal to Angel and his season-long struggle to accept his role at Wolfram & Hart—because it's Lindsey, in the end, rescued from an eternity of torment in a special Hell dimension (suburbia, which is quaint, and has heart-rending demons in the basement), who makes the wake-up call to team Angel, pointing out just how they're serving the interests of the Senior Partners.

It's a wake-up call they *need*, and it's one that only an insider like Lindsey could give. Because Lindsey has never been entirely one thing or the other, and his enmity with Angel is almost sibling-like in its intensity.

Lindsey is still the bright, dark light of the show.

Michelle Sagara West lives in Toronto with her long-suffering husband and two children, who, unlike her friends' cats, don't sit on her face in the morning when they want to be fed. She was a finalist twice for the John W. Campbell Memorial Award for Best New Writer, and has published four novels under the name Michelle Sagara (the four books of the Sundred), eight novels under the name Michelle West (the Sacred Hunt Duology, and the six books of The Sun Sword), a number of short stories under either name (or a mix of the two) and an intermittent review column for The Magazine of Fantasy and Science Fiction, *edited by Gordon Van Gelder. She is currently working on a West novel called* House War, *and has finished and turned in her first Sagara novel in a very long time, tentatively titled* Cast in Shadow, *to the newly formed Luna Books.*

Marguerite Krause

IT'S A STUPID CURSE

Among the many pleasures of the Buffy/Angelverse is its occasional foray into metaphysics. What does it meant to have a soul and what does it mean to lose it? It's easy to see Angel as a human superhero with vampire "superpowers." But then there are episodes that remind us it's not that simple, such as when Willow deliberately infects Angel with Eyghon ("The Dark Age," B2-8), to force a battle with Angel's demon. The soul, the nature of self, what it means to be human: these are all staples of Joss's universe. And then there's that curse....

THERE'S NO QUESTION THAT ANGEL is a wonderfully complex fictional character. Since the first season of *Buffy the Vampire Slayer*, everything about him has been designed to be intriguing: a vampire with a soul, a loving, decent man in search of redemption, tormented by the memory of all the evil deeds he committed in the past and determined to make amends. If conflict is the core of good drama, then Angel is the ideal dramatic character, because he is so conflicted on so many fundamental levels. He constantly strives to do good, yet he is a vampire, evil by his very nature.

Or is he?

Who *is* Angel, really? The rules of the fantasy universe created by Joss Whedon seem to present one fairly clear answer—but the actions of many of the characters over the years imply something else entirely. It's possible to shrug off the resulting contradictions and just watch the episodes as they're presented. You can enjoy the clever storylines, exciting adventures, witty dialogue and engaging characters without thinking too much about the mythology in which the universe is rooted. Except, of course, when the stories themselves are centered in the mythology— then it gets hard to ignore the truth.

To put it bluntly: The gypsies cursed the wrong guy.

There's plenty of evidence that the vampire Angelus is a creature of pure, remorseless evil. Angelus is mentioned as a particularly cruel and dangerous vampire in the reference books Giles has at his disposal, and people who knew him during his reign of terror—the Master, Spike, Darla, Drusilla, and Holtz, to name a few—can and do provide eyewitness corroboration of the terrible deeds he committed. If any demon deserves eternal torment for his crimes, it's Angelus.

Unfortunately, the one who suffers most from the punishment of the gypsy curse is not Angelus, but Angel.

Perhaps you're thinking, "Angel, Angelus, what's the difference? Two names, same person." But that's not true, according to the mythology of the *Buffy*verse.

One of the first and clearest explanations of the nature of vampires is provided by Giles in the season one *Buffy* episode "Angel" (B1-7). Giles says, "A vampire isn't a person at all. It may have the movements, the memories, even the personality of the person that it took over, but it's still a demon at the core. There is no halfway." Later in the same episode, Angel tells Buffy, "When you become a vampire, the demon takes your body but it doesn't get your soul. That's gone."

If we accept that Giles and Angel know what they're talking about, there is a clear distinction between a human being, who possesses a soul, and a vampire demon, which achieves physical existence by inhabiting a body after death has caused the human soul to leave. None of the episodes of either *Angel* or *Buffy* have gone into much more detail than that regarding the exact process of becoming a vampire. The few slim hints we've been given provide some room for speculation. For example, in *Buffy*, the Slayer went out on patrol almost every night, frequently to the cemetery, where she would wait at fresh gravesites to stake new vampires the moment they rose from their coffins. This suggested that many, if not all, of the people killed by vampires in Sunnydale would turn into vampires themselves if Buffy didn't dust the demon at the first opportunity. However, other storylines in both *Buffy* and *Angel* implied that a vampire has to consciously choose to "turn" a victim or "bring across" a new vampire. Some humans are just a meal, while others are welcomed into the vampire community. This was particularly evident in the *Angel* episodes "Darla" (A2-7), "The Trial" (A2-9) and "Reunion" (A2-10) when Darla, resurrected as a human, learns she is dying and seeks desperately to become a vampire again. In "Reunion," both Drusilla and Angel refer to an actual "ritual" used in the creation of a new vampire. But we don't see Dru's carefully arranged "birthday party" for Darla because Angel arrives, hoping to stake Darla before she rises as a vampire. The result is a knock-down, drag-out fight among Angel, Darla and Dru in place of the planned ceremony.

But whether it is common or uncommon for existing vampires to create new ones, the essential steps in the process seem to be pretty straightforward: A vampire kills a human, the human soul departs and a new vampire demon takes up residence in the corpse to begin its "afterlife" as an undead monster.

Even though the human soul is gone, the demon has complete access to all of the human's memories, behavioral traits and personal habits. Whedon and the other writers of *Buffy* and *Angel* may not think of it in these terms, but the implication is that memory and personality are stored in the physical body. This, of course, is part of what makes vampires such disturbing monsters. When someone is killed by a vampire, their surviving friends and relations are confronted with a double horror: the grief of losing someone they loved, plus the agony of facing an utterly evil being who looks, sounds and acts almost exactly like the person they once knew. This is shown with particular poignancy in the *Angel* episode "Warzone" (A1-20), when Gunn has to confront and then kill his younger sister Alonna after she is turned into a vampire. Although Alonna tries to tempt Gunn into joining her in her new existence, Gunn's heartbroken "I was supposed to protect you. You were my sister" shows that he understands what has happened. His sister is gone, and all that he can do now is destroy the demon that occupies her dead body.

In a neat and orderly world, conflicts between good and evil could be resolved by following a few reliable rules, such as, "Humans are good;

demons are evil. Save all humans; kill all demons." But Joss Whedon's universe is not that simple. For one thing, vampires are just one of the many kinds of demons that exist in the world. Not all of the non-vampire demons that our heroes encounter appear to be evil, or even dangerous. Not all demons deserve to die. For instance, no one ever shows a serious desire to rid the world of droop-eared Clem. Other random demons in various episodes are accepted by Angel and his companions as informants or even allies—morally ambiguous in nature, perhaps, but fundamentally harmless.

Then there are the offspring of human-demon relationships—people like Doyle—who possess traits from both sides of their family. Demon powers . . . and a human soul. You could argue that Doyle's desire to do good arises from his human half. But then, what about Lorne? Can a pure demon have a soul? Lorne represents yet another shade of gray in Whedon's subtle moral spectrum: He is a good demon. In fact, the only reason to consider him a "demon" at all is that he comes from what the humans call a "demon dimension." In reality, from what we see of his home dimension, Pylea ("Over the Rainbow," A2-20; "Through the Looking Glass," A2-21; "There's no Place Like Plrtz Glrb," A2-22), his people seem to be no more inherently "evil" than humans are. Some are kind, some are cruel, some are loyal, some are cowardly; they have hopes and dreams, family ties and family conflicts. In other words, except for the green skin and horns, there doesn't seem to be anything fundamental to distinguish them from humans.

And never forget the fully human employees of Wolfram & Hart, who routinely commit base, reprehensibly evil acts worthy of any soulless demon.

So what is a soul, exactly? In the world of *Angel* and *Buffy*, answers to that question are frustratingly hard to find. We are told that, by definition, humans have souls and vampires do not. (The fact that Angel and Spike have souls is highly unusual.) People who possess a soul are presumed to share certain common traits: For example, it is the soul that enables an individual to feel remorse and guilt, to seek forgiveness and achieve redemption. Everyday emotions and behaviors also are categorized according to who, theoretically, is capable of experiencing them. "Soulful" emotions include love, devotion and self-sacrifice. But demons are not without emotion. Demons of all kinds, vampires included, are shown to be capable of feeling pride, fear and anger, but are presumed to be incapable of the "gentler" emotions.

Such generalizations, however, prove to be less than reliable. The truth is, the distinction between beings with souls and those without is nebulous at best. Although Drusilla and Spike, in season two of *Buffy*, are pure demon, without souls, they also are obviously, devotedly in love with one another. In fact, when the Judge first meets them ("Surprise," B2-13), he complains that they carry a "stink of humanity" about them. Despite the fact that they are undeniably demons, and capable of great evil, Dru and Spike also are capable of loyalty, devotion, tenderness, concern, love—all traits commonly associated with human "goodness" and the possession of a soul. Spike carries this un-demonic behavior to the ultimate extreme when, during *Buffy* season five, he falls hopelessly in love with the Slayer—not at all the proper way for a vampire to behave.

The problem, I believe, arises from the fundamental nature of vampires. Not all demons are created equal. We have already noted that different kinds of demons display different levels of morality—good, neutral or evil. But even among the specific, inherently evil demons that become vampires, some appear to be more powerful than others.

An average vampire wears its host body the way a human wears clothing. The original personality and mannerisms of the dead person are visible, but the individual characteristics and fundamental nature of the possessing demon shine through. Most of the vampires encountered on a routine basis by Angel and his team, or Buffy and the Scoobies, seem to be of this type. The primary trait of a common, garden-variety vampire is the demonic urge to kill and destroy, with the remnants of the human personality providing little more than window dressing over a core of insatiable evil.

In contrast, when a relatively weak demon rises as a vampire, whatever individual personality the demon may have originally possessed is overridden by the personality of the human body it inhabits. Drusilla, Harmony and Spike all seem to be vampires of this type. The human Drusilla had visions of the future and was driven insane by Angelus, and both of these factors continue to dominate her personality as a vampire. The personality of vain, dim-witted Harmony seems completely unaffected by her transition from human to vampire—the influence of the demon is discernible only when she actually vamps out and tries to bite someone. As for William, it might be tempting to think that his original human personality, the sensitive, emotionally needy young man and bad poet, has been totally replaced by a powerful vampire persona, the callous, snarky Spike. But in fact, Spike's evolution over the years has proven the opposite to be true. Flashbacks that show Spike's origins as a vampire (for example, "Lies My Parents Told Me," *B7-17*, and "Destiny," *A5-8*) reveal that William's loving and generally eager-to-please personality remained dominant after he died. "Spike" is the result of William's gradual reinvention of himself; a tough-guy protective shell for someone who's a softie at heart. Yes, the vampire Spike is a cruel, callous murderer, evil in many ways . . . and yet, time and again, the lingering force of his humanity influences his demonic behavior. You could argue that his love of Dru, or his alliance with the Scoobies after the Initiative's chip negated his ability to harm humans, are simply expressions of self-interest and self-preservation. But that doesn't explain why he falls in love with Buffy, or why, while he is still an undead demon, he chooses to regain his human soul.

One more piece of evidence supporting the theory that not all vampire demons are alike falls into place when Spike's soul is restored. His transformation from soulless demon to vampire with a soul doesn't change his personality one bit. Spike with William's soul is indistinguishable from Spike the demon: In either form, he projects a cocky, "who cares?" cover for uncertain, insecure sweet William.

What happens, then, when an exceptionally powerful demon takes possession of a human body to become a vampire? The demon dominates, and few if any traces of the human host remain. Which is exactly what we see when we compare the personalities and behavior of Angel and Angelus.

Angel, the human soul, is a compassionate, considerate, serious-minded person. When Buffy and her friends first meet him, they wonder about his aura of mystery but soon decide that, whatever his motivations, he is working on the side of good. Therefore, they are completely unprepared for the revelation that he is a vampire, because his personality and actions don't match what they expect to find when they are dealing with a demon. According to Giles' research, one hundred years ago, Angelus was like all vampires, "a vicious, violent animal" ("Angel," *B1-7*). But that is not the individual they know as Angel. Giles acknowledges the distinction again in "Passion" (*B2-17*), noting, "Since Angel lost his soul he's regained his sense of whimsy."

Angel's human friends are not the only ones to recognize that the man with a soul and the soulless vampire are two distinct, separate beings. In the episode "Angel" (*B1-7*), the Master, remembering Darla's vampire child, says, "He was the most vicious creature I ever met. I miss him." Darla wants Angel to acknowledge his vampire self, but clearly sees that he isn't the demon he used to be. Speaking to Angel about his relationship with Buffy, she says, "You love someone who hates us. You're sick. You'll always be sick." Even mad Drusilla knows the difference between Angel and Angelus. In the *Angel* episode "Reunion" (A2-10), after Darla's human self has died, Drusilla waits eagerly for her to rise again as a soulless vampire. Angel arrives, intent on staking Darla, and Drusilla, on seeing him, complains, "It's not Daddy, it's never Daddy. . . . It's the Angel beast."

The same distinction is drawn between other human souls and the vampire demons who later possess their bodies. In "Lies My Parents Told Me" (B7-17), Spike describes how he made his mother a vampire, in hopes that they could be together forever. But it didn't work, because by killing his mother, he lost her. "I had a mother who loved me back. When I sired her, I set loose a demon, and it tore into me. But it was a demon talking, not her. I realize that now." Buffy makes a similar point later in the same episode, after Robin has tried to kill Spike: "I'm preparing to fight a war, and you're looking for revenge on a man who doesn't exist anymore."

Perhaps the clearest and most heartbreaking example of an innocent human soul evicted from its body by a possessing demon is the death of Fred in "A Hole in the World" (A5-15). When Illyria takes over Fred's body, there is never any question that she is a demonic entity separate and distinct from Fred. Early in "Shells" (A5-16), Angel and Spike briefly hope that Fred's soul can be recovered and somehow returned to her body, but Dr. Sparrow reveals that her soul was destroyed in the process of resurrecting Illyria. Fred is gone forever; the only thing left of her is a shell, inhabited by Illyria, and a few residual memories that Illyria absorbed as Fred died.

Even more so than for Illyria, the demon that is a vampire has access to its host body's memories and habits. In the *Angel* episode "Epiphany" (A2-16), Angel has had sex with Darla, and Darla assumes this has removed Angel's soul. Thinking she has freed Angelus the demon, Darla says, "The soul is gone, but it leaves a bitterness. But it will pass." To Darla's disappointment, Angel's soul remains in place in his body and so, presumably, his vampire demon self continues to suffer the bitterness that comes from sharing a body with a human.

Is this the punishment that the gypsies intended to inflict on Angelus? In the *Buffy* episode "Innocence" (B2-14), Jenny Calendar explains,

"Angel was supposed to pay for what he did to my people." As Angel describes it in "Angel" (B1-7), "The elders conjured the perfect punishment for me. They restored my soul."

If that was as far as it went, this could have been a pretty good curse. To be trapped, helpless, within the body of a determined do-gooder like Angel must be the height of torment for a demon like Angelus. But the demon is not the only person affected by the curse. What the gypsies failed to take into consideration (or considered, then chose to ignore) was the effect the curse would have on the innocent human soul who would be trapped, along with the demon Angelus, by their vengeful scheme.

And here we reach the heart of the matter, clearly established by the mythology of the Buffyverse, but consistently ignored by most of the characters: Angel is innocent of any of the evil deeds committed by Angelus. The young Irishman Liam died, and his soul departed before the vampire demon Angelus took over his body and began to torture and murder people. While Angelus is in control, Angel is gone—absent—completely uninvolved. Where was the soul during those years? In "Passion" (B2-17), we are told that the Orb of Thesulah summons a person's soul from the ether. Presumably, the gypsies' curse acted in the same way, retrieving the unaware, blameless soul of Angel from wherever it was and returning it to a body stuffed with memories of all the evil acts perpetrated by Angelus while Angel was away.

Angel, the human soul, isn't a complete innocent. Before he became a vampire, Liam seems to have been a lazy, self-centered jerk. And in the decades since his soul was restored, there's no doubt Angel has made some morally questionable decisions; imprisoning a crowd of Wolfram & Hart lawyers in a room to be killed by Darla and Drusilla ("Reunion," A2-10) is one good example. But the gypsies knew nothing of young Liam's sins or of the moral dilemmas Angel might face in the future. Their single-minded goal was to punish Angelus.

The gypsy curse trapped Angelus. It also trapped Angel. In the blink of an eye, Angel, a human soul capable of feeling guilt and remorse, was burdened with the intimate memory of decades of bloodshed, rape, pillage and a host of other creative demonic atrocities. Angel wasn't responsible for any of those acts, but, apparently because of the connection between memories and physical form, once his soul returns to his body Angel remembers everything Angelus did—and, as illogical and unjust as it may be, takes the blame onto himself.

In fact, it seems that Angel never questions whether or not he deserves to suffer for things he didn't do. When he first describes his situation to Buffy in "Angel" (B1-7), their conversation goes like this:

ANGEL: The elders conjured the perfect punishment for me. They restored my soul.

BUFFY: What? They were all out of boils and blinding torment?

ANGEL: When you become a vampire, the demon takes your body but it doesn't get your soul. That's gone. No conscience, no remorse. It's an easy way to live. You have no idea what it's like to have done the things I've done—and care.

Angelus did the deeds, and never cared at all. So the gypsies retrieve Angel's soul, placing the terrible burden of the demon's actions on his human shoulders.

Jenny's Uncle Enjos admits that the way they chose to punish the vampire who hurt them would not be considered reasonable by most people: "It is not justice we serve, it is vengeance." For an average non-gypsy, he says, "Vengeance is a verb, an idea, payback, one thing for another, like commerce. Not with us. . . . Vengeance is a living thing" ("Innocence," B2-14).

Up to this point, I suppose I could accept the gypsy curse, despite the blatant unfairness of it all. The gypsies wanted Angelus to suffer, and if the blameless soul of Angel has to get dragged into the mess, too, well, as Uncle Enjos said, justice was never their top priority.

But then the gypsies had to add another clause which makes no sense at all.

According to the curse, Angel is meant to suffer, not live as a human being. Therefore, if there occurs "one moment where the soul that we restored no longer plagues his thoughts, that soul is taken from him" ("Innocence," B2-14).

And what is the result? As soon as the human soul is out of the way, the demon Angelus is free to pick up his previous unrestrained violent, vicious vampire habits where he left off. No one with an ounce of common sense or foresight would consider that punishment for the demon—it's a reward!

No matter how you look at it, this is a really stupid curse.

Fortunately for the fate of the world and the welfare of humankind,

Willow is able to retrieve Angel's soul from the ether again ("Becoming, Part 2," B2-22), and the status quo is restored. Angelus the demon is trapped, and Angel resumes his quest for redemption.

Does it ever occur to Angel that his present existence is little more than a byproduct of an ill-conceived, short-sighted act of revenge? Most of the people around him, most of the time, either fail to recognize or can't seem to remember the distinction between Angel and Angelus, and the same is true of Angel himself. For me, it's a frustrating flaw in Whedon's universe: to have explanations of "how things work" clearly presented in some episodes but totally ignored in others.

But of course, without this illogical, dangerously flawed curse, Angel as we know and love him—conflicted, tormented, brooding, noble hero—would not exist. He continues to struggle to come to terms with his life, to figure out his place in the greater scheme of things. Thanks to the curse, he doesn't dare seek true happiness, and can never achieve it, anyway: The moment he has it in his grasp, his soul is exiled to the ether and a powerful demon is unleashed on the world.

So, he seeks meaning in other ways. Part of the ongoing storyline in *Angel* hints that he may someday find redemption and be rewarded by becoming completely human again. Presumably, Angel would regain sole possession of his body, and the demon Angelus would be banished to wherever vampire demons exist when they don't have human bodies to inhabit. However, in recent years, Angel started to doubt the effectiveness of the Powers That Be, and Spike's presence as a second vampire with a soul threw the Shanshu prophecy into question.

But doubts and uncertainty will not keep Angel down for long. In "Epiphany" (A2-16), Angel says, "If nothing we do matters, then all that matters is what we do, 'cause that's all there is. What we do. Now. Today. I fought for so long for redemption for a reward . . . but I never got it. I want to help, because I don't think people should suffer."

A noble aspiration: try to help, try to prevent human suffering. We can count on Angel to do his best, to fight evil, to protect the innocent, to help the helpless. Maybe there's a certain karmic balance in the face that a great champion of the innocent should be an innocent victim of such profound injustice himself.

But it really is a stupid curse.

Marguerite Krause's favorite activities involve the printed word. In addition to writing, she works as a freelance copyeditor, helping other writers to sharpen their skills, and for relaxation loves nothing better than to curl up with a good book. She is married to her high school sweetheart; they have two children. You can find more of Marguerite's writing in the anthology Seven Seasons of Buffy; *her two-part epic fantasy,* Moons' Dreaming *and* Moons' Dancing, *co-written with Susan Sizemore; and her fantasy novel,* Blind Vision.

Peter S. Beagle

THE GOOD VAMPIRE: ANGEL AND SPIKE

There are Angel-lovers and there are Spike-lovers, revolving, of course, around who Buffy should really be with. But there's much more to Angel vs. Spike than who should be Buffy's boytoy. (Astronaut or caveman, anybody?) Peter Beagle explains.

I DIDN'T PAY MUCH MIND to *Angel* at first, for a lot of reasons, the major one being that vampires bore the bejesus out of me. They do *talk* so, for one thing. Anne Rice's bloodsuckers natter on endlessly—*endlessly*, you hear me?—in mournful self-justification, and Whitley Strieber fell in love with his Miriam Blaylock far too early to give her a chance to be anything but lusciously rapacious. Dracula himself is scariest offstage (where he actually spends the major part of Bram Stoker's novel), but at all events, he spends no time in *apologia pro vita sua*. In Joss Whedon's universe, humans are, in the words of *Buffy the Vampire Slayer*'s Spike,

"Happy Meals on legs," and that's the end of it. Beats the hell out of whiny old Lestat.

The only vampire I've ever been able to enjoy on a regular basis is Spike himself, primarily because of his elegantly insolent humor and his complete lack of somber self-importance. Whatever Spike does, he doesn't *brood* about it; and *brooding* is the word most often applied to Angel—lord knows how many times it'll come up in this anthology. Perhaps that's why I've never been able to feel the same affection for him that I do for Spike. Brooders are black holes for affection.

Angel and Spike have exactly one thing in common, apart from being vampires: they both possess human souls. Since vampires are, by definition, soulless walking corpses—night horrors nourished by blood, rejoicing in evil for its own sake—and since with a soul inevitably comes a conscience, comes shattering memory and ultimate self-loathing, one might imagine these two unique beings sharing at least a certain sympathy. This, as we have seen, has not largely been the case.

Buffy's creators originally dealt well with Angel. The whole notion of an ancient, conscience-hounded European vampire falling in love with an American adolescent, whose destiny is to destroy him and everything like him, was classically romantic to begin with. And by adding the brilliant extra twist of Angel's not daring to risk a moment of true happiness with Buffy for fear of reverting immediately to the monster he was, the show reached a level of genuine courtly love achieved by no other episodic television drama that I can think of. It was that tension that made Buffy and Angel's relationship as honestly haunting as it was.

David Boreanaz, who plays Angel, tends, for my taste, to be much more convincing as a monster—especially as a relapsed monster—than he is as an almost-human boyfriend. The Angel of *Buffy* knows how to be evil; he's still, for all his cool savvy, more than a little shaky on his newly-noble pins. When, having at last become Buffy's first lover, he does turn back into the soulless fiend Angelus, glorying more than ever in his absolute fiendishness, he is truly terrifying and despicable—the more so for his new understanding of the internal workings of goodness. Killed by Buffy one fateful split-second after Willow's witchcraft has restored his soul, hurled into a hell-dimension and eventually spat out on earth to make the tortuous journey back to humanity, his character inevitably takes on a quality of victimhood, absolutely fatal to a hero. Let alone a boyfriend.

The only cure for this particular fungus, as every writer knows, is humor. Perhaps because his sidekicks on *Angel*—Wesley, Cordelia,

Gunn, Fred and Lorne, the horned green nightclub Host from another world—all have distinct and individual senses of humor, Angel begins to develop one himself, as he never did on *Buffy*. It's dry, completely dead-pan and rather bleak; but what else would you expect from someone who's done what Angel remembers doing, every moment of his life-in-death? Wiping out families, ravaging entire towns and villages, sadistically seducing the innocent and turning them into gleefully undead horrors like himself . . . immortal as he is, Angel understands that there is no way for him ever to atone for his crimes. All he can do is devote his eternity to trying.

Spike's situation, through the first six seasons of *Buffy*, is a good bit simpler. Except for Buffy—and, by extension, her mother and younger sister—Spike truly despises human beings; even more so, once a chip implanted in his brain made it impossible for him to chow down on any of them. Unlike Angel, Buffy's dark knight-errant from the beginning, Spike fights his growing love for her (tooth and nail, you might say) as long as he possibly can. Not only is he poignantly aware of the hopelessness of his suit, he struggles equally hard against being drawn to the side of goodness. Angel wants desperately to be good; Spike just wants Buffy. And if his only chance of winning her must come through being good—even giving his life for her—then so be it. Long before he finally set out in search of a soul, Spike was reluctantly growing one.

But Buffy will not—cannot—ever love Spike as she loved and still loves Angel. Whatever lovers (including Spike himself) might follow, a call from Angel, or the faintest sense of Angel being in need, will still bring Buffy flying across the world, not to mention television networks. Nor is it simply, as has often been suggested, a matter of Buffy's continuing attraction to bad boys, to danger, to the edge. In the end, it is Angel's lonely, unending pain that will always speak to her. She cannot help him—nothing and no one can help Angel—but she will never be able to resist trying.

It's hard to overstate just how much Angel and Spike hate each other. The hatred dates all the way back to the days when they were rampaging through nineteenth-century Europe and Asia together, in company with Spike's mad vampire lady Drusilla and Angelus's own Darla. Angelus, considerably the elder, regarded Spike then as a boastful, troubleseeking punk kid, constantly—and often deliberately—drawing the wrong kind of attention down on his companions. For his part, Spike saw Angelus's brutal siring of Drusilla as the direct cause of her growing insanity, which he never gave up hope of curing. Even in those pre-soul, pre-Buffy days, Spike seems always to have been capable of loyalty and even love.

Over more than a century and a half, Angel's basic contempt for Spike never changes, no more than does Spike's bone-gnawing jealousy of Angel. It's not simply a question of Buffy's sexual and spiritual allegiance, nor a consequence of the period when Spike was temporarily crippled, and Drusilla took up with the reborn Angelus, flaunting the affair before Spike's eyes. Nothing Spike can do—including capturing him and turning him over to a jovially insane torturer—will ever impress Angel; not even the remarkable fact of Spike's having gone out and *earned* a soul, while Angel, after all, merely had his handed to him, courtesy of a gypsy curse. Spike's peculiar but quite real sense of justice is perpetually affronted by the unfairness of it all.

Yet over time, despite the constancy of their mutual antagonism, Angel and Spike have reversed roles in a number of ways—most notably, Angel has become the romantic that Spike used to be in his human life. Spike was William then: a curly-haired, pitifully earnest Victorian mama's-boy, completely inept socially and much given to writing appallingly bad poetry to whatever woman was currently disdaining his timorous advances. He was as hungry for the gift Drusilla's fangs could offer him as she was for his blood; and even the later, Buffy-besotted Spike gives no indication that he ever regretted the deal. Or that he ever wrote another poem.

He is as deeply lonely as Angel, but he keeps the loneliness at bay primarily with liquor and sex, whether with Harmony (as stupefyingly, almost touchingly dim as a vampire as she was during her years at Sunnydale High) or the moment when he and a heartbroken Anyanka, left at the altar by Xander, took brief advantage of each other. There was Robo-Buffy, of course, the android programmed to love and desire him as long as her batteries held out; but even Spike could never have remained content with such a pathetic relationship. Sex with the real Buffy was another matter: It was mutually intense and violent, crossing more borders than the one between vampire and Slayer, and Spike—knowing far better—was willing to imagine it love. Buffy wasn't. That time, the loneliness did break through; ironically, it also gave rise to Spike's quest for a soul.

Angel, on the contrary, admits fairly freely to his own isolation, and his impossible wish to end it. He will always love Buffy and find security in the knowledge that his love will always be returned; but he doesn't pine for her, as Spike—to his shame—can't keep from doing. Eventually he allows himself to fall in love with Cordelia, and, consequently, develops a raw jealousy of the Groosalugg, her adoring flame from the alternate world of Pylea. (The more recent seasons of *Angel* are plagued by a streak of baroque soap opera; we'll get back to that.) The Groosalugg, being a true hero, eventually chooses to return to his own country, sensing Cordelia's feelings for Angel before she does. But the relationship can never be consummated, even if that were possible, because Cordelia—who has surely come the furthest from Sunnydale of any of the major characters—keeps being assumed by the Powers That Be into ever-higher states of being. Here today, astral tomorrow; you spend a lot of time canceling dinner reservations. So Angel—the romantic, as opposed to Spike's snarky realist—remains alone.

Alone, that is, except for his handful of friends and his many enemies. It's interesting to consider that though Spike, given his own horrendous record, is undoubtedly on the "To Do" list of a fair number of people—demons and vampires as well, thanks to his alliance with Buffy. But nobody's ever hunted *him* vengefully through the centuries, like Holtz, whose wife and daughter Angelus killed so long ago that he can barely remember the occasion. Nor does Spike have an entire satanic law firm apparently devoting itself, almost from the show's first episode, to destroying or manipulating him (it's hard to tell which at times). As mentioned, he is half Angel's age; yet Spike leads a surprisingly tranquil life, for a vampire, mostly boozing in his crypt and watching TV. Only as he begins to regard himself as Buffy and Dawn's protector, and to take their dangers for his own, does his bitter serenity abandon him. Now Angel is the one who goes looking for trouble, and Spike is the guardian in the shadows. It suits both their natures better.

Angel has friends. Spike has none. Angel rescues people who need rescuing quite urgently. He's their Lone Ranger, their Zorro, their Catcher in the Rye, their Dark Avenger (as Cordelia once suggested billing him), and he deserves to be seen so—he's worked at it hard enough. Spike, by contrast, has only occasional allies. Even the ragbag demons with whom he sometimes plays cards for kittens plainly can't abide him; while Xander, who has fought at his side—and roomed with him, which is even more surprising—will always hate his guts. Willow, Oz and Tara did have a bit of a kindness for him; but it's entirely possible that the only person who has ever truly *liked* Spike in his long, bad life was Joyce Summers, Buffy's mother. Granted, she hit him with a fire axe on their first encounter, but later, meeting him in his human guise and taking him for an ally of Buffy's, she guilelessly invited him in for cocoa. (I've thought often that Spike fell in love with Joyce well before he ever began having nightmares about his fatal attraction to Buffy.) As regards loving . . . people love and have loved Angel, for good or ill, and undoubtedly will again. No one has ever loved Spike. Spike doesn't want love, or friendship either. He wants Buffy—nothing more.

Angel is one of those heroes who flourish on frustration, who thrive on never achieving their hearts' desire. Richard Wagner would have understood him very well. In one of the best early episodes, a chance encounter with the blood of a demon results in Angel regaining ordinary human mortality. This means, to his joy and wonderment, that he can walk out under the sun like anyone else. He can cast a shadow, eat a hamburger, feel his human heart beat and spend a glorious day loving Buffy without fear. It also means that his supernatural strength, quickness and resilience vanish, and that he is less than useless to Buffy in a battle with a demon. In the end, he entreats the mysterious (and rather snotty) Powers That Be to take his mortality back: He needs the curse to do his job—or to fulfill his penance. The final irony is that for the Powers to do as he asks means that his one day of happiness will literally never have happened. Buffy won't remember anything about it; only Angel will. There isn't a lot more that needs to be said about Angel's character and fate.

Angel's big structural mistake, to my mind, lies in having tied the arc of the entire show so immediately and so firmly to developments at Wolfram & Hart, the evil law firm, and—at least during seasons three and four—those characters' relationship with Holtz, the vampire-hunter, and *his* to Angel's son Connor. The word "baroque" doesn't cover it; between the various prophecies, the talismans, the portals to different worlds and dimensions and the ongoing romantic *pas de cinq*, it becomes reminiscent of Noel Coward's lyric about the wrought-iron screens of New Orleans being "dreadfully overwrought."

Commendable as it was for Joss Whedon and David Greenwalt to attempt to create a world truly different from Sunnydale for Angel to inhabit, I can never escape the nagging sense that he deserved to face off against better, more stylish baddies. Granted, you can't come up with a Glory or a Mayor every day, but where's the Master when you need him? Where are the Gentlemen? A Linwood, a remarkably tiresome Lilah, a Justine . . . it's just not the same. There's the Beast, yes, and the Beastmaster, at one point inhabiting Cordelia, but one misses the depraved delight, the wicked music. When the *good* guys start getting all the good lines, where is civilization?

One grand exception to the general villainous lethargy—one clear stroke of Whedonian genius—was the return of Angel's worst and oldest enemy: Angelus himself, summoned back out of dreadful necessity by the good guys to keep the world from ending. Crouched in his basement cage, cool and smiling and soulless once again, he is a figure out of that nightmare everyone knows, the one in which a beloved face turns in an instant to the face of a betrayer, a tormentor, a murderer. And we can believe that the nightmare is not merely that of Angel's friends, but of Angel himself, because we know him by now, and we can *feel* him in there still: voluntarily vulnerable, risking his very existence for the sake of others. How Angel of him.

Then, of course, there's Connor, Angel and Darla's son, who counts as a sort of occasional, now-and-then enemy. Leaving aside the really intriguing question of whether two undead beings can create life, let alone a mortal soul, the concept of Angel as a father was one of those great ideas that should have died at the pitch meeting. That he would unquestionably *want* children (as Spike just as certainly never would) is beside the point: Angel has no more business raising a child than he would have conducting an orchestra. Some human joys, some exalting experiences, must always be forbidden to him, or they detract from his solitude. And Angel without his ancient solitude might as well be Captain Kirk.

As for Connor himself, stolen by Holtz as a baby and raised in a dark, nasty dimension to loathe all vampires, and to work forever for their total destruction . . . Connor, however you consider him, is impressively unlikable. He has *no* humor; he's given to enough sulking and pouting to make Achilles look like Mr. Rogers; and for all the peaceful, playful interludes when he's once again on goodish terms with Angel, he simply can't be trusted. Imprisoning his father (who does have a tendency to lecture him) in a steel box, like a genie in a bottle, and then sinking the box to the bottom of the ocean, was ill-mannered enough; but to then knock up Cordelia (presumably between assumptions and ascensions)—*Cordelia*, who's practically his aunt, if not his nanny—and promptly father a monstrous being whom everyone immediately regards as a rapturously beautiful goddess of blissful world peace, and never mind the vague smell of putrefaction . . . . Somewhere around here, the soap opera hits the fan. Spike would watch it from the cold comfort of his slab and laugh himself silly.

(*Angel* got rid of Connor eventually, by virtue of a plot twist not quite as jaw-droppingly ridiculous as *Dallas* deciding that one whole season had actually been the heroine's dream, but close enough. The waste of time and character is regrettable, but the fact remains that Connor was a mistake. Angel doesn't need children or grandchildren—he needs grief, he needs long, lonesome tragedy, under which he bends his neck and goes on. His power comes from sorrow, even more than from blood.)

That earlier Wagner reference might be worth elaborating (even though I generally side with Mark Twain's observation that Wagner's music "isn't nearly as bad as it sounds"). Wagner was quite consciously attempting to create—or to recreate—a myth of the Germanic gods and their people, and to make it accessible to his own generation and those to follow. (If Hitler and the Nazis drew inspiration equally consciously from his saga, so did J. R. R. Tolkien.) Every pantheon—the Greek, the Hindu, the Southeast Asian, the Celtic, the Native American, the Haitian Creole, even King Arthur's Round Table—fills the sky with great quarrelling figures, all related in dizzyingly incestuous ways. They form alliances as naturally as they double-cross one another; they shapeshift, they drink, they laugh, they weep, they go to war—and they are constantly raiding one another's beds to father or mother everything from Cyclopses to giant wolves to multi-headed demons to Helen of Troy. Their general emotional development is barely on the level of Sunnydale High.

Yet, just as in the great soaps, the pure *size* of their foolishness—and of their generosity, and even their cruelty and lust—somehow remains eternally engaging and creatively provocative. They survive through the millennia precisely because they are bigger than we are, because their lives and passions are (or seem) grander than ours; because their stories so often seem more real than our own. And whether this is true or not is not at all the point.

I wonder increasingly whether Whedon (whom I really am, warily and enviously, willing to regard as a bloody genius; the little rat even writes fine songs) and Greenwalt might not have such a cosmology in mind for *Angel*. For all its obvious fantasy and horror elements, *Buffy* was always a more realistic epic, specifically wedded to late twentieth-century popular culture both in its episodes and its tone, as well as in its progression. The members of Buffy's "Scooby Gang" (early on, Willow proposed brightly that they call themselves the "Slayerettes") grew older and changed, inevitably developing lives apart from Buffy's mission. None of them, from Buffy on down, have any notion of enlarging into divinity: Willow herself, easily the potential goddess of the group, has a real terror, not unlike Angel's, of what she is, and what she might become—*did* become, for one dreadful time. As for Spike . . . attaining to a soul, dealing with the agony of having a soul and being Buffy's true champion for a little time is as close as he cares to come to the celestial. Spike isn't going anywhere that doesn't have beer and dog-racing.

Angel's associates, on the other hand, while revolving almost exclusively around him (barring the occasional intramural romance) seem gradually to be developing into timeless minor deities on their own. Darla's gallant gesture of staking herself so that her human child could emerge from a heap of dust is as operatically mythical as anything Joseph Campbell could have desired, let alone Wagner. Wesley, the once-prissy, self-righteous scholar and failed Watcher, so aggravating on *Buffy*, has grown into a variation on Loki: never really in league with the bad guys, but more and more involved with his own agenda, which is not necessarily Angel's. Little Fred, the shy, brilliant scientist whom Angel rescued in Pylea and brought home, was evolving into a kind of woodsprite, still fragile as a dragonfly's wing, but tender and loyal, surprisingly strong, and with a diffident understanding of how the world and the universe actually work (fairly rare among this group of self-made specialists) . . . at least until God-King Illyria, a full-blown divinity in "her" own right, burned Fred out of house and home. Gunn is the warrior: Gunn is Siegfried, perfectly capable of riding through a vast ring of flames to Fred's aid, and eager for the chance. Street-smart and cynical he may have begun, but he's become as romantic a hero as Angel—Gawaine to his Lancelot, Enkiddu to his Gilgamesh. Love will do that to man or vampire, as even Spike knows.

Paradoxically, Angel himself has changed the least of any of the major characters on either show. He remains pretty much what he was from his first encounter with Buffy: a good man trying urgently to be better, rescuing the weak from the Wolfram & Harts of this world as desperately as though he were rescuing them from himself, from terrible Angelus, who never dies. In a certain sense, Angel has always reminded me of T. H. White's Sir Lancelot, who, in *The Once and Future King*, bends over backward to be regarded as the kindest knight at court, because he so deeply fears his own native cruelty. Angel has far more reason than

Lancelot to mistrust himself, and the doubt never leaves him. What if "Angel" turned out to be a mask, after all, and Angelus the mocking, eternal truth? It does make for a lot of brooding.

Angel is emotionally weary, physically without fear, tirelessly patient and resourceful in his pursuit of evil, injustice and brutality—in fact, he matches perfectly Raymond Chandler's classic description of the private detective walking down the mean streets, except for one additional element: the deep hopelessness that sets him apart from every other television protagonist. He's definitely the one you want with you on those said streets, but his sadness, over the long haul, may very well come to bore you. Saints *can* bore you, and Angel may yet end his series run in the odor of sanctity. Many real saints have begun worse than he.

Spike is no saint, and never could be. Spike isn't remotely in Angel's league as a man, except when it comes to Buffy and her family. He's just more fun—and even in his moments as an ensouled hero and champion, he remains somehow wild, ambivalent, unpredictable, in a way that Angel could never afford to be. Call them *Vampire Yang* and *Vampire Yin*, if you like; but they won't ever fit quite properly into that classic black-and-white symbol. Or into an Anne Rice novel, either, thank the Powers That Be.

I like them both. I care about them in a way rather unusual for someone who never saw a single episode of *Friends, Seinfeld, Will and Grace* or *Mad About You,* and hasn't cared about a television character since *Hill Street Blues'* crazy, brave, lonely Mick Belker. But I *worry* about Spike.

Peter S. Beagle is the author of The Last Unicorn, A Fine and Private Place *and* The Inkeeper's Song *among other works of fiction and nonfiction. He was born in New York City, now lives in Oakland, California, and has recently completed a new novel entitled* Summerlong.

Candace Havens

TO ALL THE GIRLS HE LOVED, MAIMED AND BANGED BEFORE

The weregirl. Electric girl. Ex-liason Eve. Kate (the cop). Drusilla, for God's sake. Not to mention Darla, Cordelia and Buffy. Let's face it: If anyone ever needed dating advice, it's Angel.

DEAR MR. ANGEL,

I received your request regarding the possibility of finding true love. In compiling your report it was necessary to go back several centuries in order to get a clear picture of what your future might hold. Past behavior is an excellent barometer of what is to come.

By looking at what you've done wrong for the last two centuries, we get a good vision of prospects for everlasting amour. As we go along we will rate each woman on our true love indicator, with 1 being not such a good choice and 5 the real thing.

Those hundreds of farmers' daughters, courtesans and bar maidens you banged before you became undead are not included. Consider them a sexual bonus and unworthy of our test.

125

We begin, therefore, with your tryst with Darla that night in the alley behind the pub, when she gave you the eternal kiss and sentenced you to a life of damnation. God bless her. She knew how to have a good time.

It was Darla who encouraged you to eviscerate your father, the man who believed you to be a bum who would never be worthy of existing, thus sending you down a long road of plundering and gorging on tasty human snacks.

The relationship with Darla was absolutely your longest to date. I mean, come on, 140 years? That's pretty much it for anybody. And she was so hot. True love? No. But admit it: You had fun terrorizing Europe with that sexy wicked woman.

The main problem was your propensity for making the wrong decisions whenever she was around. You should have just said no to the young gypsy girl when Darla offered her up as a flavorsome morsel. Then you would have never been cursed and could have lived out your days gnawing on humans and whatever else was around with no guilt at all.

But you didn't say no, and you chewed up the Gypsy girl. Got cursed. Then you woke up whining about all of your nasty deeds over the last century. Darla dumped you faster than a vampire runs from sunlight, right after she tried to stake you.

Is it a coincidence that you killed or tried to kill Darla more than once? I think not. No guy likes to get dumped. Or staked for that matter.

She's so good at coming back from the dead that perhaps it will happen again and the third time will be a charm. She'll whisk you off your feet and into the sun-drenched horizon, and watch as you burst into flames.

Darla's true love potential score: 2

(In the future you may want to steer clear of women who drain your blood to turn you into their boytoy. You can do better.)

Remember that fling with Drusilla in the nineteenth century? That had definite possibilities. The pasty chick was one sick puppy from the get go, and the things you two did would make the Marquis de Sade blush. Who needs true love, when you can have wild, nasty sex?

She and those virgin sisters of hers, you just couldn't resist. You made her watch as you killed her family and the nuns, and as she slowly went mad you turned her into a vampire.

Hey, there have been worse starts to relationships.

You lost interest once she began spending so much time with Spike, but that didn't mean you guys didn't slip a little fun in every now and then over the last 200 years. She gave new meaning to the term crazy ex, but you've got to give her her due. She's good with the torture, but it's never a good idea pursue relationships with women who would rather hang you from your fingernails than do the mattress dance.

Dru's true love potential score: 1

Of course all that craziness flew out the window when your soul came to visit. You never had a single romantic inclination until that fateful day you first encountered Buffy. (And if you did, down there in the sewers with the rats, I don't want to know about it.)

Former cheerleader Buffy Summers was and is a cutie patootie. How many nights did you stand in the shadows throwing tortured looks her way before you made your move?

In the beginning she had a hard time with your being a vampire, not difficult to understand since she was a Slayer of your kind. But she grew to adore you and eventually you made sweet, tender and passionate love. Perfect and sensuous, it was downright toe-curling.

How were you supposed to know that experiencing true happiness would send your soul on a hike, and that you'd run around the next few months killing and torturing Buffy's friends and family?

Things just weren't the same after that. She had to send you to hell, and you came back all animalistic and smelly. Realizing you could never do the big nasty again sort of put a damper on the relationship. Not that you two kids didn't try. Unfortunately, when the Buffster realized she would never hear the pitter-patter of little vampire/Slayer feet it was over.

That was a sincere effort, about as close to true love as one can get. But some things just aren't meant to be.

Buffy's true love potential score: 4

So you did the only thing a broken-hearted vamp could do: you moved to L.A.

Here's a place where millions of women reside, many of them quite evil (you do have a tendency, you know). A virtual demon and freak warehouse, a plethora of choices for your bed.

True love around every corner—or at least some good one night stands.

I had hopes for you when you met electric shock girl last year. Whoosh, she was a fun one. All that electricity really had you revved up. Too bad she didn't stick around for a little hide the electrode. Women leaving you, it's a definite theme.

Electric shock girl's true love potential score: 2

Detective Kate Lockley was a nice broad. She was almost as dark and broody as you. That first meeting, where she thought you were a serial killer, upped the tension and made a possible union exciting. Admit it, you had a thing for her in a big way.

She never really trusted you though. Being undead has caused a lot of problems in your relationships.

Your standing in the door when the bad guys killed her father didn't do much in the way of improving the communication between you two either. In fact, she never forgave you and would have been more than happy to stake you given half a chance. Not really the positive vibe you need to keep a good thing going. She really hated you, something many of your former friends who are girls have in common.

Kate's true love potential score: 1

You had that fun fling with Rebecca, the famous actress who wanted to be eternally young. She drugged you so she could have her way with you, and you still didn't go through with it. At the very least you could have practiced some kind of intimacy.

But no, you tossed her around a bit and made her realize that spending an eternity with you might not be such a wonderful trip, and she moved on. Dumb, dumb, dumb.

Once again your altruistic side got in the way of hot sex. (Yes, we know the quest is true love, but a little fun on the way never hurt anyone. And if you don't try out the merchandise how will you ever know if it's going to fit?)

Rebecca's true love potential score: 2

From your first few days in Los Angeles, Cordelia was there for you. Always in the background keeping things running.

In Sunnydale your relationship with the then-cheerleader was adversarial at best. She didn't care for your being a 200-year-old dead guy, and you couldn't stand her acerbic, self-centered, snobby cheerfreak ways.

Things were different when you two went into business together. The universe shifted a little to the left and you became friends.

It took years for you to discover you had more in common than the need to make some extra cash. She began to see you as a champion of good, and you saw her as . . . well, hot.

The bones (no pun intended) for a positive, healthy relationship were there. Cordy had true-love potential written all over her.

That freaky night at the ballet where you two were living vicariously through some ghosts ended up being one hell of a time. Sexy, sexy.

Then things got weird. Darla came back pregnant with your son, and the timing was oh-so-bad. Cordy was really angry that you had done the nasty with Darla, and she couldn't forgive you for screwing things royally (pun intended, this time).

But Connor's birth made everything seem right in the world—you had a tiny being you loved, who loved you back. Cordy saw that soft, loving father and went all gushy for you.

For a few weeks anyway.

Then Connor was kidnapped, taken to some hell dimension. Came back as a teen, who, in the way of teenagers, hated you and constantly tried to find a way to impale you with daggers and stakes.

Do you see a theme here? Why is it that the people you love almost always want to kill you?

It was that pesky boy of yours that kept you from meeting Cordelia so that you two could talk about how you really felt. He locked you in a cage and dumped you in the bottom of the ocean to live out eternity with the fishes.

As angry as you were with the young man, you understood his actions. You tried to make him see that you only had love in your heart for him, but it wasn't a message he wanted to hear.

At that same time when you were deep-sea fishing, Cordy was lifted heavenward to take her place with the Powers That Be. Another bump in your not-so healthy relationship. She came back, and couldn't remember why she loved you in the first place. Then she slept with your son, and that was pretty much the end of that.

She did love you, and called in her final favor to put you back on the path of the righteous. She loved you, you loved her. That passionate kiss before the phone rang was absolutely yummy.

It was perfect true love—for about a minute and half. Then she died. Poof, gone.

Angel loses again.
Cordy's true love potential score: 4
(Ouch. That has to hurt.)

One of your more interesting relationships, though not really romantic, has been with Faith. She fits into our report because you have, on occasion, tried to maim and kill her. Through the years you two have tried to redeem each other in one way or another, usually with some success.

You were there when she hooked up with the bad guys and tried to murder you. She begged you to do her in, but you wouldn't. In your stoic but understanding way, you made her realize she had worth in the world.

Years later she did the same for you. She risked her life in order to save you from being Angelus. (Now, I know, Angelus: evil demon, murderous ways. But at least he gets to have sex before he kills the women he wants.) She drank the poison then you gave her a bite, turned back to Angel and there you go. Faith went off to fight the good fight in Sunnydale, you and she destined to be friends for life. And you seem to be okay with that.

Faith's true love potential score: 3
(You might want to give her a ring.)

Don't forget that darling Fred. A woman who worshipped the ground you walked on back in Pylea and followed you back home like a puppy on a short leash. Brilliant, beautiful and innocent. Ripe for the picking. But did you notice? Hell no. Yes, having sex with her would have turned you into an evil beast, but at least you would have gotten a little tail in the process. And she didn't seem to mind your demonic side when you guys hung out in the cave.

But no goodie-two-shoes for Angel.

When Fred died and turned into that sexy Goddess, I thought, "Here we go big boy." And you've always had a thing for older women. Er, demons. But she was more interested in destruction than love. Not really true love material.

Fred's true love potential score: 1

Now keep an open mind with this next suggestion. Over the last 150 years or so I've noticed you have a great deal of chemistry with one person, who is hotter than hot. This person is bad, but has a tendency to fight on the side of good. The energy sizzles when you two are in a room together, and the intensity when you two stare into one another's eyes . . . whew, I get hot just thinking about it.

Yes, Spike is a guy, but if you're looking for love. . . . I know, I know, it's enough to make a grown man puke. But think about it. Maybe it means a lifestyle change or two, but you boys could do it. It's just something to think about. Don't go getting homophobic on me; I'm only here to give you options.

Spike's true love potential score: 3

(Just think, the love of your life might be a man. Stranger things have happened.)

So that brings us to your current stable of bad girls, which, let's face it, are extremely doable. Eve, who you got jiggy with behind the couch, is a great example. She's beautiful, smart and a bad, bad girl. She's tried to kill you several times, but that sort of thing quite often turns you on.

Eve's true love potential score: 2

(Oh, but the fun you could have if Lindsey were really out of the picture.)

If Willow weren't gay, she'd be an obvious choice. She's both bad and good and always has to keep that balance. You could ask her to make her eyes and hair turn all black and get her in a grumpy mood before you do it. But I'm fairly certain that whole lesbian roadblock is going to be a tough one to cross. Best not to even go there.

Willow's true love potential score: 0

(She's having none of that, thank you.)

Oh, and regarding that cute little werewolf you saved: She's only considered "bad" when she's in wolf form, so that's entirely up to you. We certainly wouldn't judge you in any way should you decide to go all beastie on us.

Werewolf girl's true love potential score: 2

Mr. Angel, I am sorry to say that, having looked closely at the whole of your romantic dossier, you can rest assured that as long as you continue to screw only the bad girls, you should live a long and disturbingly violent life, filled with unfulfilling sex.

If you are still desperate to find true love, please proceed to the nearest stake and ram it into your heart. Because it isn't happening in this lifetime, big boy.

Best Regards,

The Love Goddess
Consultant
Wolfram & Hart

Candace "Candy" Havens is one of the nation's leading syndicated entertainment columnist for FYI Television. She has interviewed hundreds of celebrities, including the entire cast of Angel, *and covers everything Hollywood for publications around the world. She is the author of* Joss Whedon: The Genius Behind Buffy, *and can be heard weekday mornings on 96.3 KSCS, which broadcasts in the Dallas/Fort Worth area.*

Jacqueline Lichtenberg[1]

VICTIM TRIUMPHANT

Of all the differences between Angel *and* Buffy *(and sometimes I think the producers tried a bit too hard to make* Angel *"not-Buffy"), the greatest was in the characters of their respective heroes. Buffy, confronted with countless horrors, always seemed to take the initiative. And when she stopped doing so—in much of seasons six and seven—it really hurt the series. Angel was always much more reactive. But the difference is more profound than that. I didn't really get it . . . until I read this essay.*

THE COMMERCIALS ADVERTISING *Angel's* first season named Angel a hero. But do you believe everything commercials tell you?

Angel's certainly the man in charge. He headed Angel Investigations, and then had his own branch of a law firm, not to mention the most lines, the most scenes and the best close-ups. He's likeable enough

---

[1]With research assistance from Cherri Muñoz and Chris Jacobs (creator of Writercon, a convention about Fanfiction as Literature In the Whedonverses, www.the-sandlot.com/writercon/), who both identified scenes I could only describe. Websites: vrya.net/bdb/, buffyguide.com and tvtome.com/BuffytheVampireSlayer/

to be a hero and apparently has a worthwhile goal—preventing the destruction of the world. He also faces seemingly overwhelming odds as a goal-directed hero must.

But as heroic as Angel may appear on a weekly basis, he does not fit the profile of a goal-directed hero because he's no hero. The goal he pursues in each episode—whether saving a child or a half-breed demon, the city of Los Angeles or the whole world—is not his own.

Note that it took the appearance of Doyle and his pipeline to the Powers That Be before Angel started doing significantly more than taking out a few vamps at some L.A. bars. A hero has to act. And Angel doesn't act—he never has. He *reacts*..

He doesn't scheme, plot and orchestrate events to achieve his personal goal. He doesn't even stumble across trouble in classically heroic, single-minded pursuit of his own goals. He doesn't go looking for trouble. Trouble finds him, whether in the form of gypsy curses or regular missives from the Powers That Be. The Powers assign him goals and he achieves them, hoping for the ultimate reward: redemption and restored humanity

A classic action hero plot (and *Angel* has been consistently billed as an action show) goes like this: "A hero gets his fanny caught in a bear trap, and has his adventures getting it out." Vampirism is certainly a formidable bear trap, and adding back the vampire's soul sharpens the teeth of that trap with barbs of guilt and remorse. The adventure comes in finding ways to atone for all those regretted sins. But Angel doesn't actively search out ways to atone. His desire for redemption has never played a driving role in the show. At most, it's a low hum in the background.

Angel accepts that his ultimate reward—becoming human—is not within his power to achieve. Until the Powers deem him worthy, he feels he must play by their rules, doing their bidding like a horse after a carrot on a stick.

This is diametrically opposed to Buffy's attitude. Buffy is a classic hero with her fanny in the beartrap of being the Slayer. This prevents her from living a normal life. Almost every episode is, in some way, about her struggle to achieve normality.

Buffy gets manipulated by circumstance and higher powers as much as Angel, and deserves it even less. But her response is to assert her own agenda and choose her own goal. Handed a nasty job, she does it not because it was given to her but because it needs doing. She does it not because she seeks to be given a reward but because she can do it. Then she returns to her original objective: living a normal life. Her heroism lies in her ability to take the cards she's dealt and refuse to play the hand. When faced with an unacceptable choice, she doesn't choose the lesser of two evils—she finds another way. Buffy is a hero because she makes her own rules.

This was never better demonstrated than in her show's final episode, "Chosen" (B7-22). Finally an adult, Buffy rejects the fate laid out for her by the Council of Watchers and a couple of old men millennia ago. She changes the rules of the spell that creates Slayers, sharing her power with dozens of potential Slayers around the world. She finally achieves her goal of normality—not by denying her own nature, but by making others like her. She changes the very definition of normality.

In contrast, Angel's strategies rely on his ability to accept others' rules and play the hand he's been dealt. He's not any kind of hero. He is a very talented *victim*.

Angel is a veritable paragon of victim-hood, a true role model for those beaten down by life's events. He was made a vampire without his informed consent, as all vampires must be—how could any mortal be informed enough to understand what it means to exist as a vampire?

Imagine Angelus, for the moment, as innocent. Look at him as a victim not only of his sire, Darla, but of his own nature as well. Angel began as a man who was nothing more or less than the product of his time and circumstance. Because he conformed to the norms of his society, he had done nothing to deserve being stripped of his conscience, handed enormous physical power and turned loose with the inability to feel joy without causing pain.

Angel's response to being put in this position was to perfect the art of being a soulless vampire. He used the intelligence that now serves him so well in his fight against evil to become the de facto head of his small family of vampires—the planner, the group's most skilled and zealous victimizer. As the First Evil reminds Angel in "Amends" (B3-10), "That's what makes you different from other beasts. They kill to feed, but you took more kinds of pleasure in it than any creature that walks or crawls."

A century later, Darla victimized Angel again. Her birthday present to Angelus in 1898 was a gypsy girl she had caught and bound for his pleasure ("Five by Five," A1-18). But the gypsy family retaliated against Angelus, not Darla, restoring his soul and turning every moment of his existence into his own personal hell.

The initial shock must have been utterly deranging, as it was for Spike when he regained his soul by a different mechanism ("Grave," B6-22). But once that shock wore off, Angel could have tried to rid himself of his soul again to escape the constant pain. Instead, he accepted it and chose to elevate his existence as a vampire with a soul to a fine art—long before he ever laid eyes on Buffy. (As he says in "Lie to Me," B2-7: "[I spent a] hundred years, just hanging out, feeling guilty. I really honed my brooding skills.").

Step by step, Angel accepted his victim-hood, played by the rules others dictated and perfected his own character. Later, with Buffy, and eventually at Angel Investigations in Los Angeles, he was ready to accept the role of Champion of other victims.

But what are the Powers' intentions regarding Angel? How much of his fate were they responsible for, and how much did they simply take advantage of? We know they sent Whistler to bring Angel to Buffy, but as Whistler informed her in "Becoming, Part 2" (B2-22), "It wasn't supposed to go down like this. Nobody saw you coming. I figured this for Angel's big day. But I thought he was here to stop Acathla, not to bring him forth. Then you two made with the smoochies . . . ."

Angel would have followed the path laid out for him if not for Buffy's influence. But was his move to Los Angeles already predestined? Had the Powers been grooming him from the beginning to go up against the Senior Partners at Wolfram & Hart? How much of seasons two through four—Darla's return, Connor's birth and kidnapping, Cordelia's pregnancy—did Jasmine orchestrate? And why did Wolfram & Hart put him in charge of their Los Angeles branch?

It seems as if Angel has been manipulated from the moment he became a vampire. But I would also say that Angel's love for Buffy changed him so much that he became unpredictable to the Powers. He likely also learned from her indefatigable response to the forces manipulating her. Many of those forces were mortal, though more than a match for the high school girl, Buffy. Most of the supernatural forces manipulating Angel's life are likewise more than a match for him, even with his formidable allies.

But these supernatural forces have discovered that Angel has become an even more slippery target since Buffy entered the picture. Every plot against him, whether for good or evil, tends to do the instigator more damage than it does Angel. Sending Angel to Sunnydale backfired. Jasmine's plans to birth herself into the world ended with her death.

Connor didn't kill Angel. Presumably, whatever plans the Senior Partners have for Angel will go equally poorly.

The blows aimed at Angel ricochet precisely because Angel has perfected the art of being a victim. He has responded to his repeated victimization by accepting his fate as if it were an opportunity. As Angelus, he sharpened his ability to scheme, plot and out-think others; as Angel, he perfected his self-control, self-denial and discipline, as well as developing a strong moral sense he never possessed in life.

Now The Powers and the Senior Partners have discovered that anything they throw at him makes him that much stronger.

That's why we love Angel. That's why we identify with him so easily. As a victim, he exemplifies a life pattern that is far more common than that of the hero. Very few of us are in a position to make our own rules, to fight back against the fate or circumstances that hold us down. But almost every one of us has been, in some way, at some time, a victim.

Angel reveals that life's victims—not heroes, but people just like us—are all that stand between us and annihilation.

Even if you're a victim, you don't necessarily need rescuing, you don't need to transform yourself into something you're not and you most certainly don't need to knuckle under to anything more powerful than you are. You don't have to consent to your own undoing.

You have other options. You can follow in Angel's footsteps, develop the attributes that lie dormant within you, perfect the art of living as a victim of fate, and become stronger for it.

The victim's true triumph is to thwart the victimizer, not by direct confrontation the way a hero would, but by living with style, grace, humor, honor, dignity and loyalty, without losing self-worth, compassion or the courage to champion other innocent victims.

Angel may not be a hero, but he *is* a champion who has used his victim-hood against the forces of darkness far more effectively than he could have used classic heroics.

Romantic Times *award-winning author Jacqueline Lichtenberg is the primary author of* Star Trek Lives!, *the Bantam paperback that revealed the existence of* Star Trek *fandom and looked in-depth at the motivations behind fan-involvement in the television series. She is featured in the docudrama film* Trekkies Two. *Her first published novel,* House of Zeor, *was the first novel in the legendary Sime~Gen Universe—a series that sparked its own outpouring of fan activity. She has two occult/sf novels in print, titled* Molt Brother *and* City of a Million Legends, *and BenBella Books has recently reprinted her vampire romance* Those of My Blood *and its companion novel* Dreamspy. *www. simegen.com/jl/ provides details.*

K. Stoddard Hayes

WHERE HAVE ALL THE GOOD GUYS GONE?

Who else thought Angel had lost it during "Power Play" (A5-21)? That a more laconic Angelus had somehow been raised from the depths of Angel's psyche? That Wolfram & Hart had been drugging Angel's blood supply? Turns out he was just using Wolfram & Hart's own tricks against them. K. Stoddard Hayes probably saw it coming.

I N A CITY WHERE A DEMONIC BEAST can darken the sun, where the most prestigious law firm caters exclusively to demons, vampires and other hellish spawn and where a goddess can take control of the entire human race just by smiling on television, only the mightiest champions have any hope of defeating the darkness. On *Angel*, these mighty champions are Faith, Wesley, Spike and Angel himself. The rest of the team are all good guys—they just don't have the same clout. Whether it's Wesley working his magic, Faith hunting Angelus, Spike dueling the Reaper or Angel taking on the Senior Partners themselves, we know that these four will always find a way to win. We'd back them to beat any evil they go against. What makes them the champions they are? They've all been bad guys.

In Angel's world, the only way to become a champion is to start out as the enemy—or at the very least, sleep with the enemy for a while. Faith enters Angel's world as that scariest of bad girls, a Slayer run amok, ready to hire on as a paid assassin or commit murder, torture and mayhem just for the thrill of it. Wesley first shows his dark side under the influence of Billy Blim's woman-hating magic, when he becomes a terrifying sexual predator stalking Fred ("Billy," A3-6); he then plunges into the dark by betraying Angel, kidnapping Connor and having an affair with Lilah. Spike has only just regained his soul and his conscience, after more than a century of vampire evil that earned him the nickname William the Bloody. And Angel is the poster boy for bad guys turned good. Not only did he live a century and a half as Angelus, the most vicious vampire in history, he still carries Angelus with him every day—a demonic split personality just waiting for its chance to emerge.

Naturally, having been evil isn't what makes these four champions of good. Each of them had to decide to walk away from the dark side: to admit they had been evil and to start living like good guys. And that was only the first step. To become champions, they had to do more than turn their backs on the dark. They had to dedicate their lives to fighting it. Faith and Wesley both take this final step naturally: Wesley was brought up to be a Watcher, instilled at an early age with the kind of dedication to Goodness (however misguided the Watcher's Council might have been at times) most people never achieve, and Faith, as a Slayer, was born with the calling to serve. Spike, however, fights the good fight at first only for Buffy's sake. He doesn't truly commit himself to the war until his encounter with the mad Slayer Dana forces him to look at his own past and recognize that his crimes were truly evil ("Damage," A5-11). And he's moving quickly, compared to Angel. For a hundred years after Angel regained his soul, he hid in the shadows, tormented by guilt for his crimes and doing only whatever good deeds came directly in his path (saving puppies, rescuing submarines, convincing other people they were better off leaving him alone). He had to see the heroism of another champion, Buffy, before he could take the final step of dedicating his own life to helping her cause.

Former monsters make much better champions than the average, pure-as-the-driven-snow good guy. (Even Slayer powers are rooted in the demonic.) Because they know the dark side intimately, they are uniquely qualified to fight it.

Evil's power is not so much what it can do to your physical body— though what it can do is still nothing to laugh at. Its real strength is its ability to overwhelm—with pain, with terror, with hopelessness. Angel and his comrades are not cowed by the horrors of the dark, because they've been those horrors. They know exactly what evil can do because they've done it themselves. When Spike, in his bad boy days, hires the psychopathic vampire Marcus to torture Angel, both he and Marcus expect Angel to break. They should know better: Angel has all the memories of Angelus, who devoted his life to torture and terror for over a century. Marcus can only cause Angel physical pain, while Angelus could drive a young woman mad with horror. Angel's grasp of torture is so far above his torturer's that he can even make Marcus believe he's breaking long enough to get his feet on a handy stake ("In the Dark," A1-3).

Those who have been evil and turned away from it also have a unique way of destroying it: They know how to lead others along the same path. They can see the potential for good in (some of) the bad guys and bring them to redemption—and the day every bad guy becomes a good guy is the day the champions can lay down their swords and stakes.

When it comes to redemption, Angel has reached out to more bad guys than everyone else put together, because he understands not only what it means to act out your pain on other people, but what it's like to be in love with your own cruelty—and what it's like to hate yourself for it. He has a couple of lifetimes worth of experience in both. Sometimes he succeeds, as he does with Faith and, before she was re-vamped, Darla; sometimes he fails, as he does with Lindsey and initially with Connor (who is saved not because he chooses to reject the darkness but because Angel buys him a life without darkness; only after he has lived this life is he able to turn his back on the memories of the old life).

For the same reason, when Angelus must be captured so that Angel's soul can be restored, Wesley is certain that no one but Faith can do it without killing him.

FAITH: There's no way I'm giving up on him.
WESLEY: That's why it had to be you. ("Salvage," A4-13)

The Slayer whom Angel saved from her dark side is the only one who will be totally committed to rescuing Angel from his own.

But there's a more ominous reason that makes *Angel's* fantastic four the champions they are: they all fight darkness with darkness. Not only do they know all the weapons of evil—violence, terror, black magic, deception—they don't hesitate to use them. We expect all four to be awesome, kick-ass fighters, and so they are; each can fight any number of bad guys single-handed, wield any weapon, take on any monster or demon.

But more than that, *they fight dirty*. Faith captures Angelus by letting him bite her—after she has injected herself with a dose of the mystic drug Orpheus, which knocks him out cold within seconds of his first gulp ("Release," A4-14, and "Orpheus," A4-15). Angel pays back a treacherous employee by handing him over to a restaurateur who will carve him up to be eaten alive ("Unleashed," A5-3). And Wesley gets information from a junkie by driving a dagger through her shoulder ("Release," A4-14). Good guys aren't supposed to do things like that, even to the bad guys. They're supposed to treat their prisoners decently, fight the villains face to face in fair combat and turn human criminals over to the law.

This kind of heroism brings up a moral ambiguity the size of California. If *Angel's* champions use the methods of the bad guys to fight for good, can they still be champions? While *Buffy* only touches on the ambivalence of the Slayer's violent fight against evil, *Angel* plunges right in. Our hero himself is the darkest of the dark champions, whose vicious alter ego is not merely the demon who moves in when his soul moves out, but an integral part of himself. In his very first scene, we see Angel thirst for human blood, and since then we've seen him fire his friends for opposing his dark plans ("Reunion," A2-10), jump into the sack with his vampire lover Darla ("Reprise," A2-15) and even deliberately raise Angelus to help him fight the Beast ("Awakening," A4-10). Talk about using the dark to fight the dark!

The challenge here is that the good guys still have a bad guy inside. The champions still have their darker moments: Angel locks a party of lawyers into a room with a hungry Darla and Drusilla ("Reunion," A2-10); Wesley shoots an underling who didn't get the message that the whole office should be trying to save Fred ("A Hole in the World," A5-15) and stabs Gunn when he finds out Gunn was inadvertently responsible for Fred's death ("Shells," A5-16). And the twist of logic that allows our heroes to use the tools of evil for the side of good is dangerous in and of itself. It doesn't only convince the characters; it can convince the audience as well. When Wesley skewers the junkie in "Release" (A4-14) to make her talk, a part of us may be shocked—but part of us is also cheering him on for doing whatever it takes to save Angel.

In the fifth season, Joss Whedon and his team bring this moral ambivalence to center stage, when they make Angel the CEO of the L.A. branch of the company from Hell, Wolfram & Hart. Now, at last, the characters are arguing every week about whether it's right to use the methods of evil to fight evil. Angel may terminate—with a sword—any employees who think it's okay to massacre humans on the job or off, but he also has to kiss up to demon warlords, win court cases for the nastiest demon gangsters and make a profit for the Senior Partners.

Is it really possible for Angel and his comrades to fight the good fight from within the belly of the beast, and use the beast's own teeth and claws as their weapons? More than that, is it possible to do so without compromising their moral higher ground? The show's final episodes take Angel straight into that beast, as he becomes, at least as far as the rest of the group is concerned, the kind of creature Wolfram & Hart likely wanted him to become. He sacrifices a baby to win the favor of a demon overlord, ruins the life of a senatorial candidate with accusations of pedophilia and kills Drogyn, who is not only a mystical guardian on the side of good but also a friend. And he does it all to gain access to the most evil secret society this side of the dimension portal. Until he lets his friends, and the audience, in on his plan, he is utterly indistinguishable from Holland Manners, or Lindsey, or anyone else he's ever fought against.

In the end, the baby is rescued, and Angel has succeeded in bringing Wolfram & Hart and the forces behind it to their knees . . . at least temporarily. But some things cannot be undone, like Drogyn's death. Was it worth it? When the finale ends, leaving Wesley dead and Angel and Spike, with Gunn and Illyria, bracing to fight an onslaught of demons, that question is not yet answered.

Would a sixth season of *Angel* have resolved the moral ambivalence of having heroes who fight evil with evil's own methods? I think it never intended to. Because *Angel* isn't about resolving that ambivalence; it's about the struggle of living with it. *Angel's* real theme is redemption. It's about bad guys becoming good guys, about making up for all the wrong that's been done, about living as if you are a hero and a champion, even though your entire resume says you're a monster. It's about making the choice to fight the dark.

A sci-fi TV junkie since the first season of the original Star Trek, *K Stoddard Hayes finally validated her addiction when she sold her first article to* Babylon 5 *magazine. Since then, she has written about many genre series, including* Farscape, The X-Files, Star Trek *and of course,* Buffy *and* Angel. *She is also the author of* Xena: Warrior Princess: The Complete Illustrated Companion. *When not programming her VCR to catch the latest episodes of current TV genre series, she likes to take her family to the beach or the movies, volunteer at the Rhode Island International Film Festival and add to her small but growing collection of comic books.*

Amy Berner

THE PATH
OF WESLEY
WYNDAM-PRYCE

Wesley's come a long way since his first appearance on Buffy.
*In fact, you could say he's changed more than almost any other
character on either show. Or has he?*

Funny thing about black and white: You mix it together and
you get gray. And it doesn't matter how much white you try
and put back in, you're never gonna get anything but gray.
                                      –Lilah, "Habeas Corpses" (*A4-8*)

T HE LAST THIRD OF THE FINAL SEASON of *Angel* was jam-packed with
major plot happenings. Character deaths, new arrivals and, oh yes,
the requisite Last Stand. Amidst all this, there was another event
that you'd think might have received a little more attention: In "Shells"
(*A5-16*), Wesley stabbed Gunn in the gut. Calmly. Without a glimmer of
remorse.

And yet, nobody was really all that surprised about this, were they?
I wasn't. Momentarily shocked and saddened, yes, but not truly sur-

prised. Taking a step back, I have to wonder why that is. Why weren't we surprised? Shouldn't we have been? How is it that a character can be that brutal to a former friend and comrade-in-arms without a huge out-cry from fans? The wound intentionally wasn't fatal, but that fact doesn't explain this silence away completely.

A part of this is certainly our anger at Gunn. He made an incred-ibly poor judgment call in order to get his legal knowledge reinstalled, one that led to the death of the woman Wesley loved. Actions have consequences. If they didn't . . . well, it wouldn't be a Joss Whedon show, would it? This has always been one of the main tenets of his work. There's no such thing as a free lunch, free resurrection or free instant law degree. Ever.

But that isn't the whole story. A big chunk of our lack of surprise comes from having watched Wesley's development of the years. Most of the attention might be paid to the undead on *Angel*, but for my money, the most fascinating character on the show is Wesley Wyndam-Pryce.

How did Wesley transform from a bumbling rookie Watcher to a composed and ruthless man? During the third season of *Buffy the Vam-pire Slayer*, the name "Wesley Wyndam-Pryce" would elicit little more than an eye-roll or a snicker. What caused such a drastic change? How much of this was in the Wesley that we originally met? I believe that the pieces were there, and that circumstances over the years just brought it to the fore.

THE GREATER GOOD

Wesley has always leaned on a guiding principle: do what is best in the context of the Big Picture. He looks for the "greater good," the best case for everyone who might be concerned, and acts accordingly. This is a logical goal, one that should ensure as little failure as possible. It can't usually be faulted. Knowing this, he has often been ruthless in pursuit of that goal.

Let's look at the earliest example of this viewpoint. The Scooby Gang was faced with a choice in the appropriately named episode, "Choices" (B3-19): save the captured Willow or destroy the Box of Gavrok, ending the threat of the Mayor's imminent ascension. Wesley alone was willing to sacrifice one person in order to ensure the safety of the entire com-munity. He supported what he saw as the lesser of the two evils.

If you step away from the affection that we have for Willow (be-cause, really, who doesn't adore Willow?) and look at the situation objectively, he was correct. Even though Buffy and her army of fellow students stopped Mayor Wilkins shortly after he became a giant demon-snake, many still died on Graduation Day, including Principal Snyder, Larry and Harmony. These deaths could have been averted if they had sacrificed Willow. And, had they not succeeded in stopping him post-ascension, the death toll could have been far worse.

Another obvious example: As the newly-appointed leader of the rebels on Pylea, he knew that his guerrilla warfare strategy would be fatal to some of the fighters under his charge. As he told Gunn in "There's No Place Like Plrtz Glrb" (A2-22), "You try not to get anybody killed, you wind up getting everybody killed." He risked the fighters to save Cordelia, but also to help them win their battle, which he believed would help the fighters as a whole, as well as the rest of Pylea's human population.

Then there was the time Wesley kept Justine prisoner in his closet, which was not a choice that resembled anything close to a "good" act. In its own strange way, it did have a just purpose: She was the key to finding Angel. Wesley used her in his "good" quest to find Angel and return the Champion to the world. By bringing Angel back from the bottom of the ocean and helping him regain his strength, Wesley also partially repaid Angel for the theft of his son, slightly easing his own self-loathing for his failure.

After breaking Faith out of prison—also not normally considered a "good" act, but one that was necessary to stop Angelus—Wesley assisted Faith in using a dangerous drug to bring Angelus down when he understood far better than Faith the enormity of the risks involved ("Orpheus," A4-15). Wesley was willing to sacrifice Faith to stop Angelus. Of course, he himself was the one who had suggested and arranged for the removal of Angel's soul ("Awakening," A4-10) in an attempt to serve the greater good.

You see the problem: this "greater good" thing gets a bit tricky. Instead of being a safe rock that Wesley can cling to, serving the pursuit of achieving the greater good has led him astray as often as it has guided him well. Rather than following his heart, Wesley follows his head. This is the way he was raised, but it hasn't always worked out for the best. Plus, as is always the danger, his interpretations of "greater good" aren't always the same as that of his colleagues, and this was a fact that Angel knew only too well. As Eve asked Angel in "Lineage" (A5-7), "Are you worried about the next time Wesley betrays you trying to do the right thing?"

THE EFFECTS OF FAILURE

When we first met Wesley, he was Buffy's new Watcher—a Watcher like his father before him, and probably his father before him. But he never won his father's respect or approval; there are even references to abuse in his early life, emotional or otherwise. Wesley's self-image was incredibly negative, and the failure to please his family was only the start of a string a failures—some mainly self-perceived, some not—that plagued him over the years. He doesn't easily forgive himself for anything, and his self-loathing increased with each failure in his lifelong quest to Do Good.

Wesley failed as Watcher to Buffy and Faith, and more importantly, he failed Faith completely. Here is a man who we first see dropped into a near-impossible situation in "Bad Girls" (B3-14) as a rookie Watcher sent to oversee two Slayers who don't want him there. He makes the mistake of over-asserting his authority over both Slayers. After Faith committed murder, his attempt to capture her and return her to the Council was what pushed her over the brink and into the Mayor's camp in "Consequences" (B3-15). It wasn't until she tortured him a year later that he realized the enormity of this first major failure ("Five By Five," A1-18).

Wesley failed Connor. His attempt to save Connor's life and protect his "family" was a plan he didn't share due to extreme bad timing. Cordelia was on vacation, Fred and Gunn had their budding relationship and Angel was the perceived threat. Wesley treated with the enemy in order to ensure Connor's safety, and he had every intention of caring for the child himself until Justine and Holtz double-crossed him. Wesley's judgment calls resulted in Connor spending his childhood in a demon-dimension, far from those who loved him ("Sleep Tight," A3-16). Wesley's exclusion from what was likely his first-ever close social group compounded his self-recrimination and resulting bitterness.

Wesley failed Lilah. Their relationship began as a fulfillment of mutual needs—first physical, and then more. Despite being on opposite sides of the war, they found a commonality in each other and grew to care for one another in a strange way neither of them ever understood. Lilah was killed in the supposed safety of the Hyperion ("Calvary," A4-12), and then, more importantly, he could not save her eternally damned soul ("Home," A4-22). Some contracts are just too binding for anyone to break. Even Lilah herself was touched by Wesley's efforts to burn her contract with Wolfram & Hart. She explained the futility of his action: "Flames wouldn't be eternal if they actually consumed anything. But it means something that you tried."

And, finally, the proverbial last straw: Wesley failed Fred. After years of yearning and watching her become involved with other men (first Gunn, then Knox) he'd finally found love with the girl of his dreams. Of course, in Joss Whedon's grand tradition of No Happy Endings, she died in his arms one episode later ("A Hole in the World," A5-15). He was helpless to save her and helpless to bring her back. Worse, he was left with a walking, talking image of her, to whom he agreed to act as guide. What reason would he have to help the being that robbed Fred of her life? He admits that he did so because Illyria looked like Fred. It was one last chance to not fail her.

With each failure, with each loss, his anger at himself grew. He might have purged some of his internal torment by apologizing or seeking forgiveness, but as both Lilah and Angel have observed, Wesley was not a man who used the word "sorry." Instead, the worse things got for him, the more quiet and composed he became, and the less we saw of the goofy young Watcher we first knew. As time progressed, only his actions and his intensity revealed any of what was below the surface.

We'd seen this behavior in Wesley before, long before his life fell apart after Connor's abduction. In "Billy" (A3-6), Wesley was infected with magic that brought out a primal anger in males which targeted women. Wes, unlike the other victims of Billy's magic, was frighteningly calm and methodical as he stalked and threatened Fred. He recognized that this anger came from a well within himself, and it was his extreme guilt at what the magic had caused in him that hamstringed his efforts at a romance with Fred early on.

Since then, his anger has manifested in similar ways without magical inducement. In "Lineage" (A5-7), Wesley received a visit from a cyborg masquerading as the elder Mr. Wyndam-Pryce. When this non-father threatened Fred, Wes didn't balk or hesitate. Calmly, and truly believing that he was killing his own father, he emptied the gun into the creature's chest. It was as if he poured every ounce of stored-up anger and resentment into his faux father with those gun shots, but none of that emotion reached his face. Fred's destruction caused Wesley's anger and pain to reach a level comparable to what he experienced under Billy's magics. The Wesley we saw in "Shells" was able to shoot an underling for poor prioritizing skills, kill the unarmed yet incredibly culpable Knox and stab Gunn while staring him straight in the eyes. And so, when he stabbed a man whom he once thought of as family, there's a part of us that understands how he got there.

With Knox dead, non-fatal vengeance enacted on Gunn and the Fred-like demon Illyria asking for his guidance, Wes was at a crossroads. What was left for him? The good and just path became unclear, and he didn't trust himself enough to believe that he could teach Illyria about "what's right" ("Shells," A5-16). The black and white categories of his Watcher days had become irrevocably gray, his view of himself with them.

Wesley should have given himself more credit. Illyria, a former god-king who regarded humans as insects, not only grew enough as an individual to participate in the final battle but also exhibited feelings for Wesley himself. This demonstrates the kind of person Wesley was, even if he no longer believed it himself: a good man, still able to effect positive change on the world around him even in the depths of despair over losing Fred.

Wesley readily agreed to Angel's proposal to eradicate the Circle of the Black Thorn, fully knowing the risks. He saw the impact that this plan would have in serving the greater good. Would he have been killed if the series had not been canceled? Signs point to no, but with the series drawing to a close, it was the only way he could find peace. His death was tragic and staggering, but in some strange way, it was right. This was a man with little left to live for. Until six years ago, he had focused his entire life upon serving as a Watcher, but when tested, he'd failed. Since his arrival in Los Angeles, he had formed ties only to watch them unravel. How many times over the years have they shown Wesley sitting alone in his apartment? He had few chances at happiness. By the end, Angel no longer fully trusted him and never would. He and Gunn would never have the brotherly bond they once shared. Lilah, who understood him better than anyone, was long dead. Fred had been destroyed, leaving Illyria as a pale imitation. By the final episode, the fight was all that he had left. He did not enter that last situation with a death wish, but he was simply outmatched. It is a credit to him that he kept fighting for as long as he did, both in this battle and overall.

Wesley was a good man who wanted to do what was right. We loved with him. We grieved with him. We witnessed him repeatedly continue the good fight when he could have walked away. We watched him be just and we watched him be good, if not necessarily at the same time. Wesley always strove for the light, even when he did so from a dark place.

Amy Berner has a not so slight obsession with quality genre television, with Angel *and* Buffy the Vampire Slayer *topping her list of favorites. Using what spare time her "day job" and her cats let her have, Amy pops up all over the place with reviews, essays and short stories. She is also a regular columnist for Dark Worlds (www.darkworlds.com) and lives in San Diego, California.*

Nancy Holder

DEATH BECOMES HIM: BLONDIE BEAR 5.0

Pick your favorite Spike:
- ❑ *Big Bad Spike (Buffy seasons two and three)*
- ❑ *Emasculated, Snarky Spike (Buffy seasons four and five)*
- ❑ *Lovelorn but Getting Some Spike (Buffy season six)*
- ❑ *Puppy Spike (Buffy season seven)*
- ❑ Angel *season five Spike*

My character has better arcs than any character, except for a lead, has in any other project, movies or theater. One of my favorite things about the role is that it hasn't stayed in one place. It's gone all over the map. I like to say that I started out as a super-villain and went to wacky neighbor for a season and then the wrong boyfriend for a couple of seasons and then the redeemed man. That's kind of like four roles in one.

—James Marsters, "Undead Again," *BTVS Magazine*

BEFORE THE OPENING OF *ANGEL'S* FIFTH SEASON, there was a great deal of fan anxiety and speculation about which known "version" of Spike the show's producers would bring to *Angel*. But season five viewers actually saw a fifth—and therefore, new—version of Blondie

Bear. Now that the series has ended, we can easily see how Spike was transformed from the snarky, dangerous villain of "School Hard" (B2-3) into a true Champion willing to give his life for the cause.

We saw most of Spike's transformation on *Buffy*, but it was not until he was removed from *Buffy's* world and made a fulltime inhabitant of the *Angel* mythos—a mythos that had itself undergone a brilliant retrofit during its fifth season, courtesy of Team Whedon—that he was capable of taking the final steps toward his transformation.

First, some backstory. In the spring of 2003, worse news for *Angel* fans than the end of *Buffy the Vampire Slayer* was that *Angel* itself might also go off the air. *Angel's* ratings had dropped, and "the suits" were talking about canceling it. With *Buffy's* move to UPN for seasons six and seven, while *Angel* remained on the WB, Whedon was in a vulnerable position. Ratings were dropping; he was no longer Hit Show Guy. Upon the cancellation of *Firefly*, Joss aficionados grew even more alarmed.

Fundamental changes were required if *Angel* was to survive. *Buffy* veteran David Fury, who had served as Consulting Producer on *Angel* since season one, was officially brought on board as Co-Executive Producer and charged with helping to reshape the show. Team Angel's efforts were successful and cancellation was averted.

Assured that *Angel* would have a season five, rumors began to fly among fans regarding exactly what Joss & Co. had promised to do differently in order to stay on the air. There was talk that a *Buffy* cast regular would join the *Angel* cast; and for a time, many fans assumed it would be Willow, who had already appeared in a trio of episodes ("Disharmony," A2-17, "There's No Place Like Plrtz Glrb," A2-22, and "Orpheus," A4-15). Additionally, she was engaged to (and later married) Alexis Denisof, who played Wesley.

The reshaping commenced with the finale of season four. Fans eagerly tuned in to get hints about the shape of things to come. They learned that Angel's surly son, Connor, was (probably) history; that Cordelia, who had gotten progressively stranger (and rounder), was (probably) being written out; and that Wolfram & Hart would (definitely) reclaim the dark spotlight as a force of evil to be reckoned with. The implied promise seemed to be that the show was going to return to its earlier incarnation, that of Angel and his cohorts working on individual cases to help the helpless—but with more resources at their disposal, and in some new and different way. Left behind would be the show's increasing preoccupation with the love lives of the quick, the dead and the very green.

Shortly before the *Buffy* finale, James Marsters was identified as the *Buffy* character that would join the cast of *Angel*. Though Spike would heroically sacrifice himself to save Buffy in an immolation scene worthy of a Wagnerian opera, the Big Bad would be back.

It came as no surprise to fans that Spike could and would be resurrected after such a spectacular death. Actors on Whedon shows like to joke that dying is no indication that a part is over, and it's even possible their role will expand.

Additionally, on *Angel*, the notion that once a vampire was staked he/she/it was destroyed had already been thrown out the window: Angel had staked Darla, the future mother of his child, during season one of *Buffy* ("Angel," B1-7), yet she was magically brought back to life—literally, as a human being—by Wolfram & Hart during the *Angel* season one finale ("To Shanshu in L.A.," A1-22). She was revamped by Drusilla in season two ("The Trial," A2-9), then staked herself in season three ("Lullaby," A3-9) to protect her son. Yet she reappeared on this plane a third time, in season four ("Inside Out," A4-17), to plead with Connor to spare the life of his intended sacrificial victim.

As longtime online fan Mariann Palmer ("AngealEire") recently remarked, "You know there are no easy exits in Jossland."

So, speculation swirled in chat rooms and on fan sites about what Spike would be like when he came back. Would he be human again, like Darla? Would he still have his soul? Would he appear only in flashbacks?

But a more basic question began to be asked: Would he be the beloved "Snarky Classic Spike" of the earlier seasons of *Buffy*, or would he remain the unloved "Schmoopy S7 Spike," Buffy's wimpy lapdog (as described in the Spike section of televisionwithoutpity.com)?

It could go either way. Marsters himself had discussed some reasons for the versatility of his role as it had unfolded on *Buffy* in a 2002 interview:

> Being a vampire is both good and bad. . . . It's good because they can't make Spike hump the plot around. . . . He walks into the darkness, which means I am a dab of color rather than a main character who you are going to experience the story with. The heroes are the daylight characters, and those are the people the audience wants to be. I am not one of those. . . . If you ever redeem my character, he will become a patsy.
>
> —"Crossroads," *Cinescape*

Marsters made this statement midway through *Buffy*'s sixth season, and it was precisely this turn of events—the theme of ensouled Spike's redemption—that annoyed many fans of "snarky" Spike. Spike was originally intended to be a "disposable villain" who would appear in a few episodes, be evil, then be gone (beginning with "School Hard," B2-3; next were "Halloween," B2-6, and "Lie to Me," B2-7, his intended arc probably concluding with "What's My Line, Part 1," B2-9, and "What's My Line, Part 2," 2-10). But fans liked the smart-mouthed vampire with an attitude, and he was retained as a cast regular. It was thought for a time that he would take over Cordelia's role as brutal truth-sayer, but that didn't fit, and Anya the former vengeance demon took over that function.

Because he was no longer just "a dab of color," Spike was redrawn as such that he became more of a "daylight character." First his humorous and kinky obsession with Buffy was spun as a deep, tragic love. Buffy was shown responding to him, and began to have sex with him, although it was clear to viewers that she was using him and did not return his love. But any longstanding relationship with the main character naturally gave Spike more "real estate" in the Whedon mythos.

Next, pushed beyond his limits by his need for Buffy, Spike attempted to rape her. Realizing that he was still a monster, at least in Buffy's eyes, he left Sunnydale to win himself a conscience—a soul—so that he would never do such a thing again.

The burden of his soul drove him mad, and as season seven unfolded, Buffy became his caretaker, treating him with brusque firmness as if he were an Alzheimer's patient. Once he pulled himself back together, he strove to do good, but primarily to win back her love. Over the course of the season, his hesitancy and reluctance to take action were directly related to his need to appear good in her eyes.

With Spike's obnoxious aggression diluted to such an extent, his fans were concerned as they prepared to watch his debut on *Angel*. Some felt that the original concept of Snarky Classic Spike had been irredeemably undermined during the last three seasons of *Buffy*. By series' end, not only did Spike have a soul, but he had just saved the world: What more could he do to but become even more "schmoopy"? Answer: Join *Angel* and work with a bona fide Champion in a show themed around redemption.

But as previously noted, *Angel* was undergoing a major overhaul. Bringing Spike on board was only one of the significant changes that

Whedon and his creative staff effected to keep the show on the air. Another was to plop Team Angel into the belly of the very first beast they had encountered in Los Angeles: to hand them control of Wolfram & Hart.

Angel's availing himself of the vast resources of the evil empire—even if to do good—threw Angel's heroic status in jeopardy. That status had been jeopardized before, in season two, when he fired his friends and went on a private mission of vengeance. But taking over the offices of Wolfram & Hart was not portrayed as a personal dark night of the soul; it was a group consensus to walk on the dark side, agreed to by all the members of Angel Investigations, and signaled a change in direction for the entire show, not just the main character.

Thus, the "ordinary world" of Angel's hero's journey was redefined as a much grayer, murkier landscape than in previous seasons.[1] The rules under which all the characters would now operate were new, because their world was new.

It was also a world in which Buffy would not be able to function. Though she had broken rules to protect people she loved, she was, at the core, a force for justice. Her world was far more black and white than Angel's ever had been. In *Angel* season one, when renegade Slayer Faith asked Angel to help her return to the light—to seek redemption—Buffy couldn't fathom a world that would permit that.

Yet Buffy's sharply defined world was the one Spike had previously operated in, either as a supervillain or as a redeemed man. Though the world of *Angel* has always been more ambiguous than Sunnydale, moving to Wolfram & Hart painted that world in many more shades of gray. During the opening episode, Gunn opts to get a "brain dump" of all law, including demonic variants thereof, without consulting the others. Fred is in charge of the same lab that created the retrovirus threatening the destruction not only of L.A., but of the world.

> ANGEL: [S]ooner or later they'll tip their hand, and we'll find out why they really brought us here. Meanwhile, we do the work our way, one thing at a time. We deal with whatever comes next. ("Conviction," A5-1)

What comes next is Spike, reassembling pixel by pixel from his death scene in "Chosen" (B7-22) on *Buffy*.

---

[1] Please see my essay in *Seven Seasons of Buffy* for a more detailed discussion of the hero's journey.

As Marsters has pointed out, it is the lead character in an episodic television series who carries the plot. But a vampire is the one who "humps the plot around" on *Angel*. As the central focus of his show, Angel is the main actor, literally. It is left to other characters to react to events Angel either sets in motion, or which occur because Angel exists. Since he is not the main acting agent of either show, Spike has always been one of those reacting to the lead character, first to Buffy, and now to Angel. And, in season five, Angel's world has significantly changed.

Although Spike cannot serve as the focal point of the series, he is the central focus of his own grand entrance. In this case, it is left for Angel, Wesley and Harmony to react to his arrival, giving fans a few clues about how the others will deal with him. Two other objectives were also accomplished in that first glimpse: Spike was introduced to returning *Angel* fans as someone who had an important connection to Angel (and who had guest starred in season one in "In the Dark," A1-3, at the height of Spike's snarkiness). He was also introduced to brand new viewers as the last of the cast regulars, shots of whom flashed on the screen during the theme song.

After the season premiere, fans were sanguine and, in many cases, already aware that Spike's arrival had been saved for the last few seconds of screen time. It lay for succeeding episodes to unveil his characterization.

The revelations began immediately in the second episode, "Just Rewards" (A5-2). To fill in viewers who had not watched the finale of *Buffy*, Spike's pivotal role in averting the Apocalypse was shown. With sweeping music and heroic fervor, Spike's sacrifice was manifested as he exploded in white light.

But as the transcendent scene pulls back into Angel's office (nineteen days later, the viewer is told), Spike is described as a monster:

> WESLEY: William the Bloody. He's a vampire. One of the worst recorded. Second only to—
> ANGEL: Me.

Later during the same episode, the relationship between Angel and Spike is underscored:

> GUNN: So he's a good-guy vampire like Angel?
> ANGEL: He's nothing like me.

And then Spike himself reveals the good news: Houston, we have Snarky.

SPIKE: You heard me! You left town in the nick of time, didn't
    you before the death and mayhem? Abandoned the wom-
    an you claimed to love.
ANGEL: She made the call. It wasn't my choice.
SPIKE: And this, bloody hell, it wasn't mine. I'm not you. I don't
    give a piss about atonement or destiny. Just because I got
    me a soul doesn't mean I'm gonna let myself be led around
    by—

So much for redemption. With that notion tossed out the window,
Spike can get his snarky mojo working again. As Marsters states in his
interview in *BTVS Magazine*:

He went in there willing to die to back Buffy up. I don't know
if he cares about saving the world. You know, Buffy? Yeah. Save
her. She's cute.

During that episode, Spike discovers that he's incorporeal—something like a ghost, but not even a ghost. No one in the show knows what
he is—just like the viewer. He can't physically interact with his surroundings, so he can't change the new world that has been established
(at least not yet.) He's not quite there—an apt metaphor for his transition from the world of *Buffy* to that of *Angel*.

As the second episode unfolded, viewers learned that Spike was unable to leave the city limits and kept winding up at Wolfram & Hart.
They learned that Angel was less than pleased to be haunted by him,
and wondering if he, Angel, was the one who was supposed to wind
up as Spike had, since he had originally planned to wear the amulet.
Thus, he would have been translated into the incorporeal being Spike
had become.

Spike echoes the flipside of Angel's perspective:

SPIKE: You got it too good. You're king of a thirty-floor castle,
    with all the cars, comfort, power and glory you could ever
    want. And here I save the world, throw myself onto the
    proverbial hand grenade for love, honor and all the right
    reasons, and what do I get? Bloody well toasted and ghost-
    ed is what I get, isn't it? It's not fair.

In typical Whedon fashion, the episode confronts the expectations
of fans who have wondered if Spike will be "good" or "bad." Spike ap-

pears to side with the villain of the episode, a necromancer, who promises to reinstate Spike as a corporeal being—for a price. But later on, it is revealed that Angel and Spike have concocted a sting in which, when the necromancer attempts to put Spike's essence into Angel's body, Spike inhabits the necromancer instead, killing him. But Spike prolongs the deception long enough to "get a few licks in" during the ensuing fight with Angel.

So Spike has proven to be a loyal member of Team Angel, yet with his snarkiness in place. This is interesting territory and, one may argue, old territory at that: On That Other Show, although Spike was chipped, he snarkily but willingly helped the Scoobies. He also tried to kill himself to put himself out of his misery. But Spike is chipped no longer; he is ensouled, he is not looking for death and he is still willing to help his old nemesis and rival for Buffy.

In the following episode, "Unleashed" (A5-3), Fred again reminds us that we are seeing a new version of Spike: something "unique." In addition, he has a new problem, one which will help "hump the plot along"—moving from B story to A story—in future episodes:

> SPIKE: I know what's down there—where it's trying to take me—and it's not the place heroes go. Not by a bloody long shot. It's the other one. Full of fire and torment. And it's happening. And I'm terrified.

Spike's losing his presence in this reality, and his purpose in this episode is also weak: He serves as Snarky Exposition Guy, spouting such lines about the girl werewolf in jeopardy as:

> ANGEL: All I care about is the girl.
> SPIKE: That's rough. 'Cause here on out, she's in the kill-or-be-killed club.

And:

> ANGEL: So, what do we do now?
> SPIKE: We wait for the show. Should be a good one. Everyone on pins and needles, dreading the moonrise, then pop goes the werewolf.

The werewolf girl dealt with, the episode ends with Fred's agreement to make it her priority to halt Spike's disappearing act. This places Spike back in an important role in the series, once more focusing the viewers' attention on his unique situation.

In "Hell Bound" (A5-4), the next layer of Spike's new characterization is cleverly layered in:

> FRED: I've been working on a theory. Well, more of a hunch, actually. But I think I'm getting close.
> SPIKE: To making me a real boy again?
> FRED: Heh. As real as a vampire with a soul can be. It won't be like Angel's thing with the prophecy, but . . . .
> SPIKE: What prophecy?
> FRED: The shan-shoe-ha something or other. It says that if Angel helps enough people, he gets to be human again.
> SPIKE: Oh, really?

Spike's interest in the prophecy prompts Angel to re-examine it, despite his assertion that he doesn't believe in it and that it wouldn't matter if he did. Angel has come to believe that the Shanshu Prophecy was part of the elaborate hoax perpetrated by Holtz in order to kidnap Connor. But now another ensouled vampire has appeared on the scene, and that vampire is interested in living as a "real boy"—anything to escape the fires of hell that threaten to consume him, if he continues to lose his purchase on this dimension.

The careful viewer realizes here that a new Spike dynamic is being set up. Since Spike is not the main character, his main source of motivation is to react to Angel. Where Spike was moved by love to act in Buffy's world, his situation in *Angel* has become one of self-preservation . . . and self-promotion. In "The Cautionary Tale of Numero Cinco" (A5-6), Wesley discusses the Shanshu Prophecy with him.

> SPIKE: When you say, "plays a major role in an apocalyptic battle," you mean like, um, heroically closing a hellmouth that was about to destroy the world?
> WESLEY: The text isn't specific about the battle.
> SPIKE: But it's specific about the name of the vampire with a soul.
> WESLEY: No, I imagine it could be any vampire with a soul. Who isn't a ghost.

However, two episodes later ("Destiny," A5-8), Spike is a ghost no longer: After receiving a "bit of flash" in an envelope, he becomes corporeal. And suddenly "that ghost pal of Mr. Goodfang" is a force to be reckoned with—in more ways than one. His newly physical existence is disrupting the order of things: there are now two vampires with souls who qualify for the title of champion.

Initially, Spike snarks over this development. But he stays to help avert yet another apocalypse, despite the fact that Europe is where Buffy is. So unless one argues that he remains at Wolfram & Hart to protect Buffy, his priorities have shifted. He is now reacting to the agenda set in motion by the main character of his new show, Angel.

The pivotal moment where Spike's characterization makes the full leap from being as he was on *Buffy* to a new version of Spike, never before seen, comes in this scene, when he and Angel are battling over the cup that will be drunk by the vampire of the Shanshu Prophecy:

> SPIKE: You never knew the real me. Too busy trying to see your own reflection. . . . Take a long look, hero. I'm nothing like you!
> ANGEL: No. You're less. That's why Buffy never really loved you. Because you weren't me.
> SPIKE: Guess that means she was thinking about you, all those times I was puttin' it to her.

That last line tells the tale: It is more important to Spike to one-up Angel than it is to defend Buffy. He is, in essence, betraying all the soft emotion he had for her in his eagerness to deal Angel a blow. This is a Spike who no longer acts and reacts out of love for the Slayer; this is a Spike who will do anything, say anything, to diminish the vampire he once called his Yoda ("School Hard," B2-3).

To make sure the lesson has been heard, the writers offer it one more time. Again, from "Destiny" (A5-8):

> ANGEL: So ask yourself: Is this really the destiny that was meant for you? Do you even really want it? Or is it that you just want to take something away from me?
> SPIKE: Bit of both.

The episode ends with the revelation that Eve is in cahoots with Lindsey, the Wolfram & Hart lawyer who drove off into the sunset in season two ("Dead End," A2-18). The "cup of destiny" was a ruse to pit

Angel and Spike against each other. For the purpose of this essay, that's not material. What is important is that Spike's characterization has now fully shifted from the weakened, redemptive version of Spike from the last episode of *Buffy*—Version 4.0, as it were—to a new Spike: snarky, bordering on evil (or at least immoral) and more interested in competing with Angel than doing good for Buffy's sake.

When evil attorney Lindsey makes his move, he does so by taking advantage of this very change in Spike's characterization: Lindsey tries to convince Spike to take over Angel's destiny by recreating the circumstances that called Angel to his role as a champion. Lindsey calls himself Doyle and claims to have been sent from the Powers That Be directly to Spike. Via painful visions, he will send Spike on missions to save the helpless.

Lindsey/Doyle demonstrates a strong familiarity with Spike's past, referencing Buffy, and that plus his assurance that he was responsible for Spike's recorporealization catch Spike's attention. Why? Because Angel is on the side of evil now, having agreed to run Wolfram & Hart. As Spike explains to Gunn and Wesley: "A place like that doesn't change . . . you sign on, it changes you."

Just as becoming a champion doesn't completely change Spike:

GIRL: Thank you! That thing was going to kill me!
SPIKE: Well, what do you expect? Out alone in this neighbor-
    hood? I got half a mind to kill you myself, you half-wit.
GIRL: *What*?
SPIKE: I mean, honestly, what kind of retard wears heels like that
    in a dark alley? Take two steps, break your bloody ankle.
    ("Soul Purpose, A5-10)

Spike fans, of course, are watching to see which way the champion wind blows—especially after Angel echoes the sentiment that sent him over to the dark side in season two's "Reunion" (A2-10), when he abandoned the elite of Wolfram & Hart to the mercy of Darla and Drusilla: "Let's kill them all." If Angel opts out of the championship season, it may fall to Spike by default.

Spike's championship moments are played against Angel's fever dreams of inadequacy, caused by a parasitic demon Eve and Lindsey unleashed on him. In scene after scene, Angel dreams that he has been found wanting, and been pushed aside—even by Buffy, who is talking about the Prom and having children with Spike while Spike is making love to her. In Angel's nightmare, Spike is the new champion. And Spike reaps the ultimate reward: The Blue Fairy from *Pinocchio* descends and turns Spike into a real boy, fulfilling the Shanshu prophecy.

In the end Spike does save the day, guided by Doyle's "visions" to remove the parasite from Angel's chest.

The arc to champion is complete . . . which is underscored in the opening of the next episode, "Damage" (A5-11); when both Spike and Angel arrive independently at the mental hospital to offer help with the escaped Slayer, Dana, Spike explains that this is what he does now, though Angel clearly resents his interference.

By "You're Welcome" (A5-12) Angel has totally lost his sense of mission, and tells Cordelia that the Powers That Be aren't in his corner anymore: "It looks like Spike is their new champion. . . . He's got a soul now. And he's saving the world. And he's out there on the streets. You know, helping the . . . helpless."

But when Spike learns that Lindsey has been impersonating Angel and Cordelia's old friend, Doyle, he recedes into the background as Angel regains his good-guy mojo, and by "Smile Time" (A5-14), Angel and Spike's rivalry has resolved itself into a squabbling, big brother-little brother relationship that reaches its comedic zenith in "A Hole in the World" (A5-15), when they nearly come to blows over whether cavemen or astronauts would prevail in battle.

But the cancellation of the series had already been announced, and "A Hole in the World" signaled a new arc, the show's last—the ramifications of Fred's death lead directly to the finale's apocalyptic fight.

Despite Angel's announcement that he wants Spike to leave, possibly to head up a new office, they join forces when Illyria possesses Fred. When the Keeper of the Deeper Well states that a champion is required to defeat the ancient being, Angel replies, "You've got two of those right here."

Two champions, indeed. Though Fred is lost, Spike elects to stay after all. As he says to Angel in "Shells" (A5-16): "I don't really like you. Suppose I never will. But this is important, what's happening here. Fred gave her life for it. The least I can do is give what's left of mine."

In the very next episode, he is the only member of "Angel's Avengers" to show up for an important meeting Angel has called. In fact, he's brought a briefcase . . . with a beer in it. And he willingly goes to hell with Gunn and Angel, to save Lindsey. Spike has been accepted as full team member, taking responsibility for testing the range of Illyria's powers and continuing his brotherly bickering with Angel.

At the start of "Power Play" (A5-21), with only two episodes left, it remains to be seen how Spike's season on *Angel* will end. The writers offer a recapitulation of his beginning, as he says to Illyria, "Still, you can't enjoy haunting this place. . . . Believe me, I've been there." He has another stint as Exposition Guy, identifying the latest demon as a Boretz, and then continues his champion arc, volunteering to kill the Boretz . . . and inviting Illyria to join in the fun. Later, he insists that he's "not missing the fireworks" when Wesley, Gunn and Lorne decide to question Angel about his recent erratic behavior, specifically the murder attempt on Drogyn.

And when Angel asks them to vote themselves into the house they will set on fire (taking on the Black Thorn) Spike is the first one to announce that he's in—and even he seems a little surprised.

In the last episode of the series ("Not Fade Away," A5-22), Spike's characterization goes through a recapitulation as it has been portrayed on the retrofitted *Angel*, not as it began and played out on *Buffy*: His dodgy relationship with Angel is underscored when Angel says, "One of you will betray me," and Spike raises his hand. (It's not him, but he still asks, "Can I deny you three times?") Later, he asks Angel what he thinks will become of them vis-à-vis the Shanshu prophecy: which one of them will become human? Angel's reply: neither of them, because they're both going to die. Spike's response is, "Well, long as it's not you." His role as savior of Sunnydale is tinged with humor—"First off, I'm not wearing any amulets. No bracelets, brooches, pendants, pins or rings" and he tells the baby he saves, "Lucky for you I'm on a strict diet."

On what may be the last day of his life, Spike drinks some Dutch courage, then faces the rabble—as he reads his paean to Cecily at the Poetry Slam—and receives a standing ovation. This is the completion a very old arc, at least in terms of Spike's history, as it was his rejection by Cecily that drove him into the arms of Drusilla, who sired him.

The last battle, set-piece for champions, is about to commence. In the alley of the Hyperion, Spike is the first to arrive after Angel, and he makes a snarky comment about finally getting a decent brawl. His concern for the mortally wounded Gunn is palpable. He is propping up a wounded comrade, preparing for a battle he does not believe he will survive.

At the end, he stands on Angel's right side, ready to fight an unwinnable fight. Not for Buffy, not for Angel, but because Spike has become a champion in a champions' world. In *Buffy*'s world, the most he could aspire to was to give his life to save the Slayer; in *Angel*'s, he could finally become his own person—poet and fighter, schmoopy and snarky, hero and champion, in a seven season character arc that rivals that of even Angel himself.

Nancy Holder is a four-time Bram Stoker Award-winning author, and was nominated a fifth time for one of her Buffy *novels. She also received a special award from Amazon.com for* Angel Chronicles Volume 1. *She has written or co-written over three dozen projects in the* BTVS *and* Angel *universes.* The Watcher's Guide, Volume 1, *coauthored with Christopher Golden, appeared on the* USA Today *Bestseller List and was described in* Entertainment Weekly *and the* Wall Street Journal *as "superb." She lives in San Diego with her eight-year-old daughter, Belle, who has decided against taking ballet lessons for the time being because she is "working on her own moves." Truer words were never spoken.*

Josepha Sherman

ANGEL OR DEVIL

Playing with Mythology and Folklore in the Angelverse

Vampires, blind child prophets, ghosts, zombies and beasts; the Angel *universe is filled with creatures taken from folklore—or at least seem to be. Folklorist and author Josepha Sherman sorts it out for us.*

L ike its predecessor, *Buffy the Vampire Slayer*, the television show *Angel* has made free use of the world's folklore and mythology, often (as with *Buffy*) with tongue firmly in cheek. Demons are not always evil, ghosts like Spike can become tangible through sheer will-power and Armageddon is somehow always kept at bay, often through impossible twistings of reality—for instance, a vampire can have a son who saves the world and then is given a brand new set of memories in order to live a happy life. Yet all the variations on mythic and folkloric themes in both *Buffy* and *Angel* are perfectly valid, since there is no such thing as one "right" or "wrong" mythic or folkloric variant, and

167

both enrich the shows and add little shivers of enjoyment to the viewer's pleasure.[1]

Angel himself is obviously a folkloric being, a vampire. But he is also definitely an odd variation on the traditional vampire theme. In most of the world's folk beliefs, a vampire has been portrayed as an evil, hideous, blood-drinking spirit that has inhabited a dead body to more easily stalk its living human prey. *Buffy* kept to that idea—at least at first—portraying vampires as bloodthirsty demons that inhabited the dead, particularly those unfortunate dead who rose out of the cemeteries of that doomed town of Sunnydale, there on the Hellmouth.

But Angel is unique. He is a vampire with a soul. This is an idea that is definitely not found anywhere in folklore, although of course all religions and mythologies around the world feature the existence of the soul. The demon that possesses Angel's dead body is kept in check by the soul's presence and has been personified as Angel's evil side, Angelus, who is demonic but definitely a part of Angel. This dual nature seems less closely related to traditional vampire lore than it is to characters such as the evil Mr. Hyde, the dark side of the nice but foolish Dr. Jekyll in Robert Louis Stevenson's classic nineteenth-century work, *Dr. Jekyll and Mr. Hyde*. All vampires in the *Buffy/Angel*verse have their human and their vampire faces, which makes this shift between the dual personae of good and evil, living and undead, even more obvious.

Another character with a dual nature, or at least a dual ancestry, is Doyle. Doyle, Angel's appealing if slightly seedy sidekick for the first part of season one, turns out to be a demi-demon—that is, a man who is half human, half demon. The idea of a demi-god or demi-demon appears in both folklore and myth, though demi-gods are more common in the world's mythology than demi-demons. These demi-gods are generally heroic figures, and include such larger than life characters as the Greek Herakles (or Hercules), whose father, Zeus, was king of the Greek pantheon and whose mother was the mortal woman Alcmene, and the Polynesian Maui, whose father was divine and whose mother may or may not have been mortal (depending on which island people are telling the story), and who is said to have done such hero feats as fishing up

---

[1]A brief stop for defining terms: "Mythology" is used to mean the major issues such as creation, birth, death and major themes such as the hero's journey. "Folklore" includes the folktales, such as "Cinderella" and folk motifs, such as "Cinderella's slipper." It also includes "folk beliefs" and "folk customs," which refer to the beliefs in beings such as vampires and fairy folk.

islands. But demi-demons also exist. They are described in particular—and in an unflattering light—in the writings of the Zoroastrian religion of ancient Persia as those who seem human but who are truly demonic in thought and deed.

Doyle, who does his best to overcome the dark side of his nature, is similar in his inner struggles and dualism of nature to Angel. But then, the brooding hero with a dark past has become a classic figure in literature and modern fiction and has been one at least since Charlotte Bronte invented the handsome, tormented Heathcliff of *Wuthering Heights*.

Doyle is soon shown to have painful, prophetic visions that warn Angel of impending danger. The gift—or curse—of prophecy turns up in myths and folktales around the world. Most famously there is Cassandra of ancient Greece, who promised the god Apollo she would sleep with him in exchange for the gift of prophecy, but breaks her promise, leading Apollo to curse her. No one will believe her prophecies after that, not even when she warns of the fall of Troy. Doyle's painful but useful gift is later transferred to Cordelia, and finally, briefly, to Angel himself, almost like a contagion. The idea that the gift of prophecy can be transferred this way is a concept that is unique to *Angel*. Prophecies, however, play a major part throughout the entire series, with many of them centering on Angel or, later in the series, around both him and his son Connor, the boy who is born of two vampires.[2] One of the specific prophecies that concern both father and son is the one that warns that Angel will destroy his son. Though the prophecy itself turned out to be fake, this is a powerful theme that can be seen in such varied places as the Old Testament story of Abraham and his son Isaac, whom Abraham is willing to sacrifice if God so wills it, in the Greek myth of Kronos, who swallows his children so that they can't supplant him on the throne, and in the *Star Wars* conflict between Luke Skywalker and his father, Darth Vader.

Doyle also unexpectedly takes on a powerful mythic role. He becomes the willing sacrifice in the episode "Hero" (A1-9), the one who gives his life for the salvation of others. Later in the series, there is a second willing sacrifice: Darla, the vampire mother of Angel's son, who gives up her life for the sake of her son. Angel also willingly chooses a form of self-sacrifice when he signs away his chance to become human in return for the opportunity to save the world ("Not Fade Away,"

---

[2]Other, lesser prophets and prophecies appear throughout *Angel*, including such minor characters as three blind children who appear only once.

A5-22). There are obvious parallels regarding this theme of willing sacrifice, from Christianity to Norse mythology and the self-sacrifice the god Odin makes to gain wisdom. Odin, chief of the Norse pantheon, gave up an eye in exchange for a drink from the Well of Knowledge, and to gain knowledge of the runes, which were full of magic and symbolism, hung himself as a sacrifice from the World Tree for nine days and nine nights, a hangman's rope about his neck and wounded by his own spear. He died and was reborn in the same night with the wisdom of the runes.

Angel also confronts the viewer with the startling idea that there can be demons, at least in the *Angel*verse, who are not evil. For the most part, these relatively peaceful demons are pictured as wanting to simply live an undisturbed, almost ordinary life—just like the humans among whom some of them live. Lorne, for instance, or the family of demons in "Bachelor Party" (A1-7), aside from their out-of-character attempt to return to ancient tribal traditions by eating Doyle's brains, are rather nice folks. This concept of harmless or at least not actively dangerous demons is completely opposite from the Christian view of the demon as a creature of utter malevolence. Instead, this idea is more closely akin to the Jewish folkloric (though not religious) view of demons not as evil, but as amoral beings who are more like nature spirits than soulless monsters. There are Jewish folktales about demon women suing mortal men for divorce, or demons complaining about humans stealing from them, but none about demons deliberately doing evil.[3]

Some demons in the *Angel*verse are, at best, ambiguous in nature. Illyria, a demon from a very ancient time, has outlived her/its worshippers, and with no other purpose left, turns her powers to helping the friends of the woman whose body she/it has taken over. Possession by a god, demon or spirit is a very common phenomenon in the world's mythology and folklore. In Jewish folklore, a person could be possessed by a dybbuk, an amoral spirit which could be reasoned with and which could be argued into leaving, or by a gilgul, a human spirit returning and possessing a living body in order to complete some unfinished task. In Christian folk belief, a person might become possessed by a true devil, and the ritual of exorcism would be needed to banish the intruder. In the

---

[3] One example that sounds like a demon that could appear on *Angel* is the Jewish tale of a foolish young man who places a ring on what he thinks is a finger-like twig but is actually the finger of a female demon. She sues him in court and claims that he married her, and the case is only solved when she agrees to a legal divorce.

case of Illyria, though, the possession seems more truly science fiction than folklore: With little of Fred left, Illyria possesses a human body that is hers now in every sense.

Illyria also does a riff on the Orpheus theme, going into hell to retrieve Gunn ("Time Bomb," A5-19). In the tale of Orpheus, his beloved wife Eurydice dies, and Orpheus goes down to the Underworld to win her back. His music is so magical that Hades, god of the Underworld, agrees to let Eurydice go—if Orpheus can keep from looking at her until they reach the world of the living again. Orpheus looks at her too soon and loses her forever. The idea of going into hell and coming out again is less of a problem to a true demon, of course. But Illyria's journey there and back again is also an echo of a British folksong in which a woman who is carried off by the devil but is so fierce that he begs her to go back to earth. The song ends with a tongue-in-cheek salute to women because they can "go down to hell and come back out again."

Angel's pantheon of supernatural creatures is not limited to cariations on the demon, of course. In the first season episode "Rm W/ a Vu" (A1-5), Cordelia comes across another one of the most common folkloric characters: the ghost. Ghosts are perhaps the most worldwide of the supernatural phenomena and are portrayed in as many different ways as there are human emotions, from vengeful to helpful. Cordy's "roommate" Dennis seems to be more of a friendly helper than a supernatural entity, and smacks more of the amiable "Casper the Friendly Ghost" than he does any truly folkloric figure. One element consistent with the folklore in Dennis's story, however, is that he, like more traditional ghosts, is bound to the place of his death—in this case, the apartment in which Cordy lives.

Angel also features a more unusual ghost. In the spectacular last episode of Buffy ("Chosen," B7-22), Spike had quite heroically died saving the world. But characters seldom die for good in either the Buffy- or the Angelverse. Spike reappears in Angel as a ghost—but one who is able to make himself (at least somewhat) material by sheer will-power, an idea unique to the series.

Spike's reappearance, notably, is due to his essence being hidden in an amulet and then released. In many folktales, it is the heart (or soul) of a powerful being, usually the villain of the tale, that is hidden. For instance, in Russian tales featuring the evil supernatural character Koshchei the Immortal, Koshchei remains immortal only so long as his heart stays safely hidden. In all these folktales, the villain's heart (or soul) is discovered by the hero after a high-speed quest and is destroyed, which slays the villain.

Another folkloric being that makes an appearance is the zombie, in the play on words episode "Habeas Corpses" (A4-8). (The legal term, *habeas corpus*, refers to the right of a prisoner to file a petition if he or she claims wrongful imprisonment, but it literally means "you have the body.") A zombie is a creation of voodoo (or voudon) belief, primarily found in Haiti and other Caribbean islands, and in such southern states as Louisiana, particularly in New Orleans. While the actual enslavement of a reanimated dead body is folklore, there are some arguments that drugs could be used to turn a living person into the equivalent of a zombie.

In a cleverly named episode called "Long Day's Journey" (A4-9)—taken from the Eugene O'Neill play, *Long Day's Journey Into Night*—Angel and company learn that there is a demonic plot to blot out the sun. In the real world, of course, the loss of the sun would be the end of most life on Earth. However, in myth and folklore, there are countless tales dealing with the loss, theft and/or restoration of the sun. In one of the most common myths found in many of the Pacific Northwest tribes, from Alaska down to northern California, the creator-trickster being Raven, in the long-ago days of darkness, learns that a greedy old man has a golden ball that he keeps in a cedar chest. Raven turns himself into a pine needle and is drunk by the old man's daughter—who becomes pregnant and eventually gives birth to Raven in the form of a human baby. Raven whines and screams until the old man gives him the golden ball—whereupon Raven turns back into a bird and flies off with the ball, which he tosses into the sky to become the sun. In Japanese mythology, the sun goddess Amaterasu is insulted by her brother and promptly hides her light away in a cave. Before the world dies, she has to be coaxed back out by the other gods with the promise of a wonderful party. And in Polynesian mythology, the trickster-hero Maui lassoes the sun, which until then raced across the sky, and forces it to agree to move more slowly and evenly across the heavens.

Another folk motif that turns up in *Angel* is the idea of magical—or in this case demonic—blood. Such blood can grant new powers to the person touching, tasting or being infected with it. When the hero Sigfried of Teutonic lore accidentally tastes the blood of the dragon Fafnir, whom he has just slain, the hero magically gains the gift of understanding what the birds are saying—and takes a warning from the birds that saves his life from a treacherous enemy about to murder him. In a variant of this motif, the Irish Celtic hero Finn mac Cumhail (also spelled Finn mac Cool) accidentally burns himself on fat from the roasting Salmon of Knowledge. He sticks his burnt thumb into his mouth to soothe the pain—and magically gains the salmon's wisdom. In Angel's case, the demon blood that infects him in "I Will Remember You" (A1-8) gives him the mixed blessing of mortality.

A folkloric object that appears early in *Angel* is the magic ring: the Gem of Amarra from "In the Dark" (A1-3) is described as a ring that renders its vampire wearer unkillable. Magic rings turn up in many a myth and folktale from Europe and Asia, some of them major items, others possessing only minor powers. Both Jewish and Arabic folklore claim that King Solomon of Israel was a magician as well as a wise man, and that he possessed a magic ring inscribed with the six-pointed star commonly known as the Star of David, which let him rule over the genii (the plural of the more familiar geni, or genie), and other supernatural beings. Magic rings are almost as common in fantasy fiction as they are in folklore, the most obvious of which are the magic rings of power and the perilous One Ring in J.R.R. Tolkien's *Lord of the Rings*.

In the fifth season, Angel and Spike fight over another mythic object, the Cup of Perpetual Torment. Magical or holy cups and cauldrons can be found throughout the world's mythology and folklore. Perhaps the most famous, at least in Western literature, is the Holy Grail, the cup from the Last Supper that is said to have caught Christ's blood at the Crucifixion and then been hidden away in a mysterious British castle surrounded by a wasteland. The quest of King Arthur's knights for the Holy Grail was the subject of works written by authors such as the twelfth century Chretien de Troyes and the fifteenth-century Sir Thomas Malory, and the cup also turns up in the 1975 comedy *Monty Python and the Holy Grail* and the 1989 fantasy adventure *Indiana Jones and the Last Crusade*.

However, earlier than the stories of the Holy Grail are those of the Celtic cups and cauldrons of never-ending plenty. The most powerful of these is the Cauldron of Rebirth that turns up in the story of the giant hero-king Bran in the Medieval collection of ancient tales known as the *Mabinogion*. Bran gave the cauldron of rebirth to the Irish king who married Bran's sister, Branwen. But the marriage was a disaster, the

Irish declared war on Bran's kingdom and the cauldron became a deadly source of warriors, until it was shattered when a living man threw himself into it.

The episode "The Shroud of Rahmon" (A2-8) is actually named for its mythic element, a dangerous, mild-altering shroud which has absorbed the power of the demonic Rahmon. This artifact was probably inspired by the very opposite type of artifact, the real Shroud of Turin (which is said in Christian folk belief to hold the image of Christ's face), but it also has a great deal to do with magical artifacts of folklore and folk belief from magic carpets to sentient swords. The idea of an arcane object imbuing its possessor with good or evil powers falls more into the category of modern folk belief—and of course of fantasy fiction. In *The Lord of the Rings*, it is the One Ring itself that has an almost sentient malevolence to it and which destroys all who wear it. The same idea of an artifact taking over a character turns up in movies such as the 1994 *The Mask*, in which Jim Carrey's character is imbued with the persona of Loki, described in the movie as "the Norse god of mischief." (Loki is actually closer to a trickster figure, like the American Southwest's Coyote, a being who works change just for the sake of change.[4])

Several times in the series, a magical portal, the arcane doorway between two dimensions, appears. In folklore, this is often a doorway that allows a human to pass into some form of Faerie realm. The most common form appears in Celtic folktales, and presents itself as an opening in a hollow hill—a clear misunderstanding of Neolithic burial mounds. The portal between dimensions can also be interpreted as a psychiatric motif, one in which the mind passes through the stages of its development, or a shamanistic one, in which the shaman is said to travel into the spirit realm. In *Angel*, an opened portal is more likely to lead into a hell dimension, or at least a demonic one—which is not always the same thing in the *Angel*verse. Aside from the fact that humans are treated as cattle, Lorne's home dimension looks almost agreeable, like some medieval setting or a version of our own Western frontier.

Related to magic portals is the concept of different and unpredictable flows of time. In *Angel*, Angel's son Connor is taken to a hell dimension

---

[4]Norse scholars also don't all accept Loki as demonic, either. They suspect that the final tale of Loki, in which he brings about the death of the gentle god Balder, is a later addition to the Norse canon, one that dates to the arrival of Christianity—and the concept of the devil—to Scandinavia.

as a baby and returns in what seems like only a short time to the mortal world as a young man, an angry teen. Time traditionally flows differently between mortal and immortal realms, such as Faerie—and Hell. There are many folktales from lands as far apart as Britain and Japan that concern humans who think that only a day in Faerie—or another, similar supernatural Otherworld—has occurred, and who then return to mortal realms to find that years have passed. In the most extreme versions of these tales, there is a tragic ending, and the unfortunate human, touching mortal soil once again, then collapses and dies of extreme old age or even dissolves into dust. The story of Ossian of Ireland is a typical tale of this type. Ossian, the son of the Celtic hero Finn mac Cumhail and a fairy woman, goes off to live in the fairy realm. When he returns to Ireland after what seems to him only a short while, he instantly becomes an ancient man and dies.

In a visit to Las Vegas, Angel becomes involved with yet another folk motif: the stolen soul. In this case, it is people's destinies that are being stolen, and stored away in gems for sale on the black market ("The House Always Wins," A4-3). In the folklore of Cornwall and other British regions, there is the concept of the Soul Cage, a magical device in which a stolen soul can be trapped. In modern folk custom in Pakistan, it is caged birds that represent such captives, and the bird sellers beg passers-by to pay to free the birds—and save their own souls from captivity at the same time.

A similar Christian motif is the deal with the devil, in which a character sells his soul and then has to be rescued from the deal when it comes due. This was the central point of Stephen Vincent Benet's mid-nineteenth century short story, "The Devil and Daniel Webster," in which the real-life lawyer argues and wins a case against the devil. In *Angel* it is the streetwise Gunn who has to be rescued from the deal with the devil ("Double or Nothing," A3-18). Later Gunn makes a similar trade to retain his legal knowledge ("Smile Time," A5-14). He suspects that there will be a price, but not the one which is eventually paid: Fred's life and, more importantly, her soul.

Angel also uses a great many religious folk and mythic motifs. One twist on a religious theme is introduced when Cordelia suddenly (and rather strangely) undergoes a mystical apotheosis, ascending up out of the mortal plane to a higher level of existence. Religious figures such as the Jewish prophet Elijah and the Islamic prophet Mohammed are said to have ascended to heaven without dying.

The major religious mythic element running through *Angel*, however, is the theme of the Apocalypse, the final battle between Good and Evil. In the Christian view, it is clear that after the Apocalypse the world will end for good. In Norse mythology, however, there is a different conclusion. In the Norse final battle, called Ragnarok (the doom of the gods), after the Norse deities battled with the forces of evil, the universe itself would die—but then would be reborn into a new golden age. This cyclical view of a destroyed and rebuilt universe also appears in Hindu religion, in which the earth is in a constant cycle of destruction and rebirth.

The Beast, the demonic creature that turns up in season four, is definitely related to the mysterious "beast" mentioned in the Christian texts of the Apocalypse. Who or what the texts' beast may be is never clearly explained, nor is the nature of the Beast. Jasmine herself fits the description of the Anti-Christ, whose objective is to deceive people into following him just as Jasmine does, hiding her ugliness behind a mask of beauty.

Cultures constantly borrow from one another, adopting ideas and stories that resonate and disregarding those that don't. In *Angel*, all these disparate elements—religious motifs, mythic objects, folkloric creatures—have been woven together to create a new story, a new mythology in its own right: a mythology that will live on in the show's fans long after it is gone.

Josepha Sherman is a fantasy novelist, folklorist and editor, and has written everything from Star Trek *novels to biographies of Bill Gates and Jeff Bezos (founder of Amazon.com) to titles such as* Mythology for Storytellers *(from M.E. Sharpe) and* Tricksters Tales *(August House). She is the winner of the prestigious Compton Crook Award for best fantasy novel and has had many titles on the New York Public Library Books for the Teen Reader list. Most current titles include* Star Trek: Vulcan's Soul: Exodus *with Susan Shwartz, the forthcoming reprint of the Unicorn Queen books from Del Rey and the forthcoming* Stoned Souls *with Mercedes Lackey, for Baen Books. She is also editing* The Encyclopedia of Storytelling *for M.E. Sharpe. For her other editorial projects, you can check out www.ShermanEditorialServices.com.*

When she isn't busy writing, editing or gathering folklore, Sherman loves to travel, knows how to do Horse Whispering and has had a newborn foal fall asleep on her foot. You can visit her at www.JosephaSherman.com.

Laura Anne Gilman

TRUE SHANSHU

Redemption Through Compassion, and the Journey
of Cordelia Chase

Cordelia played an important role—more important than most people recognized—in the first three seasons of Buffy. *But in* Angel *she wasn't important; she was essential. Her departure (which really was at the end of season three) left an unfilled hole in the show. We were reminded of just how big a hole it was when she briefly returned in "You're Welcome" (A5-12). It was almost painful, because it reminded us of just how much we missed our Cordy.*

I N MANY WAYS, *Angel* was never about Angel. The vampire with a soul provided the action, but it was those he interacted with who mattered: the people he helped—and those who traveled with Angel on his road to redemption.

So, we have a show that, at least on one level, isn't about the redemption of the titular character but instead those who, at first glance, might appear to be secondary. Welcome to Joss Whedonland, where nothing is ever as it seems. Both the redemptive successes (Wes, Darla) and the

179

failures (Lindsey) were notable, but none more so than Cordelia Chase, the poor-little-formerly-rich-girl who had come to Los Angeles not only in search of a career but to escape the hell of Sunnydale—and who, in the very first episode, found herself instead smack in the middle (again!) of the fight against evil.

So let's take a look at Cordelia Chase, lately of Sunnydale High School and the Hellmouth.

BABY STEPS

In the first episode, "City Of" (A1-1), we see Cordelia as an extension of who she was during her run on *Buffy*: not quite a victim, not quite a "Scooby." She makes an error in judgment in getting "trapped" by a vampire posing as a casting agent, but puts the clues together and tries to escape on her own. Her inability to do so, and subsequent rescue by Angel, isn't presented as a failure on her part, but merely one person needing another's help to get by. This is consistent with the presentation of victims throughout the series: people who weren't stupid or, with a few exceptions, in any way "deserving" of their fate. They merely made mistakes.

Where Cordelia differed from those other people in need was two-fold: One, she knew even before the casting director showed his (literal) fangs. And two, she went on the offensive as soon as she realized what was going on.

But Cordelia wasn't important to *Angel* because she was a warrior, however reluctant, for the Good. She was important because she was *human*. Unlike Angel, the vampire (however souled), or Doyle, the half-human, half-Brachen demon who brought purpose with his visions of those in need, in the opening episodes of *Angel*, Cordelia Chase was the everywoman we could relate to. Beautiful, yes. Smart and sassy and with the ability to protect herself as much as any human could against demons, but still vulnerable. In another show, she might have been the perpetual bait. But on *Angel*, she was Angel's right hand woman—his partner, however unadmitted, in the search for redemption.

In fact, no character was better set up to be Angel's foil as this not-quite-so-heroic everywoman. From our very first sight of her on *Buffy* as the shallow, me-me-me cheerleader, Cordelia Chase had both magnetism and pathos. Her arrogance was both undercut and enhanced by her admission to Buffy about being lonely back in the episode "Out of Mind, Out of Sight" (B1-11):

CORDELIA: You think I'm never lonely because I'm so cute and popular? I can be surrounded by people and be completely alone. It's not like any of them really know me. I don't even know if they like me half the time. People just want to be in a popular zone. Sometimes when I talk, everyone's so busy agreeing with me, they don't hear a word I say.

BUFFY: Well, if you feel so alone, then why do you work so hard at being popular?

CORDELIA: Well, it beats being alone all by yourself.

Even then, there was something about Cordelia that resonated with viewers. And when she made a comment on the actions of others, it was seen through untinted glasses with resonance beyond that of a one-dimensional spoiled teenager. If her humor and sharp-edged observations were a shield against being hurt, Cordelia still gave a human face to the Popular Girl, the Snob, the Rich Girl, and made us cheer for her when she took on vampire after bugman after oozing demon, despite wanting nothing whatsoever to do with that world. Chase wasn't a "Scooby;" she was just trying to survive.

Survival, in fact, was always the name of her game. Cordelia Chase allowed nothing to stop her for long, reinventing herself after every loss. But where the blows that she took—the debunking of any humancentric certainties about the universe, losing the family money to her father's tax evasion, Xander and Willow's "fluking," taking a rebar through the torso—might have made someone else bitter, Cordelia went the other direction. Yes, the sharp wit and biting sarcasm remained. But the innate honesty and powers of observation which had made her observations so effective on *Buffy* were honed as well, to positive result.

THE TURNING POINT

In "I Fall to Pieces" (A1-4), Angel and Cordelia have an ongoing discussion about charging people for their services. Cordelia, predictably, is all about getting paid. She argues for making the rent, paying the bills, buying designer shoes. The same old Cordelia, right?

Except that her own actions refute such materialistic goals.

In the episode "Rm w/a Vu" (A1-5), Cordelia's combination of human practicality and compassion really gets a chance to shine, and we see the progress she has made since "City Of" (A1-1). Given the chance to move into a lovely but cheap new apartment, Cordelia leaps at it. But the apartment is haunted, and she slowly sinks under the relentless negative message of the haunting spirit, a bitter old woman who cannot stand to see anyone with promise or love or hope in her vicinity. Near to being broken by the attack, which played on her most deeply hidden fears and weaknesses, Cordelia nonetheless rallies through sheer stubborn pride. She manages to not only recover enough of her "uber bitch" toughness and strong sense of self—what she refers to as "not a cry-Buffy"—to fight off the killer's murderous influences, but is able, after all that, to not only create a home for herself in that place, but to allow another ghost, the murdered son of the original haunt, to stay with her as her roommate. Without anyone else's supernatural help, she found the strength within herself to say "no, you may not beat me down or destroy me."

And then, of course, came "Hero" (A1-9). In that episode, Cordelia, the original "ewww a demon" material girl, admitted to herself that she could maybe make it work with Doyle, even if he was short, with bad taste in clothing, divorced and as she learns here, half-demon. The change in perception might not hit quite the same level as kicking demon ass and saving the innocent, but it's another major step along her own road. It also makes the pathos of what might have been with Doyle that much more painful. There is no growth without sacrifice, as Cordelia herself knows. But this particular sacrifice is even more important, not only because of what she lost, but because of what she gained. For in "Parting Gifts" (A1-10), we learn that when Doyle kissed her before sacrificing himself, she "inherited" his visions of people who needed help.

With the events of "Hero," and her realization that the things she had once held to be essential (money, looks, status) weren't the things that were maybe most important to her after all, Cordelia is showing us through her own realization that being human isn't about being weak, or clueless, or a victim. It's about the ability to learn, and the ability to grow. Through sacrifice and pain, yes, but also through joy. Because the two sides, sorrow and happiness, are inescapably entwined.

In developing the ability to sympathize not only with people exactly like herself, but those who look nothing at all like her, Cordelia had taken another step on the road from self-interest to selflessness. Although not pleased (understatement!) with her new "gift," she is able to see the useful side of it, and perhaps in some small way conceives of it as a memorial to Doyle and what now could never be.

The effects of those visions become clear in "To Shanshu in L.A." (A1-22), when Cordelia is opened to all the sadness and need in the world by the demon Vocah. Although the plan was to distract Angel by placing "his people" in danger, this is also a test of sorts for Cordelia. The suffering of so many overwhelms her and sends her into a coma-like state where all she can hear is the pain. Only Angel's determination to break the spell brings her back to herself, but once awake again, she alone can make the decision to go on. Cordelia cannot turn away from what she now knows—that she *can* make a difference.

Her journey thereafter is a series of challenges to that decision. One of the earliest and most difficult comes in the Pylea storyline—"Belonging" (A2-19), "Over the Rainbow" (A2-20), "Through the Looking Glass" (A2-21) and "There's no Place like Plrtz Glrb" (A2-22) allow Cordelia her long-dreamed of position as an actual princess, complete with a handsome champion who lives only to serve her. And yet, she finds that the role of pampered princess no longer suits her: she is unable to not see the cost other people pay for her comfort. And with that realization, she knows that she must return home, her visions intact, to continue fighting. This is perhaps the pivotal moment for her: Given the opportunity for everything she ever dreamed of, at the simple cost of giving up her visions (and the attendant migraines), she cannot. Yes, she enjoys being useful and wanted. But that in and of itself is a major change, and one she is now forced to recognize. The old "Queen C," as she was known occasionally on *Buffy*, would not have cared about being useful or needed—others were there to need her approval, not for her to aid them. It's a radical change not only in her actions, but in her self-image as well.

Looking back at the path Cordelia Chase took in the first two seasons of *Angel*—giving up her dream of stardom for A.I., learning from Doyle about the needs of the many versus the needs of the few, being misled by her own preconceptions or flawed observations but coming back to set things right—we are shown something more than a person trying to get through each day as best she can. Cordelia Chase discovers that she, as well as Angel, has a mission.

There is sacrifice and pain, yes, but joy in knowing that she is doing the right thing. She's the one who grew up through the series, more than anyone else—not just in experience but in *learning* from her experiences, something the non-human Angel was slow to do.

THIS IS THE JOSSVERSE, AFTER ALL . . .

If from every weakness you can develop a strength, the revise is also true. With every strength, there comes a weakness.

> SKIP: You're Cordelia Chase, right? Sorry it took me so long, I . . . . Is this you? Most people go astral, their spiritual shapes tend to be an idealized version of themselves. You know, straighten the nose, lose the gray, sort of a self-esteem kind of thing. You're pretty confident, aren't you? ("Birthday," A3-11)

Confident, and therefore, in JossWhedonland, ripe for temptation and distraction. In "Birthday," Cordelia, slowly dying from the visions that allow her to help those in need, is shown a universe in which the things she wanted when she came to Los Angeles—fame, fortune, someone to take care of her problems for her—are there for the taking. More, they're being *given* to her. All she has to do is be that person again. Not so much shallow as self-concerned. Caring, but limited.

She can't do it.

Leaving aside the question of Whedon's storytelling intentions (was she being further tested? Punished? Played so that she would be in position later on to give birth to Jasmine? The possibilities are endless. Trust in Joss. Joss lies), Cordelia's decision here to take on demonic aspects in order to maintain the visions without dying are a negative turning point for her, although we do not know it until much later on.[1]

Having renounced her humanity, even if for a good purpose, Cordelia also lets go of some of the vulnerability humanity brings with it. She is protected from the effects of the visions—but that opens her up to malign influences, and it's a slow but steady descent from there into confusion and Evil, until the "real" Cordelia returns in the hundredth episode, "You're Welcome" (A5-12).

In that episode, Cordelia wakes up from her coma and is shocked and unhappy to discover that Angel and the gang are no longer fighting Wolfram & Hart, they're running it. When she realizes that Angel has lost his conviction to be a hero, she gives him the information and support he needs to get back on track—and gives up her own life to do

---

[1] Remember Buffy's refusal in "Get It Done" (B7-15), when forced with a similar decision: the power to win, courtesy of a little demon-rape, or taking her chances with her own humanity. Buffy's success against the First Evil affirmed her choice; Cordelia's fate condemns hers.

so. This time, there is no safety net below her. She is human, and the truest human sacrifice (resonating with Doyle's sacrifice back in season one, even—as is revealed in season five's "Power Play" (A5-21)—in her transfer of one final vision to Angel just as Doyle transferred his visions to her) is death: the end of growing, to enable another to learn and grow in turn.

In her humanity, we see the best points of the *Angel*verse: not the strong defending the weak, but the weak learning how to be strong. That the heart can defeat the fang. That, in the end, it's always going to be up to us as individuals to get up, dust ourselves off, and move on. That being human is not about having a soul, but using it. In the exercise of compassion and love, rather than brain or muscle. That shanshu—the prophesy that said the vampire with a soul would "live until he died"—has nothing to do with breath, but heart.

Even Angel, in his own stumbling way, learned what Cordelia by then already knew: "I guess I kinda—worked it out. If there is no great glorious end to all this, if nothing we do matters . . . then all that matters is what we do" ("Epiphany," A2-16).

And with each reinvention, Cordelia, even more than Angel, showed us what to do. How to grow into true humanity. How to, in effect, shanshu (to live until you die) with passion, compassion and joy. In short, how to be human.

Laura Anne Gilman is the author of more then twenty short stories, three non-fiction books for teens, several non-fiction essays, two Buffy the Vampire Slayer *tie-in novels and a forthcoming original novel,* Staying Dead, *out in August 2004, with the follow-up,* Curse the Dark, *scheduled for July 2005. For more information, go to http://www.sff.net/people/lauraanne.gilman.*

Jennifer Crusie

THE ASSASSINATION OF CORDELIA CHASE

How many television producers do you really trust? I don't mean trust with your life or money (answer: none), but trust with your heart. How many do you trust as storytellers, to keep the faith, to play fair so that you can unreservedly enter their worlds? It's a short list, to be sure, but Joss Whedon and the folks at Mutant Enemy are at the top. So when betrayal comes, it's that much more horrifying. . . .

A S ANY GOOD WRITER KNOWS—and the writers at Mutant Enemy, the company that produced *Buffy the Vampire Slayer* and *Angel*, are usually very good writers—the first law of characterization is "Never violate your character's core identity." You can play all the variations on her psychology that you want, you can show her growing and regressing, making huge mistakes and taking huge maturation leaps, but you cannot violate who she is at heart. As a centuries-old and wise Darla tells Angel, "What we once were informs all that we have become"("The Prodigal," A1-15). The choice between honoring character to show growth and mutilating character to serve plot spells the difference between the delighted reaction, "I can't believe she did that!" and the betrayed protest, "I don't believe she'd do that." The writers at ME have played fast and loose with character before (let's not talk about "Doublemeat Palace," B6-12), but they never sinned so deeply as they did when they destroyed the character of Cordelia Chase.

From the moment Cordelia appears in "Welcome to the Hellmouth," the first episode of *Buffy the Vampire Slayer*, she is a clear-cut character, smiling a wide, bright toothpaste smile that disguises the calculating glint in her eye. Her first act is to beam at Buffy while sharing her history book, an overt kindness that disguises Cordy's covert motive: finding out if the new girl in town is a potential acolyte or a potential threat to Cordy's kingdom. She alienates Buffy by committing the worst of all possible crimes in the *Buffy*verse, being cruel to Willow ("Good to know you've seen the softer side of Sears," she tells Willow after surveying her dress), but she doesn't care because Buffy's opinion is irrelevant to her. If Buffy can't admire Cordelia for who she is, she's obviously not worthy of being a Cordette and will just have to dwell in outer darkness, away from Sunnydale High's social galaxy, a place Cordy dominates with her implacable will and indestructible smile. Cordelia may not be Miss Congeniality, but nobody ever calls her weak.

Cordy's solipsism could easily be mistaken for stupidity, but it comes coupled with a keen intelligence and a fixity of purpose that makes her almost invincible. "I have to have the most expensive thing," she tells the Cordettes, "not because it's the most expensive but because it costs more"("The Harvest," B1-2). This seems like a lovely bit of airhead-speak, but it isn't. "Expensive," as Cordelia knows, is subjective: that new detergent might be expensive and that flawed diamond cheap. "Costs more" is finite, measurable and therefore attainable. Cordy has to have the thing that costs more than anybody else can afford, the thing that's impossible for anybody else to get, because her world is about measurable things and she intends to be the material girl at the top. And since Cordy is living in the very material world of American society that the rest of us also occupy, she's usually right: Often overlooked in the outrage at the Sears comment is the fact that Willow really does look like her mother dressed her from the you'll-never-get-a-date department, and that Willow's later demonstration of her maturity and strength is shown to a great extent in her choice of a much more adventurous wardrobe. Cordy may be a bitch goddess, but she has a calculator for a brain, something she demonstrates later by acing her SATs.

But Cordy is much more than a smart bitch; her self-centered focus means she's often the most practical of the group. When she finally catches on to the Hellmouth, her reaction is exactly what it needs to be to make her valuable: she fights back, indignant that anyone or anything can threaten her, to the point of biting a vampire who tries to drag her through the library door ("Prophecy Girl," B1-12). When Willow and Jenny are threatened by a street full of vampires in "Prophecy Girl," Cordelia saves them by picking them up in her very cool car and then delivering them to the door of the library, via the school's central hall. Even her lack of depth becomes a strength: When Buffy hears the thoughts of the others in "Earshot" (B3-18), most people's insecurities show how weak they are and in turn weaken her with their pain; Cordelia's thoughts, however, are identical to the things she says out loud and don't hurt Buffy. Not even the trials she faces toward the end of her life in Sunnydale—her loss of status because she falls in love with Xander, her betrayal by Xander (with Willow in a hot black dress), her fall into poverty because her father is nabbed by the IRS—can derail her from pursuing what she feels she deserves. By the end of her time on *Buffy*, she's stronger, she's wiser and she knows how to use a flamethrower, but she's still a self-centered beauty with a blazing intelligence, a focused practicality and a keen eye for the bottom line. She's still, in short, Cordy.

This means that she fits perfectly into selfish, superficial Los Angeles, so it made great sense for ME to send her there to pursue an acting career in the dark noir world of *Angel*. L.A. is Cordy's trial by fire: Like so many wannabee actresses, Cordelia may have been the most beautiful girl in her home town, but she's one of the crowd now. Surrounded by other gorgeous women, some of whom even have talent and training, Cordy is reduced to living in a roach-infested slum and stealing tomorrow's dinner from party buffets. When she finally reaches bottom and agrees to see a famous producer in his home, she's clearly if reluctantly planning on trading her body for her career, her focus as fixed as ever. But even in the midst of her distress over what she's going to do, she's smart enough to notice a key decorating flaw: no mirrors. Her exasperated accusation, "You're a vampire!" momentarily slows her predator, who's used to disbelief, not annoyance, but she's still running for her life when Angel bursts in to save her ("City of ," A1-1).

Other women would be grateful, and Cordy is, but her eye, as always, is on the bottom line. Angel is depressed, of course, and helping people, of course, but how is he paying the rent? More important, how can he help her pay her rent? In a better place? With better clothes? Before Angel has time to protest, Cordy is printing business cards and making commercials and, no small thing, generating real income for him. Angel may be the Romantic Hero, spiritually and literally saving others, but Cordy is completely in character as the Enlightened Heroine, making sure that the bills are paid and the electricity stays on. She grounds Angel the way her character grounds the series *Angel*, by saving them both from strangling on his darkness and nobility. The elegant part of this narrative move is that by saving Angel, Cordy saves herself, discovering that she is more than a beautiful face, a hot body and a killer fashion sense. L.A. almost destroys her by making her doubt the only thing she has—herself—but Angel and the occult give it back to her, most vividly in the episode, "Rm w/ a Vu" (A1-5). The vicious ghost of Maude Pierson, haunting the apartment where she walled up her son alive, taunts Cordy into almost hanging herself by telling her that she's a nobody, tapping into the one belief that will destroy her core identity. But then the ghost goes too far, calling Cordy "a little bitch," reminding her of who she is, the Bitch Goddess of Sunnydale come to conquer L.A. When Cordy rises up saying, "That's right, *I am a bitch*," the ghost is toast, and Cordy's back—sadder, smarter, darker and more human, but absolutely Cordy, the natural evolution of the Sunnydale Queen, made mature and implacable flesh in haunted Sodom on the Pacific.

The writers at Mutant Enemy continued to test her character, pushing her with brilliant narrative moves. They first send the visionary Doyle to be the third in the Angel triumvirate, and while Cordy rejects him in the beginning, saying "I'd rather be dead than date a fixer-upper [like Xander] again," she grows to appreciate him after he saves her from a demon while her high-rent boyfriend runs away, forcing her to realize in disgust that "All of a sudden, rich and handsome isn't enough for me. Now I expect a guy to be all brave and interesting" ("The Bachelor Party," A1-7). Her first approach to him—"Maybe you don't have zero potential"—is cut short by his sacrifice of his life, a sacrifice that he makes her a part of when he transfers his prophetic gift to her in a farewell kiss.

His death changes her, not just because she's now stuck with excruciating visions, but also because she truly did love him and, amazingly for Cordy, mourns for him when he's dead, watching the terrible advertising videos he made for her with sobering intensity and regret, finding within herself a new level of humanity.

But her newfound depth does not mean she accepts the visions. Cordy is still Cordy, and the goal of her life is still to help Cordy, not a bunch of unwashed people who show up screaming in her head. She does her best to pass on the visions, kissing everyone who walks by—"I don't care, I want it out of me, and if kissing is the only way to get rid of it, I will smooch every damn frog in this kingdom"—because, as she declares, she doesn't have anything to atone for. Her last kiss is with the empath demon Barney, who reads her mind and sticks a knife into her soul, the second test the writers send her. He tells her that she knows she does have things to atone for, that she knows she's self-absorbed and full of regret and, the unkindest cut, that she's fully aware that she's a terrible actress. "You feel it," he tells her. "You're entire being is whispering it to me right now." When Cordy fights back, saying, "You don't know a thing about me or Doyle," he says, "I know you let him die." Whether it's true or not, it feels true, and when Barney adds, "If only for one freaking second, you gave a damn about anything besides yourself," he's condemning the source of her strength, cutting into the core of who she is ("Parting Gifts," A1-10). Cordy, of course, does not give up, rallying an auction house full of demon collectors to bid higher for the visionary eyes they plan to rip out of her head by extolling her many real and imagined virtues in a scene that is the epitome of Cordelia-ness. The end of the episode is a mixed blessing: Barney appears to give Cordelia empathy as he dies, an attribute that's as toxic to her character as Kryptonite, but Cordy has also faced her inner demons—with the help of an outer one—and survived, gaining even more self-knowledge and moving into adulthood.

And she's gained something else, too. Angel saves her again, the one constant in her life now, and he takes her back to his basement apartment where he fixes her breakfast. As she tells the new third partner, Wesley, as they invite him to the table, breakfast is "one of the perks of the job. After an all-nighter of fighting evil, we get eggs" ("Parting Gifts," A1-10). The empathy Barney has cursed her with makes it possible for her to connect to others without losing her basic self-interest and distrust of humanity—without losing, that is, her core identity. As she explains in the last scene in "Expecting" (A1-12), when she faces a concerned Angel and Wesley the morning after her ordeal:

> CORDELIA: I learned that all men are evil. Oh, wait, I knew that.
> I learned that L.A. is full of self-serving phonies. No, had that down, too. Sex is bad?
> ANGEL: We all knew that.
> CORDELIA: Okay. I learned that I have two people that I trust absolutely with my life. And that part's new.

It's clear, too, that Cordelia is not alone in perceiving her community. She's the one that Angel turns to with his greatest fear, that he will turn into Angelus again. When he asks her, "If the day ever comes," Cordelia says promptly, "Oh, I'll kill you dead," and he thanks her, knowing full well that she will, that he can count on her enlightened practicality to murder him without blinking. It's one of many exchanges that cement an extremely unlikely relationship, something Angel acknowledges in "Expecting," when a friend of Cordy's says, "You the boyfriend?" and he replies, "No, I'm family."

It would have been so easy for the Mutant Enemy writers to slip at this point, to make Angel and Cordelia lovers, to make Cordelia a do-gooder, to even make Cordelia less selfish, but they stayed true to her character: Cordelia might be empathetic, she might have attached with real emotion to a man who can't give her diamonds, but she's still Corde-lia Chase. Or as she sums it up in "She": "Well, this is great now we're really—do I have to take a pay cut?—a team." The empathy and visions that lesser writers might have made A Very Special Growth Experience continue to be a pain in the brain, as Cordelia complains, "I don't just see, I feel, okay?" adding, "I hate this gig" ("She," A1-13).

It was the perfect balance of self-centeredness and responsibility, but it couldn't last because story, like life, is fluid. While Cordelia's relation-ship with Angel grows stronger, and her life grows richer, the visions grow more violent until they're literally killing her. When Skip, the de-mon sent by the Powers That Be, offers her a choice of two futures, one becoming part demon so she can stay with Angel and continue to help others and the other becoming the Mary Tyler Moore of the twenty-first century, Cordy picks being Mary and leaves the others to rot while she revels in success. But like most choices offered by the Powers, it doubles back on her, and when she's led back to Angel, now made insane by the visions, she kisses him and takes them back, because it's Angel, and she loves him, and because, at a deeper level, she can't bear the guilt that failing to save another man who loves her will bring ("Birthday," A3-11). This isn't Cordelia the Saint, it's Cordelia the Practical, risking a demon tail to go back to the place where she has someone she trusts absolutely. It's both the right thing to do for others and the right thing to do for her, and Cordy needs both as motivation now. She stays, growing even closer to Angel, accepting his son as her own and finally acknowledging her attraction to him, which, entirely in character, comes long after he's admitted his attraction to her. Her brief flirtation with Groo, the uncomplicated cartoon Angel who loves her the way Angel will always love Buffy, isn't enough for the Inner Cordy who now, as always, accepts no less expensive substitutes. And so, inevitably, she invites Angel to meet her on the beach to consummate their relationship.

It's at this point that the ME writers evidently lost their minds.

For on a busy highway, time stops, a blue light shines down and the Powers That Be invite Cordy up to be a Higher Power. And Cordy, in one of the lamest scenes in Mutant Enemy history (and my deepest sympathies to Charisma Carpenter for having to act in it), accepts without much protest ("I know it's right, I know somehow it's gonna be all right"), setting aside the fact that she was about to have cosmic sex with a supernatural hero, not even asking first if there'll be little blue boxes and great shoes in Heaven ("Tomorrow," A3-22). The Material Girl, even after great spiritual awakening, does not go where she cannot shop, but Cordelia leaped at the chance as thousands of viewers frowned at the screen and said, "I don't believe she'd do that. Must be a joke," and waited in vain for the punch line.

From there, things only got worse. Cordy came back dressed like Elvira Queen of the Night and slept with Connor, Angel's sulky son. (A good topic for another essay: Why do the Good Girls Gone Bad of the Whedon Universe—the Bad Willow, Buffy from Cleveland, Cordelia the Beastmaster and Blue Fred—always wear too much eyeliner and dress like dominatrixes? Where's the subtext, the humor, the subtlety?) That Cordy came back with bad fashion sense was a real betrayal; that she came back and cuckolded Angel with a boy she'd considered her son was just gross. Whatever hope I had of Cordelia's Ascension being a bad mistake that could be forgotten died when she rolled in the sheets with Connor while Angel watched from a nearby rooftop ("Apocalypse

Nowish," A4-7). I've been a fervid Whedon fan from the beginning, but I almost stopped watching the show at that point, convinced that Mutant Enemy had been devoured by demons, probably masquerading as network vice presidents. I tuned in again for and was delighted with "Awakening," a perfectly executed Gotcha episode, but it wasn't enough to balance what the writers had done to Cordelia, and it only got worse when the writers flashed what they evidently thought was their winning hand: The whole Cordelia-and-Connor outrage had been a Gotcha, too.

Here it's necessary to discuss good and bad Gotchas in order to understand the depth, breadth and height of Mutant Enemy's mistake. The Gotcha is a trick that writers play on readers and viewers, and it's a very dangerous move to make. Much of what makes reading or viewing enjoyable is the understanding that the reader or audience is in trusted hands, that the writers will not lie to them, make them feel stupid or fail them in any way, so any story that relies on fooling the reader walks a very fine line. Readers want to be surprised; they don't want to be betrayed. The brilliance of the Gotcha in "Awakening" rests on two important things: There are plenty of clues to show what's really happening, and the Gotcha is revealed at the end of the episode.

"Awakening" begins with the attempt to turn Angel into Angelus to get information that only the demon has. The surefire way to do this is to give Angel one moment of perfect happiness making love with a woman he loves, and since Buffy is in Sunnydale and would probably reject the idea of sleeping with Angel to bring back the worst serial killer in history, they turn to a shaman who tries to put Angel into a deep sleep. But Angel disarms him—the shaman is evil of course—and reveals secret writings tattooed on the shaman's torso (there have been stranger things in the Whedon universe) which lead them to search for a sword to kill the Beast (a little standard for ME but still possible within its boundaries), which draws them all through a *Raiders-of-the-Lost-Ark*-like maze (too on-the-nose, but I still bought it) to the sword which Connor gives up to Angel, calling him Dad and reconciling with him long enough to kill the Beast together (oh, *come on*) and ending with all the Angel crew reconciled and happy, and Cordy telling Angel that she'd always loved him best and giving herself to him, at which point I hooted and said, "What is this, Angel's wet dream?" which, by damn, it was. That is, the shaman had given Angel the dream so he could achieve his moment of perfect happiness—his friends' reconciliation, his son's love and Cordy in his bed—and as a result turn into Angelus. It was one of the most perfect Gotchas I've ever seen, the kind that earns my highest praise: "Why can't I write like that?"

Why was it so good? Because the first time I thought, *Oh, come on,* should have tipped me off that things weren't real, should have prompted me to take what I knew of the Whedon universe and put together exactly what was happening. The clues were all there, which is why it was such a delight to be Gotcha-ed; they'd played fair. More important, they hadn't destroyed character to get their effect. That is, they pushed the limits of credibility past the breaking point, but Angel was still intrinsically Angel and Cordy still intrinsically Cordy; like hypnotized subjects, they might be doing things they wouldn't choose to do, but they weren't doing things that their characters could not do. No character was harmed in the making of the "Awakening" Gotcha, so we could all return to the reality of the season without any damaging memories and with, in fact, a much deeper understanding of Angel, who has *Raiders* fantasies.

The Beastmaster-Cordy Gotcha, however, was the worst of all possible Gotchas. It piled inconsistency on obscenity, it disgusted the viewer, and it destroyed Cordy's character and viewer trust, all without giving a clue that there was something else going on. To use Agatha-Christie-mystery-ese, it didn't play fair with the viewer. Which meant that when, ten weeks later, it was revealed that the Thing in the Black Bustier was not Cordy, it was too late. The Beastmaster had spent too much time in our heads as the real Cordy, we'd spent too much honest revulsion on the debasing of her character, for us to go back to the Cordelia we once loved. It's not that she stabs Lila; the real Cordy could have done that if pressed. It's that she betrays the man she trusts above all others and who trusts her absolutely; it's that she seduces a boy she once diapered; it's that she dresses like a drag queen and talks like a *Dynasty* reject. It's that she's *not Cordy,* and what might have been fun to watch had we been let into the secret before the Beastmaster seduced Connor becomes the extended rape and death of a much-beloved character.

The result of a bad Gotcha is devastating to story: I was *angry* at the writers for what they'd done to Cordelia, and that's a break in the willing suspension of disbelief that's vital to the survival of any imaginary world. The much-too-delayed revelation that it wasn't Cordy only made me angrier. I'd been jerked around, Gotcha-ed in the worst way, and the continuing presence of Cordy's face and body on the show were a continuing violation. Sending Cordy into a coma was the best thing they could have done, but it didn't make up for the betrayal of trust, and I didn't really return to that universe as a believer until the writers resurrected the real Cordy in the fifth season episode, "You're Welcome" (A5-12).

"You're Welcome" is an episode about loss, not only Angel's but the viewers. Cordelia wakes up, self-centered as always, still caring deeply about Angel, taking a last kiss at the end because she wants it, and because oh, yeah, there are those visions to pass on. She still tells Harmony to torture Eve (and let it be said that Harmony wasn't the only one hoping Eve would make a break for it so she'd die), she still does an angry fluster when confronted with occult technology and she still says the blatantly rude but honest thing; she is, in fact, our Cordy again. Her tragic ending in no way cheapens her return because the writers play fair, foreshadowing the Gotcha to come. Cordy's in a private room, yet she gestures to a body in a bed half hidden by a curtain, and says, "That chick's in rough shape." She watches Doyle's tape and says, "First soldier down," implying there's a second. She tells Angel that Doyle "used his last breath to make sure you'd keep fighting. I get that now." And at the end she tells him, "I can't stay. This isn't me any more. . . . I'm on a different road." All of these moves not only keep the Gotcha from undercutting the emotional impact of the story, they reinforce character: This is what Cordelia would do. Because of that respect for her core identity, Cordy ends as the real thing, the character who had grown to be a vividly believable woman over eight years of stories, who acts in character and still surprises everyone with a last, honest Gotcha. I am grateful to Mutant Enemy for giving Cordelia a Good Gotcha, but I'm even more grateful that they gave her a Good Death, one that honors her character.

Watching the old episodes of *Angel* for this essay brought back to me how important character truth is to any story, but especially to an episodic story that spans years. The growth of Cordelia Chase's character was exemplary over six years, a creation of a flawed, complex, selfish character who was at the same time admirable and lovable. She grew and changed, but she was never anything but Cordelia Chase—until the writers were corrupted by the Beast and betrayed her and the viewers who loved her. As a cautionary tale, the Character Assassination of Cordelia Chase is tragically invaluable. As a great, great character, Cordelia is sincerely mourned.

Jenny Crusie began writing fiction in 1991 as part of her doctoral dissertation research at Ohio State. When the fiction turned out to be vastly more interesting than the research, she switched to the MFA program. She sold her first book in 1992 and followed that with fourteen more novels including five for St. Martin's Press that have earned her New York Times *and* USA Today *best-seller status. She thinks* Buffy the Vampire Slayer *and* Angel *are the best things that ever happened to television, and Joss Whedon is God.*

Joy Davidson

"THERE'S MY BOY..."

Let's see. He spends his early days whoring, and then invites the first sophisticated woman he meets to have a taste. Now a vampire, he engages in a couple of centuries of mutual necrophilia, sprinkled with frequent bouts of S&M and serial killing. Then he gets a soul and reforms, which takes the form of deflowering a sixteen-year-old cheerleader and spending the next few months torturing and killing her friends. Back from hell, he reforms—again—and this time abstains from women with the exception of the occasional episodes of office sex with evil liaisons and rape-play with Darla. Frankly, it would take a combination psychologist and sex therapist to figure out what's up with Angel. So that's who we got.

FROM THE FIRST EPISODE of *Buffy* to the last episode of *Angel*, I've been a captivated fan, easily losing myself in the alternate universe where every dark remnant of the psyche lives vibrantly in the flesh. Perhaps that's because as a psychologist and sex therapist, I come from what some might consider an alternative universe, too, where passions are living creatures, both wanted and feared, and the demons of shame,

199

guilt, and regret can keep us chained for a lifetime. In my universe, curses are often self-made, knitted from the wool of our own histories: our families, our lovers and our beliefs about ourselves. To the degree that my universe intersects with the *Angel*verse, I view Angel as far more than a creature tormented by blood cravings, past horrors and mystical forces. In his hulking handsomeness, Angel may be one of the small screen's most sexually confused heroes. He's torn by sadistic impulses, terrified of the consequences of intimacy and driven to redeem tortured women—all because a consuming relationship with one of them framed his destiny.

We could easily mistake Buffy for the most important femme in Angel's life, considering that they had "the forbidden love of all time." But another relationship was better than forbidden, it was formative. Of course, I'm speaking of the same relationship that is central in most men's lives—the one with Mom. Except, in Angel's case, Mother did not spit him from her womb, but bit him into bloody being.

To say that Darla "made" Angel is to tell only a fraction of the story. She made him, yes, but more than that she shaped him, molded him into her perfect consort. She directed his slaughter of his own family, wowed him with sadomasochistic thrills and showered him with otherworldly wisdom. When she abandoned him, he trailed her across continents and decades. Later, ensouled and divided against himself, Darla cast him off to suffer alone, yet Angel sought her reflection all over again in another preternatural little blond.

Now that's a doozie of a relationship!

And then there's the part where he dusted her, and where she rose from oblivion to have his baby. But I'm getting ahead of myself. Let's go back to the beginning. . . .

Angel/Angelus began life as Liam of Galway, Ireland. The son of a harsh and punitive patriarch, Liam failed to cull even a lick of warmth or approval from his self-righteous father. No surprise, then, that the rejected young man turned to rebellious womanizing, drinking and brawling. Who can help but wonder about his mother's role in his fate? Given her husband's iron will and the subservience expected of eighteenth-century women, she would have been powerless to stand between Liam and his father. We can only speculate about how unprotected young Liam felt and how he might have resented his mother's helplessness.

Enter Darla, a delicately beautiful, anything-but-helpless 150-year-old seductress, magnetized by lovely Liam's recklessness and bawdy charm. Before her own vampire-birth in 1609 Darla had been an "independent" woman—a prostitute—accustomed to the fragile power that comes with belonging to no man. From the moment of his "rebirth," the two cruelly kindred spirits are bound together, and remain so for centuries.

As a vampire, Liam finally triumphs over his nemesis, his father, when he drains his lifeblood: "Now I've won!" Liam boasts. But Darla, older and by far the wiser, reminds Liam that his brief victory pales beside his father's longstanding defeat of him. With deceptive gentleness, she imparts a truth so elegant, so pregnant, that its echoes reverberate throughout Angel's existence. "What we once were informs all that we have become," she tells him. "The same love will infect our hearts even if they no longer beat" ("The Prodigal," A1-15).

Arrogant, stubborn Liam sneers at her words. He doesn't yet understand the tug of the past or the power of unresolved yearning. It will take him another 250 years to absorb this very first lesson of his making.

Liam's denial of the longing that drives him lies at the heart of his character, for Liam the Man had possessed little more soul than Liam the Vampire. We only need explore the similarities between "soul" and "Self" to see through the entrancing darkness that envelops both Liam and his vampire alter ego, Angelus, and to comprehend Darla's power.

In vampire literature, "soul" is often equated with human conscience, but it may be more fitting to compare soul with what many in my profession refer to as an integrated or "solid" sense of Self.

Let me explain.

A solid Self is believed to evolve when caregivers consistently respond to and reflect a child's wholeness and uniqueness as he grows. In the light of this accepting gaze, a child becomes grounded in an ineffable essence of "me." This consciousness of Self allows him to appreciate the sheer "not me-ness" of another, which imparts the capacity for emotional and sexual connection, and, in turn, yields empathy. Liam never developed these qualities. His father regarded him as a derivative creature, a disgustingly flawed "mini-me" rather than a treasured other. Though Liam fought against his father's indicting perceptions of him, he absorbed them, too, leaving him developmentally impoverished and empty inside.

In the absence of solid Self, a person will struggle to divine a set of illusions, a trusted fiction to fill his inner void. Liam was doomed to seek in others this reflected, idealized vision of himself—or the opposite, a devalued, repudiated image of his shriveled Self, huddling beneath his polished veneer. This hunger for reflection made him vulnerable to Darla's uber-femme predations. Ironically, on becoming a vampire, he lost whatever sense of self-observation he might have acquired in time, symbolized by the absence of reflection in the mirror. A damaged, invisible Self does not empathize; others exist only to fill his needs and make him seem real.

One word describes this embodiment of selflessness: Narcissism.

Most of us harbor some narcissistic traits, if only because we are raised in an obscenely narcissistic culture. But the pathological narcissist virtually hemorrhages from his developmentally incurred narcissistic wounds. He is both great and puny; he is one moment indomitable, entitled by his specialness to pillage and use, and the next so lowly as to be unworthy of sucking air.

As a mortal, Liam was selfish, self-indulgent and given to grandiose displays of machismo. Once his soul was extracted, his excesses became gluttonous to the point of psychopathic extravagance. Just as Liam once searched his father's visage for a reflection he could love, Angelus seeks that reflection in his new mother's smile—and finds it. He basks in her admiration. Cruelty fills the emptiness within him that might have flowed with compassion had he experienced a different sort of upbringing.

Angelus and Darla's relationship accelerates quickly in intensity, fueled both by Darla's attachment to the boy she can shape and mold, stunningly packaged in the body of a pleasure-seeking adult demon, and Angelus's fascination with Darla's strength, beauty and lustiness. At first it seems they might love each other, but at second glace it becomes obvious that neither is capable of such generous emotion.

Before being turned, Darla had been dying of a syphilitic heart condition—perfectly symbolizing her corrupted capacity for loving. As a human she had been too desperate and self-serving to love. As a vampire, she might display loyalty or the desire to merge with a mate, but she could no more love than walk freely in sunshine. Like Darla, Angelus could love only to the extent that Liam was able—suggesting that his feelings for Darla were something else entirely.[1] In light of their damaged psyches, it would seem that love's doppelganger—obsession—held Darla and Angelus in thrall.

---

[1] We have evidence that vampires can and do love—but not more or better than they did as humans. James and Elizabeth had what Cordelia called the "big, forever love" ("Heartthrob," A3-1). Spike felt love for Buffy long before he was ensouled. But all of them had been love-struck as humans, too.

However, obsession can be an even more demanding taskmaster than love, for it positions compelling need above reason or good sense.

Obsession is trouble enough in a human. In a vampire it's . . . well, demonic. As a result, Angelus's universe collapses into a mere pinpoint of ferocious desire. Nothing matters but Darla and the satisfaction of his demented cravings.

During their first dozen years together, Angelus and Darla tear across Europe, easily besting any adversary in an escalating reign of destruction. Finally, one vampire hunter, Holtz, traps them in his barn, nearly costing them their lives. But Darla's cunning survival instincts kick in and she escapes, abandoning Angelus to near certain torture and death. Her ever-resourceful son does get away—intact if not unscathed—and eager to extract his revenge upon mommy dearest. We never actually see what happens when Angelus finds Darla, but years later they both relish spinning a tale of her betrayal and subsequent punishment to the young vamp lovers, James and Elizabeth ("Heartthrob," A3-1): "She hit me with a shovel, wished me luck and rode off on our only horse," Angelus announces.

Delighting in his recollection, Darla reminds Angelus that when he finally caught up with her in Vienna, she was made to pay for her sins, again and again. Can James and Elizabeth even begin to fathom the things that he did to her, Angelus wonders—leaving both the horrors and pleasures to their innocent imaginations. Naturally, they can't, because James and Elizabeth are "in love" and vampires in love don't brutalize one another—do they?

Even if Angelus had harbored love for Darla prior to her betrayal—twisted though it might have been—the emotion would likely have died in that barn anyway, leaving Angelus with an unquenchable, ever-soaring thirst: to find her, punish her and then have her again. Obsession is sustained by the urge to gain power over another, and here we glimpse a climactic turnabout in the power-relationship between Darla and Angelus. The son gains control; mommy luxuriates in baring her throat. Watching, we feel a mingling of disgust and erotically-tinged wonder as we ponder the things Angelus did to his lover . . . his mother . . . his betrayer.

As years pass, Angelus becomes ever more artfully depraved, the legendary master of psychological torture. And Darla continues to provide fresh flesh for their sexual sideshows. True to Darla's prophecy, the past continues to inform all that Angelus becomes, as the rage of Liam builds upon itself and is unleashed upon their victims in a whirlwind of mayhem.

In the making of their own vampire child, Drusilla, Darla and Angelus's sexual-sadism reaches a high point—or, a low, depending on one's outlook. In a scene depicting the two preparing to bring Drusilla into their fold, Darla and Angelus thrash about on the floor of a convent as Dru cowers in a corner, awaiting her fate:

"This one's special. I have big plans for her," Angelus taunts. Dru watches them, alert to the sexual repartee. "Snake in the woodshed. Snake in the woodshed!" she recites, sing song. Is she referring to Angelus's snake in Darla's "woodshed"?

"So are we going to kill her during, or after?" Darla inquires, as they continue wrestling on the floor. Darla's question reminds us that Angelus now utterly dominates in their predatory marriage, while Darla submits to his whims.

"Neither," he says. "We turn her into one of us."

Darla's eyes widen, for Dru is incontrovertibly "a lunatic," and even she is startled by the incomparable evil of subjecting Drusilla to eternal life. For Angelus, that's the beauty of his plan. "Killing is so merciful at the end, isn't it? The pain has ended." He prefers to prolong his victims' suffering. The idea, itself, is an aphrodisiac, and Angelus forcefully rolls on top of Darla, pinning her beneath him as Dru looks on. ("Dear Boy," A2-5)

This scene is thick with the syrup of passion and dependency in Darla and Angelus's relationship. A more potent elixir than love alone, their obsession thrives on this intoxicating coalescence of lust, power and insane violence.

The terrible two might have continued cutting a crimson swath across the continents if Darla hadn't one day outdone herself in procuring damsels for their erotic bloodbaths. On Angelus's birthday she surprises him with the perfect gift: a glassy-eyed gypsy girl, bound and gagged in front of the fire.

"She's not just for you," Darla teases. "I get to watch."

As Angelus lifts the trembling girl's skirt, we see the couple at their most intimate, sharing a last moment of gleeful depravity, unaware that their destiny is about to change irrevocably.

The gypsy-girl's tribe soon exacts revenge against Angelus by casting a spell to restore his lost soul, condemning him to everlasting remorse over his ugly past. What's more, the curse carries an unknown tripwire: Should he ever experience a moment of true bliss, he will lose his soul and any small measure of redemption he might have earned.

Darla is incensed by the curse. She rails, ". . . they gave you a soul. A filthy soul! No!" and attacks Angelus wildly, scratching his cheek until he bleeds. "You're disgusting!" ("Five By Five," A1-18)

Angelus is consumed by the horror of his past barbarism and despair over Darla's rejection. Once more he is the spurned and loathsome offspring, abandoned and bereft. But, Darla, too, is lost, for a century and a half ingrains a ragged need not easily slaked. She beseeches the gypsy elders to "remove that filthy soul so my boy might return to me." However, the curse remains intact and Angelus, broken and tormented, wanders alone, living on vermin to appease his agonizing craving for human blood. However, nothing can appease his longing for Darla, and in a few years he returns to her, begging to be taken in. Tempted as she is, Darla can't trust that a vampire with a soul could still be "her boy."

"I don't know what you are anymore."

"You know what I am. You *made* me, Darla. I'm Angelus."

"Not anymore," she counters, though she desperately wants to believe otherwise. Obsession is not easily burnt out, and the barest flicker of hope can reignite it in an instant.

"I can be again," Angelus promises. "Just give me a chance to prove it to you. We can have the whirlwind back."

Darla's longing supplants her better judgment. They both want to believe that their naked desire for one another will overshadow the glare of his defective soul.

"We can do anything, " Darla whispers, as their trembling lips meet. And when they kiss, Angelus morphs into his primal vamp-face—for this is not just his killing face, it is his lustful face . . . the face of passion for the woman who has been at his side nearly forever. A dark romanticism infuses the scene, and it seems for an instant that love between them is not so impossible after all.

Before long, Darla discovers Angelus has failed to keep his promise. Although he has been drinking human blood, he confines his kills to "rapists and murderers, thieves and scoundrels." For Darla, his cowardly acts strike her as merciless betrayals. Yet, she can't help offering him one final opportunity, one last test through which he can atone for his moral collapse by sinking his fangs into a missionary's baby.

Angelus—now the "Angel" we know so well—is unable to consummate the awful deed, and he bolts with the baby. ("Darla," A2-7)

The lovers do not see each other again for nearly 100 years.

If the first phase of Angel's "life" as a vampire is an exotic free-for-all under Darla's tutelage, the second phase is a nightmare of stagnation. Angel no longer feeds on even the most repugnant of humans, but subsists on subterranean vermin. Isolated from both humanity and demons, devoid of attachments or connections to the world, he hovers ghost-like among the living, unchallenged, psychologically still as stone. We see the human Liam in him—a Liam whose bravado has been knocked out—wasting away in a bed of pain and self-hatred. As self-centered as ever—even if consumed by sins rather than caprices—Angel wallows in worthlessness as he once swelled with grandiosity. He may have a soul, but he still lacks a core Self; a crippling conscience is not enough to make him whole.

Joss Whedon has suggested that Angel's need for blood is a metaphor for addiction, and that he is always one drink away from reverting. But I question the actual substance of Angel's addiction. Is it blood? Or is he hooked on something from which he cannot abstain without effecting an inner transformation: his own self-loathing?

A century after his exile from Darla, the Powers That Be finally break through Angel's desolation by assigning him a mission. The new Slayer is in danger from the Master, and Angel is entrusted with her protection. Unknown to Angel, Darla has become the Master's new hit-woman and when she threatens Buffy, her own dear boy is forced to drive a stake into her breast.

Darla is finally lost to him, it seems. Will his lingering obsession be stilled? Not quite—for he seeks her again in another little blond spitfire. The advice of a "faux Swami" on how to cleanse Darla from his psyche comes to mind: "Go out and find some small blond thing. You bed her, you love her, you treat her like crap!" ("Guise Will Be Guise," A2-6) And this he did . . . in spades.

Although his longing for Darla contaminates Angel's attraction to teenage Buffy, the relationship is just what the doctor ordered for the 250-year-old vampire. Angel and Buffy are not quite the May/December pairing they seem; emotionally, they may be closer to the same level of adolescent development. So, together they grow up, through trials and heartache and the crucible of deep caring for one another. For a while it appears that Angel might have finally begun to mend Liam's wounds. But things don't quite work out the way either of them planned, and Angel eventually leaves Sunnydale.

When Angel arrives in L.A., he resumes his brooding isolation. But the Powers again intercede. (Obviously they have big plans for this accursed boy!) Flush with the new mission imprinted upon his business cards—"we help the helpless"—he becomes the *paterfamilias* of Angel Investigations. More than ever haunted by his deeds as Angelus, he craves redemption as he once craved human blood. And hope springs eternal when an ancient prophecy foretells that a vampire with a soul, after saving the world from apocalypse, will be made human again. Unlife is good. Sort of. Except for the fact that Angel's new obsession—his quest for redemption—sweeps him into a claustrophobic labyrinth of his own making. Convinced that asceticism is the path to salvation, he accepts a joyless, passionless existence in the service of his Sisyphusian struggle. How ironic that love at its most intimate and connected—the experience that makes the rest of us most human—deprives Angel of his strongest link to humanity.

Meanwhile, the Senior Partners at the evil law firm of Wolfram & Hart, in the hopes of drawing the powerful "Angelus" into their orbit, invoke magic to bring Darla back from the dead as a mortal—with a soul. As Lindsey says to Darla: "We don't want Angel dead. We want him dark. And there's no better way to a man's dark side than to awaken his nastier urges . . ." ("Dear Boy," A2-5).

Darla's return raises some hopelessly romantic questions: Could Darla and Angel have a real chance at love? Could they be "soul mates" after all? Not likely. For a soul's installation can't wipe away hundreds of years of personal history, nor heal a damaged psyche. A soul, alone, can't sweeten a hardened, selfish heart. Darla is no more a being of innocence in her second incarnation than she was on the day she was turned by the Master.

The folks at Wolfram & Hart are certainly on the right track if they want to nab Angelus. Like any good therapist, they know that a desire buried in shame and shadow will eventually rise feverishly to the surface. And because Angel embraces the celibate path to sustained goodness, he is ever so ripe for Darla's plucking.

Darla quickly rekindles Angel's neutered sexuality, spinning irresistible tales of their past debaucheries. She croons of taking the gypsy in front of the fire until the girl was nearly drowning in her own blood, and

Angel's animal nature leaps to life uninhibited, unashamed. How different are these dreams from memories of times shared with Buffy, when the "good boy" remained ever cautious. His feelings for Buffy may have elicited true happiness, but he always restrained the full measure of his lust. As Darla conjures her hypnotic dreamscape, she slowly isolates Angel from his team, replacing the bleakness of his daily existence with a tempting illusion and leaving his waking hours choked with remorse.

In Angel's world, intense sexuality is associated with dark forces that taint love. It's a world bloated with Christian guilt, and Angel's masochistic self-hatred is rooted in the very human dilemma of being simultaneously consumed with sexual tension and terrified of its release, of yearning for love yet mistrusting its carnal expression.

Angel's reaction to his curse reflects the dynamic tension operative within the majority of modern males who wrestle with extremes of connection and separation, of merging and thriving independently. To love without fear is daunting. Fear of being enveloped, suffocated, of losing one's Self, may keep love at arm's length. Men are often caught in the wasteland between polarities, unable to achieve a balance that enables them to hold onto themselves and another.

I suspect that Angel's desire to connect, to extend himself fully, may one day lead him to the completion of his heroic journey. I'd like to imagine that love will become the antidote to his curse, and cease to be the evil potion that inevitably invokes Angelus. Of all the trials that Angel confronts season after season, his final trial, and the road to triumph over the gypsy magic, may be (almost) as simple as a commitment to love fearlessly.

Angel's relationship with Darla allows him to brush closely up against this very possibility.

The first time that a wakeful Angel encounters the human Darla, his pent-up feelings quickly ignite and he bursts into vamp-face with one passionate kiss.

"There's my boy . . ." Darla coos.

Desire ripples off the screen in almost palpable waves. The raw eroticism Angel has been holding at bay oozes through, just as it does in his dreams. Angel tries to halt the momentum, but Darla pushes him up against a pillar, nuzzling close. He grabs her arm and shoves her away as she continues to entice him. "You're hurting me," she whispers. "And I like it."

So does Angel—but his concern for Darla's precious soul takes precedence. When he warns her of the toll her guilty memories will soon take she offers a means of easing his troubled conscience: allow her to give him one delirious moment of happiness—and then give her life eternal.

Angel won't bite. "You blew the top off my head," he says. "But you never made me happy."

Infuriated, Darla strikes back. "There was a time when you would have said I was the definition of bliss! Buffy wasn't happiness. She was just new!"

Angel continues preaching. "Darla, I couldn't feel that with you, because I didn't have a soul. But then I got a second chance—just like you have."

Angel is deluding himself about the soul being his handicap, but at least he believes his own lies. And who can blame him for harboring just a flicker of a fantasy that if Darla aligns with the good in the world, they could be together again and, if not happy, perhaps the next best thing.

Darla will have none of Angel's moralizing, and once again reveals her disdain for the idea of the "soul."

"What a poster child for soulfulness you are. . . . Before you got neutered you weren't just any vampire, you were a legend! Nobody could keep up with you—not even me. You don't learn that kind of darkness. It's innate. It was in you before we ever met. . . . My boy is still in there and he wants out!" ("Dear Boy," A2-5)

Centuries earlier, Darla had recognized in Liam the very qualities she sought in a mate—ruthless cruelty and daring self-indulgence. However, Liam's darkness wasn't "evil," it was merely his own pathetically human pain turned outward, savagely visited upon the world.[2] In the grip of soulless excess, however, he became her monstrously dear boy. Now, even Darla's wiles fail to sway Angel from his redemptive path, and he holds fast to the conviction that her salvation is his as well.

Soon after their confrontation, Angel learns that Darla is dying of the very disease that nearly took her before the Master made her a vampire. To save both her life and her soul, he embarks upon a tortuous series of trials. Despite his efforts, the Powers refuse to grant her another chance

---

[2]Angel also acknowledges this point when he tells Faith that he once tried to bury his pain, "but you can't get the hole deep enough. You know there's only one way to make the pain stop. Hurt something else" ("Salvage," A4-13).

at humanity, and Angel resigns himself to the idea that turning her into a vampire is the only way to spare her.

"Maybe it would be different. We don't know . . . because, you know, I have a soul. If I did bite you . . . ."

He is reaching, searching, but Darla, too, has been changed by her short mortal life. She has been so deeply moved by Angel's sacrifices, his willingness to die to save her, that she refuses.

"Angel, I've seen it now . . . everything you're going through. I felt how you care. The way no one's ever cared before—not for me. That's all I need from you."

Darla is willing to die as she was meant to die all along, and Angel promises to remain at her side until the end. "You're never going to be alone again."

For the first time, Angel and Darla realize a depth of unselfish caring for one another that transcends obsession. They are on the verge of the healing they need, and there is a chance, finally, for a resolution to their dramatic relationship. If only this tender moment could last. However, in the mythopoetic universe created by Joss Whedon, almost as soon as love blooms, tragedy strikes.[3]

So it is really no surprise that black-ops specialists burst in, subdue Angel and force him to watch helplessly as his own spawn, Drusilla, gives Darla the eternal life she had been seeking. ("The Trial," A2-9)

In the aftermath, Angel unleashes decades—centuries—of fulminating rage. His old obsession with possessing Darla gives rise to an urgency to destroy her—and, it seems, himself. His behavior becomes erratic, driven: giving the Wolfram & Hart staff over to Darla and Dru's blood lust, setting fire to the two vampires and finally launching his own Kamikaze mission into the bowels of Wolfram & Hart's home office to wipe out the Senior Partners. He has lost hope, lost belief in anything except vengeance upon the evil that he can no longer abide—especially as it lies concealed within him. To the team at AI, he is almost unrecognizable.

"I don't even know what you are anymore," says Cordelia, noting that Angel is neither evil vampire nor good "helper of the helpless," but some curious hybrid.

"I'm a vampire. Look it up!"

Angel has no illusions about the side of the divide from which he's drawing energy. This scene is starkly reminiscent of the one between An-

---

[3]Think of Buffy/Angel, Giles/Jenny, Willow/Tara, Darla/Angel, Cordelia/Angel, Lilah/Wesley, Fred/Wesley

gel and Darla when she says nearly the same words after Angel returns to her, ensouled, promising to prove himself.

When Angel fails to annihilate either his own misery or the worlds', he returns home, defeated, more disconnected from life than ever before. And there is Darla, waiting. Too lost to wonder why she is there, Angel violently pushes her up against a wall, devouring her with his mouth.

"I just want to feel something besides the cold."

But in the midst of passion, Darla begins to giggle.

"Why are you laughing?" Angel snarls.

In spite of herself she continues to laugh, perhaps at the improbability of it all, the single turn she hadn't anticipated. Angel strikes her viciously across the face, sending her crashing through the glass doors that lead to his bedroom. Slowly, he approaches her, a predator stalking prey. Light bounces off the jagged shards of glass that surround them, reflecting his own shattered sense of meaning. He reaches for her, gently pulling her up off the floor.

"What are you doing?" She seems genuinely puzzled.

"It doesn't matter," he replies, stroking the marked side of her face where he'd struck her. "None of it matters." He kisses her again and she matches him eagerly. They fall back onto the bed, ripping at each others clothes . . . tearing at each other . . . mouths locked tightly. Angel pulls back and looks into her eyes with such blatant desire it borders on amazement . . . and, of course, the screen goes black. ("Reprise," A2-15)

Finally, we see the wreckage of 250 years of psycho-emotional torture (350 if we count the century-spent-in-hell's timeline). If Angel wakes up as Angelus, so be it. Angel has ceased to care, and like any of us when pushed beyond our capacity to bear the burden, he reverts to the most familiar and predictable form of comfort. Darla is Angel's touchstone. And for a while he is—in every way that counts—her boy.

Angel awakens with Darla beside him in an agony of "perfect despair," yet his soul is intact and he feels illuminated. While he may not have had a chance to see Darla through her illness, or been able to give her a shot at redemption, her presence in his life has both incited and helped resolve his crisis of meaning. Later, he shares his epiphany with Kate Lockley—shortly after preventing her suicide. (Angel is still run by the axiom, "if you can't save one little blond, rescue another.")

He tells Kate that he knows there is no grand plan to life, no big win. But, "if there is no great, glorious end to all this, if nothing we do matters, then all that matters is what we do—'cause that's all there is. What we do, now, today. I fought for so long. For redemption, for a reward—finally just to beat the other guy, but . . . I never got it."

Now, all Angel wants to do is help, "Because if there is no bigger meaning, then the smallest act of kindness is the greatest thing in the world." ("Epiphany," A2-16)

Angel's epiphany is the first real step in his psyche's resurrection, drawing him back to Angel Investigations where he humbly apologizes to Wes, Gunn and Cordy. He is willing to relinquish his quest for power and do what ordinary folks do . . . reach out, share, cooperate. Once again, his involvement with Darla breeds his transformation.

It also . . . well . . . breeds!

Darla discovers that she is impossibly, yet quite assuredly, carrying Angel's child. How two undead could create life is a mystery even to the shamans and mystics Darla consults to try to put an end to the pregnancy. The fetus seems magically protected, and as her due date approaches, Darla appears—where else?—but on Angel's doorstep, seeking help. As if Angel's "perfect despair" was itself a dream, the two reminisce almost longingly about the last time they were together. Angel says he can't help thinking about the episode, in spite of trying to forget. Darla needles him with her rendition of events:

"So, you threw me through those glass doors, slammed me against the wall, pushed me onto the bed and took what you wanted?"

"It seemed like the thing to do—at the time." ("Quickening," A3-6)

The wry playfulness of their banter is charming in spite of its dark underpinnings. With Darla, and only with Darla, Angel is fully realized, completely present in all his aspects. Whatever he feels, whatever he needs—be it a trick of the light or the shadows—he embodies with absolute commitment. Though Darla lies and deceives, Angel reveals to her, and thereby to himself, the truth within. He might not have a reflection, but Darla is still his pure mirror.

As Darla prepares to give birth, she realizes that she is sharing more than a belly with her baby. She is sharing a soul – his soul – and its presence infiltrates her with such maternal love that she fears letting him leave her body.

"I love it completely. I-I-I don't think I've ever loved anything as much as this life that's inside of me."

"Well—you've never loved anything, Darla," Angel reminds her.

"That's true. Four hundred years and I never did—'till now. I don't know what to do."

"You'll have it. You'll have it and then . . ." Angel begins.

"What?" Darla interrupts. "We'll raise it?"

"Why not?"

Darla's dear boy is momentarily quite mad with paternal joy and the rush of hope that arises whenever Darla reveals even a hint of vulnerability. Clearly, the embers of Angel's obsession with Darla will not die. Try as he might to snuff them out, Darla's slightest exhale wills them into flame.

Darla, as usual, is the practical one.

"It's impossible . . . . What do I have to offer a child, a human child, besides ugly death?"

She knows that she has not been nourishing the baby, that the feelings she's having are not coming from her; they're coming from him.

"You don't know that," Angel argues, hopeful of her capacity to love—logic be damned. But Darla's strength is her ability to appreciate the harshest of history's legacies. Her very first lesson to Liam echoes here: what we were informs all that we become. Darla knows who she was—and what she will become once her body no longer envelopes her baby's soul.

"I won't be able to love it. I won't even be able to remember that I loved it," she sobs, as Angel holds her close, stroking her hair and crooning "Shhhhh . . . shhhh."

Darla knows intuitively that her body is not a life-giving vessel, and that she can't carry the baby to term. But because the child is protected, it can't be C-sectioned from her, either. As long as the baby remains inside, he will die. When Angel begs her to fight for the baby, he is just as desperately begging her to fight for them. Darla swears she doesn't know how.

"My boy," she murmurs, stroking her belly. "My darling boy." Is she speaking of the child in her belly or the "child" by her side—or both? " I told you I had nothing to offer this kid. Some mother . . . I can't even offer it life."

Darla is wrong, she can and will give life.

Lying in an alleyway amidst the debris of club Caritas, Darla feels the child's life-force ebbing away. Angel squeezes her delicate hand between both of his and lovingly presses her fingers to his lips.

"This child—Angel, it's the one good thing we ever did together. You make sure to tell him that."

She reaches out with her free hand to grasp a pointed chunk of wood from the rubble and swiftly buries it in her chest. Angel looks as if his heart will break as Darla's hand disintegrates within his . . . and she turns to dust.

Where Darla had been, a naked human infant lies squalling in the rain. ("Lullaby," A3-9)

Angel carefully gathers the infant in his arms. He will later learn that he is holding the "new life" that he had heroically battled to win for Darla during the Trials—a "gift" from the Powers That Be.

Angel has kept his promise to see Darla through to her death. With her final act of unselfish love, she achieves a sort of redemption, and certainly Angel's forgiveness. Angel once told Darla that if he could redeem her—the vampire who made him—he could redeem himself. Perhaps, in forgiving her, he can finally begin to forgive himself.

The team at AI rallies around the newborn. With Darla put to rest, Angel's relationship with Cordelia deepens. But, before anyone can grow too chipper, the child is abducted by the revengeful Holtz and lost to a demon-infested world where time moves at a different pace. Soon afterward, the "baby" reappears through a dimensional portal in the lobby of the Hyperion Hotel. Trouble is, he's now an angry eighteen-year-old, hell bent on killing the father he has been raised by Holtz to detest.

Despite Angel's efforts to bond with his beloved son, Connor is driven by the hatred and bitterness instilled by his adoptive father. Just as Cordelia is about to declare her love for Angel, Connor imprisons him in a metal box, welds it shut and drops it into the sea ("Tomorrow," A3-22). Connor is anxious to see Angel suffer for the agonies of Holtz's lost family, and his death. He might have succeeded if not for Wesley, who, a few months later, drags Angel out of his watery grave.

When Angel sees Connor, his sadness seems to overwhelm any vestiges of anger. Time below has given him perspective—an M.C. Escher perspective, he admits, but, hey, he'd weathered worse when his girlfriend, Buffy, stuck him in a hell dimension for a hundred years.

The events of the last year had demanded that Angel grow in ways surpassing anything evident in the previous two centuries. We see his identity, his Self, taking shape. We see his unconditional love for his offspring shining through his pain. We see his strength, his honor. His trials have forced him to mature, and now his task is to guide his son. Weakened, blood starved, near unconsciousness after his ordeal in the sea, he confronts Connor.

"What you did to me was unbelievable," Angel says. "But I did get time to think. About us, about the world. . . . Nothing in the world is the way it ought to be. It's harsh, and cruel. But that's why there's us. Champions. We live as though the world was what it should be, to show it what it can be. You're not a part of that yet. I hope you will be." Angel moves closer to his son, looking him square in the eye.

"I love you, Connor," he says quietly. "Now get out of my house." ("Deep Down," A4-1

Angel may retain some of his old grandiosity, but he is now dedicated to ideals instead of indulgence, to loving rather than loathing. His indelible relationship with Darla has completed itself. Life has emerged from her ashes; Angel, the father, has taken the place of Angel, the son. Again, Darla's first lesson to her own dear boy ripples down through time. We feel sure that Angel's pure love for Conner will inform all that each is yet to become as their intertwined destinies unfold.

And so it does.

In the wake of Jasmine's ascension and Connor's vicious rampage ("Home," A4-22), Angel sacrifices himself again to save his son, his love proving as deep and boundless as the very sea to which Connor would have abandoned him. For his child's physical and psychic security he makes a pact with the devil, and, taking the helm of Wolfram & Hart, he delves into the magma core of the evil he once sought to destroy.

As Angel's saga draws to a close, the apocalypse that had been prophesied bears down upon the new team at Wolfram & Hart. Connor, his memories restored and cleansed of Holtz's pestilent imprint, acknowledges his father's love on the very day that could well become Angel's last. As the final battle begins, Connor appears at Angel's side—an angelic savior himself—and we see that Darla and Angel, through their extraordinarily selfless love and Angel's tenaciously forgiving efforts, have indeed brought forth a champion. Whatever cruelties Angel may have perpetrated in the past, he has redeemed himself in the fire of this singular creation, this brave and stalwart son.

However, in the Whedonverse, redemption is not an end. Even an apocalypse—that "nowish" concatenation of events—is not an end. These are merely harbingers of cycles yet to be. So, as Angel and his valiant troops gather—tragically, minus one—in exhausted celebration of a world that they hope is finally as it should be, they discover that nothing, nothing at all is as it ought to be. There is no grand resolution, no "big win."

Hideous, shrieking demons swoop down upon the wounded, weary troop, so many creatures that the odds are surely impossible. Yet, raising their weapons, fervor burning in their eyes, the team attacks the resurgent evil. Angel's words of epiphany ("Epiphany," A2-16) seem to echo silently in the darkness:

> *If there is no great, glorious end to all this, if nothing we do matters, then all that matters is what we do. Because that's all there is. What we do now . . . today.*

Joy Davidson, Ph.D., is a licensed marriage and family therapist and certified sex therapist with a doctorate in clinical psychology. A veteran writer, with dozens of national magazine articles to her credit, she has also been the relationships and sexuality columnist for Playgirl *magazine,* Men's Fitness *magazine and* MSN's Underwire. *She is the author of* Fearless Sex: Overcome Your Romantic Obsessions and Get the Sex Life You Deserve *(Fairwinds, 2004) and* The Soap Opera Syndrome: The Drive for Drama and Excitement in Women's Lives. *She also co-created the award-winning video,* Playboy's Secrets of Making Love to the Same Person Forever, Volumes I and II. *Joy lived in the City of Angels for most of her adult life, but the abundance of sunshine drove her away. These days, she resides in Seattle, where she is happiest during the long grey days of winter—which leads her friends to suspect that she is more vampire than human, and may account for her untreatable obsession with* Angel, Buffy, Anita Blake *novels and other darkly archetypal fare.*

Now Available
from BenBella Books